They shall be called oaks of righteousness ISAIAH 61

Janet W. Ferguson

Blown Together

Southern Hearts Series

Book 4

Janet W. Ferguson

Southern Sun Press LLC

Publisher's Note: This book is a work of fiction. Names, characters, any resemblance to persons, living or dead, or events is purely coincidental. The characters and incidents are the product of the author's imagination and used fictitiously. Locales and public names are sometimes used for atmospheric purposes.

ISBN-10: 0-9976587-4-6
ISBN-13: 978-0-9976587-4-3

Acknowledgments

I wanted to write something funny after writing *Tackling the Fields*, and I have these nice friends, Lisa Cantrell and Cindi Latson, who started asking me to go with them on "girls' beach trips" to Fort Morgan. Bless them forever for that kindness. This story grew in my mind on the Fort Morgan beach as a storm blew in—a lonely writer who was the queen of bad dates. That was the fun part.

As I began writing Elinor's story, the Memory Oaks Assisted Living portion of the story materialized. I realized that I was writing through part of my grief of losing my parents. My mother, like Miss Zula in the story, was a brilliant, sweet woman who was ravaged by the nightmare that is Alzheimer's. My father died only two months after his wife of 60 plus years at the age of 94. He had no short-term memory most of the time like Brother Hammill in the story. But every day after he asked how old he was, he said the good Lord had been good to him, letting him live that long. He also loved singing "How Great Thou Art" and eating cookies any time. Almost all the time. How I miss those great people. I'm dedicating this book to my daughter Mary Kristen who took such good care of her grandparents during those last years.

My thanks go out to:

God for loving and searching out prodigals like me

Meteorologist Barbie Bassett for reading through and checking the weather data

Karen Barnes who grew up in Mobile and provided a wealth of information about the culture of the city

Amy Palmer, Physical Therapist Assistant, for answering many questions about physical therapy

Tony Edwards for answering questions about wealth management

Clara McKinnon for allowing us to visit her Mobile home on the Dog River and answering many questions

Carrie Schneider for sharing about growing up in Mobile and about the Azalea Trail Maids

Elizabeth Wright, also from Mobile, who proofed the story and gave feedback

My amazing ACFW critique partners

Volunteer proofreaders, Marilyn Poole, Kathy McKinsey, Karla Patterson, Melissa Thompson

My husband, Bruce, for supporting me

Mentor author Misty Beller, Editor Robin Patchen, Cover artist Paper and Sage

My dog and cats who sit on or beside me while I write, the reason pets end up in all my stories.

They will be called oaks of righteousness, a planting of the LORD.

Chapter 1

"No way. Not now. Not ever." Sam Conrad tossed the manila folder onto his father's massive mahogany desk.

"Tiffany is a bank customer, like any other, and I expect you to grow up and take orders. Forget she's your ex-fiancée." Teddy Conrad stood to his full height and thrust out a finger. "She's waiting in the lobby, so suck it up and get out there."

Suck it up? Take orders? Bile seared Sam's throat. He'd been taking orders, trying to please the man his entire life. Working the account for Tiffany was asking too much. Another wealth manager could easily handle her money. No more. "I quit."

"What?" His father's face reddened and screwed into a familiar scowl.

"Done. Through. Out of here." Sam pivoted, crossed the extravagant office, and slammed the door behind him. His leather loafers slapped the white marble floors leading out of the bank. He refused to glance Tiffany's direction. Wouldn't give her the satisfaction.

Outside, thunder cracked and rain poured from the sky. Sam lingered a half second under the awning before stepping onto the sidewalk of the soggy town square. A man had to draw the line. And being thrown together with Tiffany was it. His father had controlled his life long enough.

Strong winds pushed torrential rain sideways, pummeling Sam's face. His vision clouded as he ran toward his Mazda. Impeccable timing as usual. Couldn't quit on a sunny day in Oxford, Mississippi. Had to quit during a storm.

Mud washed out from a freshly planted flower bed onto the sidewalk. With one long stride, he jumped over the slick patch. He landed on the far side and took another step. Into a smaller patch of mud. His foot slipped and slid forward this time. He reached for something, anything, to keep him upright, but found only air. A second later, he landed on his backside. Hard. Pain shot up his tailbone.

Shoot. He resisted the urge to look back at the bank window. Was his ex-fiancée laughing as she watched from a side window of the bank?

He needed to get up, but wow, that hurt. Water seeped through the fabric of his favorite suit as he sat in the mud. He glanced around. At least no one was on the Square because of the storm.

He closed his eyes for a moment. How could his father expect him to invest Tiffany's new inheritance? To "push away his pride for the good of the bank" and make money for her and another man? The other man.

Not happening. Sam scrambled to his feet and craned his neck to survey the damage to his backside. Mud was slathered all over his pants. He eyed his Mazda. Did he really want to sit in his car and ruin the seat?

Sam groaned as water splattered around him.

If only he still owned his little place nearby—the one Tiffany had insisted he give up for the bigger house on the edge of town.

He pulled out his phone to check the time. Cracks ran across the screen. Great. What next?

The digital numbers read five-thirty. His best friend lived close. He could borrow dry clothes from Jess and wait out the rain. Maybe ask him for advice. Sam turned and crossed the street at a jog, a slower pace than his usual runs. No need busting his behind again. Water pelted him, ran down his face, and filled his shoes, but jogging three blocks in the deluge energized his mind. He should've quit years ago. Wouldn't he love to wash away his old life and start a new one? A life where he called the shots. About his career. His neighborhood. His relationships.

Light shone in the front windows at Jess's. Good. Someone was home. He bounded up the steps onto the front porch and knocked. A piercing cry echoed through the door. *Oh, man.* He must've woken the baby.

The door flew open. Strands of Cassie Conner's red hair fell from her bun, and a baby clung to her hip. Her eyes widened as she took him in. "Oh, my, Sam. Are you okay?"

Why was one of his best clients answering Jess and Sarah Beth's door? "Just wet." And jobless. "But what are you—?"

"Thank goodness. I could use assistance." Her normally controlled voice sounded strained. "Come in and take off your coat. Then take Michael, please."

"Where's Jess's baby girl?"

"Madison Rose is in the bassinet." She pointed toward the living room with her head and held out the plump, green-eyed toddler.

After Sam removed his coat and hung it on the rack in the foyer, he held his arms straight out and caught gentle hold of the fussy child. "Where are Jess and the wife? Your husband?"

"Everyone left for a university fundraiser before the bad weather blew in. I offered to skip it and stay with the babies since they both have upset tummies."

An odor hit Sam's nose as he followed her farther into the house. "Whew. Something's foul in here." He cringed and swallowed a gag. "Hideously foul." Cassie was lucky he'd spent a large part of his life in locker rooms with smelly men, or he might've hightailed it back to his car.

Across the living room in a white wicker contraption, a dark-haired infant screeched. The black and white cat perched on the couch alongside Jess's large dog, staring at the noisy creature.

"Stomach bug going around the church nursery. You might need this." Cassie offered him a towel before opening a package of diapers.

Great. A stomach virus might be next on his agenda. At least he wouldn't have to worry about missing work. He laid the towel across his shoulder then shifted the toddler up into the crook of his arm. No sense getting baby goop on his clothes.

After pulling out a few wipes, Cassie leaned over the crib to change the diaper. "So, what's got you running around in your business suit while these summer storms ravage north Mississippi?"

"Long story you don't want to hear. I was hoping to borrow dry clothes from Jess and hitch a ride to my car once the rain stopped."

A small hand smacked Sam's nose hard enough to bring tears.

He mashed his eyes shut. "Little dude, that hurt."

Michael let out a deep belly laugh and smacked him again.

"Ouch."

"You bring out a mischievous side in him." With an arched brow, Cassie eyed him while she trashed a bunch of stuff he didn't want to see. "I'll take that little joker as soon as I sanitize my hands."

Sam scrunched his nose at the grinning boy with curly auburn hair. "More like little stinker."

After another laugh, the boy pressed a slobbery kiss on Sam's cheek.

"Aw, now. That's gross." Not that he wasn't already wet. But still.

Cassie set Madison Rose into an infant seat with some sort of contraption swinging over it. "Michael seems to like you."

"Glad someone does. But I want to get this slime off."

"Here." She handed him a wipe and took the child.

It would take more than that tiny square to get him clean. Howling winds ripped through the trees outside the window.

The electricity flickered, then cut off, leaving only silhouettes in the dim light cast through the windows.

"Crud." Now he couldn't see.

One of the babies squeaked, and the dog barked three times.

"It's okay, sweetie," Cassie's voice crooned. "Sam, I have no idea where they keep the candles and matches."

He took out his cell and turned on the flashlight. "If you tell me where your phone is, I'll get it. They'll help some."

"On the end table behind you."

He twisted, laid his phone face up, and did the same with the other. "Got it." The glow from the two cells worked for now.

Still holding the feisty toddler, Cassie sat on the floor beside Madison Rose. "Looks like we have some time if you feel like telling me what's troubling you."

Sam ran his fingers across his wet silk tie. Why not bellyache to a couple of smelly babies and one nice lady? They were friends after all. "In a nutshell, I quit my job. I'm ready to start a new life away from the bank. Away from my father."

Lightning split the dim light, illuminating the room for a second. "Hmmm…" Cassie switched the wiggling boy to the other arm. "If you're serious, I know someone who'd help you get a fresh start. What do you think about moving to Mobile for a while?"

"In Alabama, down on the Gulf?"

"That's the one. A man became my father's mentor and helped him turn his life around. Now Dad enjoys doing the same for others. I could give him a call if you'd like." Cassie paused. "If nothing else, you could get away and think about what you want to do."

This town was too small to avoid his father. Or Tiffany. Leaving for a while might be just the ticket.

Shadows swallowed the room, much like the shadows swallowing his life in Oxford. And his soggy suit clung to his skin, heavy and cold like Tiffany's fake smile and his father's never-ending domination. Could he really do this? Step out of his hometown, a successful career, the only life he'd ever known? The thought of walking back into the bank turned his stomach worse than the smell of the dirty diapers still saturating the air.

Mobile was at least five hours south. *Why not?* "Make the call."

~~~

Sinister clouds loomed over the Gulf of Mexico and Fort Morgan, Alabama, blocking the sun as Elinor Elizabeth
~~~

Bosarge turned and headed back toward her beachside cottage. She should've taken her daily walk earlier, but the words had flowed so well, she dared not leave the computer. Now, the line of storms that had brutalized Louisiana and Mississippi overnight swooped down upon Alabama. At exactly the predicted time.

Elinor picked up her pace to a jog. She needed to get home to poor Mr. Darcy. He despised thunderstorms. Who knew a cat could be so destructive?

The blowing sand bit into her skin like tiny needles as a red beach umbrella caught air and sailed toward her like a torpedo.

A frantic young mother ran after the airborne parasol, lugging a large bag while clutching a little boy on her hip. "So sorry. This wind..."

With one arm shielding her face from the sharp tips, Elinor caught hold of the umbrella with the other. Not a good day to use a flimsy piece of equipment.

The mother struggled to walk against the gale and the blasting sand, and the little boy covered his eyes with his hands. The woman needed a few more arms.

Elinor waved her off. "I can assist you." She'd seen them earlier in the week and pointed to the house behind them. "Isn't that your place? I'll put it in the carport for you."

"Thank you so much." The mother didn't waste time changing course toward the boardwalk leading to shelter.

After fighting with the strap, Elinor got the ribs closed tight and trudged through the dry sand until she made it underneath the house. A canister stood in the corner that looked to be the storage area. She secured the umbrella and started back toward her own cottage at a jog.

At least she hadn't had to pull anyone out of the water today. She'd raised a red flag on her deck to warn tourists of the unfavorable conditions, since the city didn't hoist one this far down the peninsula. Despite her repeated requests.

Only twenty yards before she reached home, she spotted him. Another crazy teen, arms waving and head bobbing, bodysurfing and caught in the rip current. He'd ignored not only the black skies and thunder, but her tidal flag as well. Her lifeguard training set into motion, the way it had since she'd been a teen herself. She sprinted the rest of the way to her fence and grabbed the equipment, her calves aching from the dense sand. The wind slowed her progress, but she pushed onward. At least he wasn't too far out. Yet.

Lord, help me.

At the water's edge, Elinor, still carrying two life belts, entered the surf at an angle to the foaming current. A few swells lapped over her head, but she swam through the churning waves. She paused and popped up, wiping the briny water from her eyes to check the teen's location once more.

Lightning lit up the sky on the horizon, sending adrenaline shooting from Elinor's head to her legs. She swam harder. Being electrocuted wasn't on her to-do list.

Almost there.

At last, she neared and held out the orange life belt. "Just hold on to the float. I'll pull us out of the current."

"Yeah." His knuckles whitened as he grabbed on.

The boy was large enough to swamp them both if he panicked.

"Don't worry. I've assisted many swimmers."

"Okay." His round eyes flitted from her to the large swells.

She glanced back and tried to give a reassuring smile. She'd save the stern lecture about the dangers of the sea and the purpose of the beach warning flags for when they reached the shore.

Thunder cracked in the west, loud enough to be heard over the waves. Her heartbeat kicked up a notch. Elinor took a gulp of air, dipped her head under, and using fierce kicks, she surged them forward. When she surfaced, they looked near enough to touch bottom. She straightened, planted both feet, and stood. Once she steadied herself, she tugged the boy closer.

"You should be able to walk out now."

When he realized he was in shallower water, he got his balance and took off. "Thanks, lady."

"Wait. See that red flag? That means don't go in the—"

Another bolt of lightning zapped only two houses away, and the teen shot down the beach. She'd better do the same. So much for educating him. She reached the shore and sprinted, the floats dangling from her hand and periodically whipping her legs.

The one palm tree beside the cottage creaked and moaned under the pressure of the fierce gusts of wind. Heart pounding, she raced up onto the back deck and slid open the glass door.

Inside, she grabbed a beach towel from the basket she kept by the door and wrapped it around her dripping swimsuit. "Mr. Darcy? Come hither, sir." Crawling across the hardwood flooring of her living room, she peeked under the furniture. "Where is my little hairless kitty?" If she didn't find him soon, the panicked cat would select another chair to slice to shreds. If he hadn't already. Apparently, destroying expensive furniture consoled his anxiety.

A loud clatter overhead began. Hail pelting the roof? Thank the good Lord she'd made it back before that barrage of precipitation. She'd intended to have the roof replaced soon anyway. Maybe this would spur her on to the wretched task. Contemplating the earsplitting sounds of men hammering for hours shot a chill up her neck almost as much as the storm.

"Mr. Darcy, where are you?"

Lightning flashed, and thunder rattled the windows. The lights blinked then went out. She poked her head up. Outside the window, the sky transformed into a murky green. Not good. Last time that happened… "Mr. Darcy, we have to get in the bathtub." Elinor sprang to her feet and darted into the bedroom to grab the pillows from her bed.

A throaty meow came from near the closet where the cat lay beside a pile of shredded straw.

"My favorite beach hat. How could you?" Groaning, she lifted the animal and a few pillows. The cat's claws dug into her arm, but they made it into the tub, and Elinor ducked and covered them both. "Please don't let it be a tornado, Lord."

A boom and a crash shook the walls. "Not an innocuous noise." But at least it didn't sound like a freight train, which meant no tornado. She squeezed the pillow tighter above her head with one arm and held the squirming Mr. Darcy with the other.

For ten more minutes, she held still and listened. The wind and rain slacked off. Then nothing. No hail. No thunder. "Whew. Only a fast-moving thunderstorm."

Mr. Darcy wriggled from her arms and hurdled the side of the claw-foot tub.

"The coast must be clear." She gathered the pillows but took measured steps out of the bathroom. A strange gaping light came from the front room, and a small stream of water trickled across the floor toward her.

"No." Her shoulders drooped, and the pillows fell from her grasp. "Not my cottage."

Her heart thudded as she scrambled down the hall, but the sight that met her stopped her in place. Water dripped through a cavernous hole in the front wall and roof. The end of a power pole protruded inside, and sparking lines draped the front porch.

Her stomach squeezed as surging panic zapped through her. She ran to find her cell phone. She'd left it by the bed. Her fingers shook as she punched in 911.

When she finished the call, sadness crept in and took the place of the panic. She loved her small yellow beach house tucked among the others of all shapes, colors, and sizes on the end of the peninsula. Though hers was a smaller home, it was free of clutter and carpet and all the other knickknacks she lived without to keep away the dust. She was one of the few owners who lived in this area year-round. Her cottage provided sanctuary. A place where she could breathe and write. What would she do without that?

Thirty minutes later, emergency workers arrived to clear the lines.

After calling her handy man and informing her insurance agent, she made a quick run to the dollar store to purchase plastic containers. Apparently her cottage was the only place damaged by the storm other than a few limbs littering her neighbors' yards—which was a good thing. She just wished her own home had escaped unscathed.

She stood in her living room, overwhelmed by the arduous task of packing. Despite the blue tarp covering the ragged roof, she'd need to protect her belongings from water damage. At least her books and paintings had been spared. And of course, herself and Mr. Darcy. *Thank you, Lord, for protecting us.* Although between the workers in the cottage and the stress of the storm, she'd had to crate the poor cat to keep him from shredding more household items. Every few seconds his howl echoed, a protest to his incarceration.

In her room, she gathered clothes into one large suitcase and dragged a smaller bag to the medicine chest. She grabbed two inhalers, all the antihistamines, nasal spray, a box of tissues, and an EpiPen. Another pen couldn't hurt. One hand rubbed the area on her thigh where the last two had been plunged in, and then she threw in her spare pen.

After all, they had pharmacies in Mobile. She'd be fine with just a few things.

Hours later and with muscles aching from packing and rearranging the furniture, she steered down the long drive of her parents' estate beside the Dog River. Not as quiet as she desired with her father's constant banter, but she could stay in the boathouse. With her cousin Darren living in their summer home for the month, what choice did she have? There were so few rentals available this time of year, much less hypoallergenic ones.

At least the summer skies had cleared. A yellow glow shone from the west where the sun sank lower. She skipped parking in the main garage and pulled around the circle drive that ran between the main house and the boathouse. She'd like to unload before dark. A red Mazda was parked near the fence. Probably the pool man. Mother and Daddy hadn't answered her calls on the way over, so she'd say hello once she got Mr. Darcy settled. With designer cat carrier in one hand and laptop satchel over the other shoulder, she strode down the sidewalk.

Her keys jangled in the boathouse deadbolt. Not even

locked. Her parents should really be more careful. Everything looked to be in order though. With the minimal décor, leather furniture, and stained concrete floors, the boathouse kept her asthma at bay. No place for dust to collect. After discarding the computer on a side table, she pulled the cat from his travel bed.

"I know you'd rather be at home, but we have no choice in the matter."

The cat gave a low growl and a hiss.

"Oh, don't be mad." She scratched at the wrinkles around his neck, just the way he liked, and a purr vibrated the creamy bare skin as smooth as toasty suede. Big green almond eyes stared at her. "You are such a sweet baby. You've been through quite a trauma today."

A spray of light cut through the shadowy room as the side door creaked open.

Her heart skipped as she spun.

A tall, blond, and shirtless man slid to a stop just inside. "Who are you and why are you in here? Holding a…a… Is that a rat?"

Oh my. Elinor froze. The clean-cut man didn't look like a robber, so he had to be with the pool service. Of all the nerve. "This is not a rat. This is a hairless cat, a Sphynx to be exact. And for your information, the pool man is not supposed to be dillydallying around in here. You must go back outside, sir."

Mr. Darcy hissed again and sprung at the man, who vaulted behind the leather couch.

"Whoa. I don't care what you call that thing, housekeepers shouldn't bring their pets to work. Big Roy wouldn't want that genetic mutation inside. And I'm not the pool man. I'm a guest." A smug smile pressed his mouth upwards. "Of Mr. and Mrs. Bosarge."

Housekeeper? She'd—

Wait. A guest? Or another mentee like Craig? The thought jarred her, and fire swept through Elinor's hands, arms, and face. "My father couldn't have taken on another project." Especially after last time.

"Project? Your father?" The man's eyes squinted as he looked her up and down. He stood taller and crossed his arms at his chest. Muscular arms across muscular chest. "I remember you from Cassie's wedding. I should've guessed with that flaming red hair."

Flaming red hair? His blue eyes sent another wave of heat to her cheeks. She forced her gaze down, but the chest was there. Oh, where to look? His ear. She would look at his ear. "My hair is not flaming, and I have to stay here." Frustrated, she picked up her laptop and carrier, then swung back toward the door. "I'll pay for a hotel nearby if you can't afford one, and in the meantime, I'll wait in the main house."

"Hey, missy." His voice stopped her at the doorway.

She jammed her shoulder back and pivoted. "Did you call me missy?" What a miscreant.

"I can afford a hotel, and you forgot your"—he made air quotes—"Sphynx."

Chapter 2

The weird cat lady's pouty lips captured Sam's attention and held him prisoner for a moment. A little cute, if he were honest. Not to mention, the red hair hanging in damp, wavy strands around her cheeks. Elinor Bosarge, huh? What was the woman blathering on about?

Unsure of what to do or say next, he trailed her and waited outside while she took the kennel into the main house of the sprawling estate and set it inside. He'd helped her catch and crate that foul beast she called a Sphynx. Hairless cat? Why in the world would someone want anything that looked like that? A shiver ran across his shoulders despite the blistering heat. He'd never liked cats, but at least he could see how someone—not him—might go for a fluffy little kitten. Once the animals grew up, they became snooty creatures that skulked around, always looking superior. A lot like this one's owner.

After she'd placed the feline in the main house, she came back outside and marched to the Lexus crossover parked nearby. A nice ride. Too nice to let an animal in it, even if it was hairless. The automatic locks clicked, and the back hatch opened. She heaved a large plastic box from the trunk.

A gentleman would help her take it to the main house. Plus, he was a guest here. Sighing quietly, he forced his heavy feet to trudge over. "Let me get that."

"I put it in the car, and I can carry it inside." Her lips pressed together.

"It'll take less time, and you can get back to…whatever it was you said you needed to do." And the sooner he could get back into the AC.

"If you insist."

He eyed her car. "Nice vehicle, but not quite fast enough

for my taste."

"It's plenty fast for a sensible person." She hoisted the box his way. "Take these first editions into the main house, and I'll get the portrait. I don't want Mr. Darcy's painting damaged."

His arms shifted as he took the weight of the container. "Why's this so heavy? And who's Mr. Darcy?"

She snapped her fingers in the humid air. "If you could try to pay attention. I said the crate held irreplaceable first editions I've collected. First editions are books, in case you're not familiar with the term, and I couldn't risk water damage or theft. There are three more crates after that one. And two smaller ones." Her body swiveled back toward the car. "Mr. Darcy is my cat." She held up a painting. "This can't be replaced either."

A huge oil painting of the ugly cat stared back at him. He couldn't stop the laugh erupting from his chest. "What on earth?" And why, for the love of all that's right in the world, would someone paint that? The sight of it gave him the creeps. He'd probably end up coming in the main house sometimes. Could he turn it to face the wall when she wasn't looking?

A smack sounded against the concrete as she stomped toward the house. "This is by an up-and-coming artist in Atlanta."

Words and a few comebacks formed on his tongue, but he held them in. He'd been working on his filter for some time now. Not always successfully, but he tried. Instead of speaking, he followed, thankful for a small breeze that stirred the leaves in the dense woods surrounding the lot on three sides.

She plodded on through the door of the mansion. "I can't wait until my parents return so I can straighten out this loathsome situation. Daddy was not to do this again."

Do what again?

Sam set his load inside and returned to the car and grabbed another crate of *first editions*. Heavy first editions. How was it possible that the sweet, down-to-earth Cassie shared DNA with this woman? The tall, white poodle he'd encountered earlier in the afternoon nuzzled his elbow. "Watch out,

Dashwood. There's a disturbed woman afoot."

"What?" Suddenly beside him, Elinor looked up at him. Her forehead wrinkled as she picked up one of the smaller containers. "How do you know my parents' dog?"

"I'm their guest." He continued toward the house, stacked the two-ton box on top of the other, and then snapped his fingers like she had. "If you could try to pay attention. Your sister Cassie and I are friends. I didn't bust out of prison or anything."

Her blue eyes impaled him. Apparently, she didn't get his humor. And he probably should've filtered.

Sam rose to his full height and attempted to keep a pleasant expression plastered on like he did with difficult bank customers. "I'm a wealth manager." *Or I was, anyway.*

With meticulous moves, Elinor set aside her load against a far wall and then stood up straight. "Why would a successful wealth manager need my father's help?"

Her chin took a defiant tilt. And here came the pouty lips again.

He should be insulted, but he struggled to contain a chuckle. "Don't you worry about me, missy. Let's just unload the rest of your valuable first editions." Back at the car, he picked up the last big crate. Even heavier. Good grief.

She edged next to him. "My name is Elinor. Or Miss Bosarge. Not missy." More daggers fired from her blue eyes. Eyes as blue as the sky after a storm.

Wait. *Get your head out of that place.* A woman like this made his ex-fiancé look like Mother Teresa. And he wasn't going down that road again. Ever.

He needed to get back to the boathouse in a hurry.

As he dropped the box beside the others, the door from the garage flew open, and the huge poodle scurried toward the sound.

"Elinor Elizabeth?" A voice boomed. The giant of a man entered the living room. "What a sight for sore eyes. Come here and give Daddy some sugar." Red and gray whiskers spread with a smile that filled Big Roy's face. He covered the distance in four long strides and wrapped his huge arms around Elinor. "How's my girl? Goodness gracious, I've missed you."

"Daddy, it's only been three weeks since we had dinner, and I'm working under a deadline."

"Three weeks is a long time for your daddy. Especially when his little girl's right across the bay. Your momma had to all but hogtie me to keep me from taking the boat over." He kept one arm around his daughter.

Mrs. Bosarge entered with a phone against her ear. "Em, I'll call you later. Elinor's here. Love you, hon." After dropping the phone into her purse, the petite woman pushed her short blond hair into place and strode across the room. "Hey, sweetie. What brings you over? I thought you had a manuscript to complete." She glanced at the boxes and the portrait. "What's all that?"

"I called you both, but no one answered." Elinor's chest shook, and a sob escaped her throat. "A storm catapulted a power pole through…" She sniffled and touched her lips. "My cottage has a hole in the wall and roof."

"Oh, sweetie." Her mother joined the hugging. "We were in our last full Krewe of Hope meeting before the Mardi Gras charity ball this weekend, and my phone was on silent. I'm sorry. That had to be terrifying."

Sam let out a deep sigh. He'd been hard on Elinor when she'd likely been scared out of her wits. Maybe that explained her crazy behavior. Didn't explain the weird cat, though. Or the painting.

With a jolt, Elinor pulled away from her parents' embrace. "But I found…" She swept an arm toward him. "This man was in the boathouse." Moisture filled her blue eyes. "I need to stay there to write, and my allergies…"

Big Roy's brows knit together. "Lands sakes alive, we got rid of all the rugs and drapes and house plants. Got leather furniture and washable bedspreads."

"I know you did, and I hate I was the cause of all that expense." The pouty lips again. "It's quiet in the boathouse, plus if I stay in the main house, the dog might bring in pollen and other allergens."

"Little missy, your momma's frazzled enough with everything she's got going on without you raisin' a ruckus about her pet."

Little missy? Sam smothered a laugh.

"Now, Roy, she's not raising a ruckus." Mrs. Bosarge patted Elinor's arm. "She's anxious about her health, plus she had a big scare today." She directed her attention to her daughter. "I loved Cassie's poodle so much, I wanted one of my own. I'll bathe her more often and keep her fur shaved short. Besides, dogs lower stress."

"What do you have to be stressed about, Mother?"

"I think I know." The words slipped from Sam's mouth before he could bite his tongue.

A stifled chuckle escaped from Big Roy. He coughed and covered his mouth with his fist.

Both women nailed the poor man with a hard look.

"Daddy, you promised not to harbor another swindler after…Craig." Elinor's mouth quivered with the words.

"I apologize for laughing, darling, but I didn't promise. And Sam's not a swindler. He's a friend of Cassie's and a professional." Big Roy turned his hands upright. "It's my Christian calling to help my fellow man."

Emotion pressed Elinor's lips together as she turned and bolted up the stairs. Was it anger? Or had it been pain?

Mrs. Bosarge gave her husband a wide-eyed stare and followed her daughter.

After the footsteps overhead echoed away, Sam cleared his throat. "Sir, I can get a place in town."

"Nonsense. Not another word about leaving. I want you here. Elinor Elizabeth was a bookish child, lived in her own world, dreaming of chivalry and romance. She's my most sensitive, too, and I always end up making an utter mess with her. Most of this drama is about Craig, and I carry the blame for that one. A slippery fellow that fooled and hurt the whole lot of us. Especially Elinor."

"Craig?"

"Long story, and no need to air dirty laundry." He clapped his hands together. "The fridge is stocked, so you make yourself at home in the boathouse. She'll be over her hissy fit soon, and I'll be out there with the information I'd like you to look through in about an hour."

"Yes, sir." Sam made his way out the back door. The last bits of sun disappeared across the river. In its place, a full moon hung large, casting an eerie reddish glow between wispy clouds. Almost as red as Elinor's hair. And lips. Sam groaned. What had he gotten himself into?

Chapter 3

"Sweetie, I know you're scared after the incident with the allergy shots." Elinor's mother followed her into the bedroom.

Incident? Elinor frowned. She'd stopped breathing during the incident barely a year ago, and it had taken the nurses at the allergy clinic two epinephrine shots to revive her. Even now she could still recall the swelling of her throat. The panic. *Calm down. Deep breaths.*

Her near-death experience wasn't the really distressing part of this whole situation. "How could Daddy take this man in after what happened last time?" Elinor threw herself across the four-poster bed in her old room beside Mr. Darcy. The firm mattress barely bounced, and the cat's eyes remained closed. "Is this new? It's hard. Almost rigid."

Her mother took a cautious seat. "It's the new hypo-allergenic one. Since you can't take the shots anymore." With soft strokes, she rubbed up and down Elinor's back. "Hon, your father thinks mentoring young men is his ministry—"

"Like Uncle Dale did for him."

"A few weeks ago, your dad told me he felt God would be sending us someone soon. It's always worked out fine, except for that Craig."

The memories of Craig flooded Elinor with a blast of anguish, like a tidal wave ripping through her insides. His jet black hair and his dark, smiling eyes. Always smiling. All the while lying. The thought sickened her. She needed to decompress. "The weather's calmed outside, and I need to swim to clear my head." Her rescue swim earlier in the day had hardly been relaxing. "Can you at least ask Daddy to keep his new mentee away from me? I have no desire to get acquainted with him."

After thirty more minutes of unloading her car and rummaging through bags, Elinor located a swimsuit. She slid on the high-neck one-piece and bounded down the stairs and out the door. Tiptoeing, she scanned the dark ground surrounding the pool for slithery movement. Chills raced across her shoulders. There'd better not be any snakes. Another trauma today might push her over the edge. One never knew around this area so near the Dog River.

When she reached the edge of the pool, she lowered herself into the warm water.

Thank You, God, for this. And for keeping me safe today. Oh, and for my parents and Mr. Darcy.

She sighed and dipped her head back to wet her hair. Her gaze went to the boathouse.

We can talk later about the dreadful oaf in there. The painful memories of the last man to stay there ran too deep for now.

With broad strokes she glided across the pool. In the water, she could move and breathe and imagine another world. A world where men were romantic and heroic and kept their word.

A world where she wasn't so lonely.

~~~

After going through mounds of statements, Sam stood. This had been a long day.

Big Roy slapped Sam's back. "I think this partnership will make us both happier than a tick on a fat dog. Even if it is temporary. In the morning we'll meet for Bible study and prayer time before we leave for the office." He glanced at his watch. "About six-thirty work for you?"

Bible study and prayer? Sam mashed his lips together. Awkward. But he'd give it a shot. The early hour would bump his run to around five-thirty. "I'll be ready."

"That's what I like to hear." A grin lifted the man's bearded lips. "After work, we'll help Miss Ruby with the Mardi Gras ball preparations at the Krewe of Hope's den. That's our storage and work place. You're gonna have a big time learning our Mobile traditions. You got a tux?"
~~~

"Cassie told me I might need one. Black okay?"

"That dog'll hunt. We'll get you the traditional white vest to go with it. Have a good sleep, and remember, help yourself to whatever you need. This is your home."

As the big man let himself out the door, a thousand thoughts ran through Sam's mind. He'd really quit his job. A job he was good at. A career where he made a lot of money. Now he was in the boathouse of a large man he barely knew whose nutty daughter wanted to claw his eyes out. And he didn't even want to get started on that creature she'd called a cat.

Sam stretched his arms and then hit the floor for pushups and burpees. Maybe tomorrow he could find a gym nearby to shake off his tension. If not, with that woman around, he might have to find the nearest bar.

After eight sets of each exercise and a hundred sit-ups, he stood and paced. Another swim would be relaxing after the drive and the chaos of settling in. If *she* wasn't still out there. He'd seen her when Roy came in, but it'd been well over an hour since she'd started her laps. Surely, little missy had long since gone into the main house to curl up with her weird pet. He threw on his trunks and crept outside. No splashing sounds came from the pool. The moon illuminated the sky, casting a shadow as he moved closer.

A silhouette floated, red hair streaming out in all directions. *Oh, shoot.* She was still there—on her back, not moving, just staring up. Slightly attractive. But creepy, too.

Was she okay? After taking one step back and two forward, he cupped his hands around his mouth. "Are you alive?"

No answer.

He stepped closer. "Are you okay, missy?"

A frantic splash met his words. "What are you doing?" Her feet plunged to the bottom of the pool, and her eyes opened wider. Once her shock dissipated, she speared him with that steely gaze again.

"I'm at a pool wearing trunks, so…"

"Didn't my father tell you I like to swim alone?"

"I'm not going to swim near you."

"Your impudence awes me. The water is where I plan my stories, and I won't have you polluting my thoughts."

Impudence? Who talked like that? "So I awe you *and* pollute your thoughts? Quite the compliment, but I'm not interested, missy. I'll take a seat in the lounge chair until you finish daydreaming."

Her hand slapped the water. "That's not what I said. I don't want you over there gawking at me."

"I'm willing to close my eyes."

"Still disturbing."

Not budging. He crossed his arms at his chest. He'd had enough bossing around from his father and Tiffany to last a lifetime. "There's nothing in that pool I want to see."

"Fine. But do not speak. Not one word."

Why did her voice have to be so shrill? And proper? Did she think she was royalty? What a nut.

A nut with cute lips.

Oh, man. Had he really thought that?

But Elinor wasn't actually alone in the pool. A ripple formed in the water behind her, casting a large shadow in the blue pool. Not an enormous spider, but not a small one either. He should let it crawl all over her. His chest squeezed with a laugh.

"Take your seat and close your eyes, then."

A gentleman would get the skimmer. Why did he have to keep thinking about being a gentleman? "Wait a sec—"

"No talking."

"But—" Sam shrugged. "Most of them aren't poisonous anyway."

With a shriek, Elinor moved faster than he thought possible, a flurry of water splattering behind her. A second later, she'd scrambled out of the pool, thrown her arms around him and jumped, leaving him no choice but to catch her. "Where's the snake? Carry me inside. What color was it? They can climb, you know."

Water dripped from the red hair, and Elinor's fingers dug

into his shoulders. Carry her inside? This chick had some major hang-ups. And pretty eyes.

"Please, hurry."

Was she trembling? "Would it make a difference if it was a spider? Not a snake."

Those blue eyes searched his face, igniting a feeling of protectiveness and a strange fire in the vicinity of his heart.

"A spider?" Her feet dropped. "You're not lying?"

"I'm a lot of things. A liar isn't one of them." Warmth spread from where her arms still draped around his neck.

With one last look around, she released him. "We are never to speak of this misunderstanding."

Sam took a deep breath and nodded. "Yes, your highness." The sooner he could forget the misunderstanding the better. "You can have the pool. I'm hitting the sack."

~~~

How could she have made such a fool of herself again? Elinor clomped toward the house. Jumping into the man's arms… Surely, someone had told Sam about her phobia. The situation was just too coincidental.

His shocked expression when she'd clung to him came to mind. A little chuckle escaped. He had looked surprised. And slightly attractive. Maybe he wasn't lying… But still, having another single man living in her parent's boathouse unnerved her. She'd never been good with people or connecting emotionally—the reason she'd much rather escape into a good book, and the reason she'd ended up writing her own love stories. When she wrote about her heroes, she knew why they behaved so strangely, what they were thinking, and their real motives. If only that could be true in real life. Sadly, when it came to reality, she had no clue. A fact that Craig had exploited all too easily.
~~~

Chapter 4

Mist hovered over the river as bursts of orange and magenta emerged on the horizon. *How majestic, Lord.*

Elinor's fingers flew across the keyboard of her laptop as she sat beside the pool. So beautiful and inspiring. Fortunate, because the deadline for this Regency romance loomed only a month away. The shawl on her shoulders slipped, and she turned her head, trying to catch the edge with her chin.

A tall profile came into view near the metal gate. Such wretched luck. Surely that man wasn't trying to monopolize the pool again. Swimming was one of the few activities she could do and still breathe without all the congestion, itchy eyes, and wheezing. Exasperating allergies and asthma.

Sam stopped and stretched a long, toned leg behind him. His arms had been a tad bit strong when he'd caught her last night during that debacle. Cassie must have told him about the snake phobia, and he'd duped her for spite. As he stretched the other leg, her neck craned to the side for a better view. Obviously, he worked out.

His head rotated her way, and his mouth turned down into that smirk he seemed to have perfected.

She held up a hand. "You're not trying to swim this early, are you?"

He waved. "What? Talk louder."

Was his hearing impaired? She pushed the words from her diaphragm. "Are you going to swim?" Perhaps he could understand that.

"No, thanks. Going for a run. Maybe later."

The intolerable oaf. "No. I don't want to swim with you."

His hand cupped his ear. "What?"

For goodness sakes. She shook her head. "Never mind."

"Still can't hear you." He jogged toward her.

Exactly the opposite of what she'd wanted.

In a few seconds, he towered over her chair. "Okay, I'm here. Why were you hollering for me?"

"I was not *hollering* for you. I am attempting to write."

"Good luck with that." He glanced beside her. "Are those snake-proof boots?"

"None of your concern." Something in his smart-alecky smile told her he'd been toying with her the entire conversation. "Three words. I. Need. Silence."

The smirk widened. "Good job. You must be a terrific writer." He bounced up and down on his toes. "If that's all you wanted, I'll go for my run now."

"Good."

"Great."

When was he leaving? Oh and which way? She hoped Daddy had warned him. "Do you even know what direction to go?"

His arms crossed his chest. "I suppose you want to instruct me on the best route."

"Yes, and if you have any sense, you'll listen."

~~~

Sam's jaw clamped shut, and he turned his back on the crazy cat girl. The last thing he wanted was another uppity female bossing him. Even though the worried look in her blue eyes picked at his resolve. Just a little. "I'll be fine. Thanks for caring so much about my well-being." He stepped through the gate.

"Wait. At least take these." From the clatter, she must've hopped up in a hurry. He wouldn't look back though.

Her feet pounded across the concrete, and some sort of cabinet opened and shut near the colossal outdoor grill. Now her footsteps thunked closer until she reached him. She held out a small plastic bag with what looked like wafers in it.

Sam stared at the bag, then his gaze dropped to her feet. She wore the knee-high camouflage boots. "Why are you wearing those snake boots?"

She huffed. "Here. Take the treats. You'll need them."
~~~

"I'm not hungry."

Her chin jutted forward. "These are not for you. They are dog treats, since you refuse any help. Not listening seems to be one of your shortcomings." She grabbed his hand and shoved them into his palm.

"Whatever." He grasped the *treats* and took off at a hard pace down the drive. Why did that woman think he wanted or needed her help? Everything she did aggravated him like a rock inside his shoe.

But it was kind of fun watching her get riled up. And her hands were soft.

Run faster.

At the curb, he jogged in place and glanced both ways. To the left, the water gleamed in the rising sun. The hum of an outboard motor drifted over the waves. Probably an angler. On the right, the road curved with trees blocking the view of the river. He turned left and resumed his stride.

Gravel and broken shells crunched beneath his feet. Overhead, pelicans glided in a V formation below wispy golden clouds. Peace washed over him—a feeling long forgotten. He covered ground with ease. Maybe coming here had been the right choice. Despite the annoying Elinor Elizabeth Bosarge.

Around a curve, the clearing ended, and a wooded lot blocked his view. Squirrels chattered and fussed in the pines. Then another noise ripped the air. Was that a snarl?

Sam's steps slowed as he listened.

From his left, a ferocious bark was followed by the sound of clawed feet tearing down a gravel drive. Uh, oh.

Sam spun to the right and walked back the way he'd come. Running could make things worse. And he shouldn't look the animal in the eye.

The clawing neared with snarling and heavy panting, and he glanced back at his predator.

A muscular Rottweiler barreled toward him. *Lord, help me.*

His hands tightened into fists. The treats. He opened the plastic bag and dumped the contents onto the street behind him. He rolled his eyes as he strode away. Maybe Elinor

Elizabeth Bosarge wasn't all wrong. But he'd never admit it to her.

~~~

This state of affairs simply would not do. That stubborn man. If he didn't leave, she'd call a Realtor to find a hypoallergenic house to rent.

Elinor tapped on the master bedroom door. "May I come in?"

"Of course, hon."

Inside the room, Elinor found her mother on a pink yoga mat at the end of the monstrous four-poster bed. An ankle weight hung near her foot as she lifted her leg up and down. The local news played on the television, the weather man pointing at a tropical storm out in the Caribbean.

Elinor's nose tickled, and she sneezed three times. She glanced up at the spinning ceiling fan. A dust rotator. Her finger flicked the switch to end the toxic breeze.

Her mother grabbed the TV remote. "Let me turn this down." She muted the volume. "I didn't want the noise to bother you, so I'm doing my exercises in here instead of the living room."

"Mother, you don't have to—"

"I've been wanting to ask you something, Elinor. And it's okay to say no. I'll completely understand." Her movement stilled, and lines crinkled her forehead.

What was troubling her mother? Elinor's rib cage squeezed at her stomach. "What's wrong?"

"It's my knees. They're giving out, and the doctor says I need to have total replacements. I've tried to ignore the pain for as long as I could, but I went ahead and scheduled the first surgery for a week after the ball."

"Oh, I didn't know. When you quit playing tennis a couple of years ago, I didn't realize it was because you were in pain." A knife of guilt embedded in Elinor's heart. She hadn't been paying attention. "You want me to stay and help you, and of course, I will."

Her mother's lips curved up, and her eyes glistened. "Thank
~~~

you. It means a lot to me. Otherwise, Roy would have to take off and cart me to the doctor and therapy. You know how scary his driving can be." She chuckled. "I can picture me with my knee bound up, getting jostled all over the car. Your sisters can't come. Cassie's got a new life with her husband, and you know Emma's…well, Emma. But, I could always hire someone."

Elinor moved to the floor beside her mother, offering a hug. "That scenario is unacceptable. You can count on me. I'll take care of you." Her parents had never needed anything from her, and she wouldn't fail them now that they did.

Chapter 5

Showered and dressed in his navy blue suit, Sam checked the knot of his red power tie in the mirror. Good enough. That ought to make an impression. He grabbed his cup of coffee and stood gazing out the windowed wall overlooking the Dog River. Sam took a long sip of the hot brew. Even with the wild beast encounter, the run this morning had been a good one. A change of scenery. A change of pace. Literally.

The door swung open at six-thirty. Big Roy stepped through, and the scent of food hit Sam's nose. "Mornin', son. I brought a couple of Miss Ruby's biscuits with homemade blackberry jam. I know there's protein bars and such in the cabinet, but sometimes a man needs something more substantial and tasty to start a new life."

Sam's mouth watered as Big Roy opened a napkin wrapping the golden bread and held it out. "Thank you, sir."

Big Roy's reddish whiskers lifted with a grin. "You have a good run?"

"You could say that. I broke a personal speed record. With a little canine encouragement."

"Met Roscoe, did ya?"

"Didn't catch a name."

"Gives a new meaning to 'if you can't run with the big dogs, better stay on the porch.'" A jolly chuckle followed as Roy slid the largest Bible Sam had ever seen on the table and took a seat. "We got a big day ahead. Sit, and let's get started right quick." The thin pages flipped under the huge man's thumb and came to rest in Exodus. "We're going to study godly leadership through men in the Old Testament. Sound agreeable to you?"

Sounded like a waste of time, but whatever. "Yes, sir." He

took a bite of the steaming biscuit dripping with blackberry preserves.

"First, how about a prayer? You pray?"

A cough sputtered from Sam's throat as he tried to swallow. "Um, I did this morning on my run, but before that it'd been a while."

"Okay, I don't wanna be puttin' on airs or anything, so I'll do my hard prayin' before I get here, and we'll only have a short one together." He bowed his head and began. "Lord, I ask for You to speak truth into my life and Sam's through Your word. Guide us to be men of honor. Help Sam with the decisions he has to make. In Jesus's powerful name we pray."

After the Bible talk in the boathouse and then a forty-minute drive through traffic, Sam stretched his legs under the extra desk in Big Roy's office. His laptop stood open beside at least a dozen files and a jump drive. His perch on the twentieth floor provided an incredible view with Mobile Bay and the port spread out below. Light shimmered off the ripples in the water where a large ship passed through. The banks on either side held massive terminals which buzzed with activity as men and machinery worked. He ran through the events of the morning. The Bible study hadn't been so bad. Actually, Big Roy had made the talk about Moses interesting. A man who made plenty of mistakes, but God still spoke to him and used him to lead. One verse even said God spoke to him as a friend. What would that be like?

Big Roy entered and clapped his hands. "Alrighty then, Sam-man, we'll meet with the whole staff in thirty minutes. Jody's picking up bagels and juice. Then I'll announce the plan to everyone."

A tinge of doubt picked at Sam. "They won't be too excited to have a consultant hanging around."

"If anyone gives you any trouble, let me know. I'll jerk a knot in their head." His tone became more serious. "Figuratively speaking, of course. Don't want any lawsuits." The man chuckled at himself and took a seat behind the executive desk. "After lunch, we'll meet with Boyd Watson, my financial advisor. He's retiring soon, so you being here is good timing. I'll need to find a new money manager."

Sam typed the name into his notes. "Your call, but are you sure you want me nosing into your personal finances as well?"

"Cassie thinks you're the best money manager in Mississippi, so I'm taking advantage of your know-how while I can. I'd like to retire from my law practice in a few years myself." He slapped the desk. "That's what I forgot to tell you. I knew there was something." He stood, joined Sam at the desk, and opened the top drawer. "Memory Oaks. The Krewe of Hope will donate money raised from the ball to the nursing home this year."

"What exactly is Krewe of Hope anyway? I know a little about Mardi Gras in New Orleans, like parades and all, but..."

"The Krewe is a Mardi Gras organization. You know Mardi Gras in the U.S. started right here in Mobile. I think it was around 1700. Anyway, our Krewe's a little different than most of the others in that we're mainly a philanthropic organization. Sure, we participate in the parade early in the year, but we hold our ball in the summer for charity. It's not so much about the revelry, more about giving to our fellow man. We also hold other events through the year—a king cake tasting to raise money for the children's hospital, a marathon for the hospice center, a red beans cook-off for the homeless…"

"And you want me to look at your Mardi Gras club financials, too?" With all this work, he'd be busy for the next year.

"No. I'd like you to take my place heading up the steering committee for the Memory Oaks renovation since Ruby's having knee surgery. Coordinate the proposal with the funds raised. Our fundraisers are highly attended by the local upper echelon, thanks mostly to my uncle Dale, may he rest in peace. We should get a pretty penny."

"Wait. I'm no expert on construction."

With both hands on the Memory Oaks file, Big Roy set the folder beside Sam's laptop. "First off, we have a couple of experts on architecture and commercial building on the committee, and we don't actually implement the construction, just make the proposal. Second, this is more important and pressing than everything else we've discussed. Research, develop, and finalize a plan the Memory Oaks board will love like their long lost huntin' dog." Roy leveled his gaze on Sam. "I have no doubt you will succeed."

The confidence the man had in him saturated his bruised heart. For all the years he'd worked at the bank, his father had hovered over him, badgering him about each decision. And nothing he'd done had ever been good enough for Teddy Conrad.

~~~

Four hours, and she'd only written five hundred words. Pathetic. Elinor stood and stretched. Why couldn't she clear the fog from her brain? The heroine's thoughts and voice tumbled out with ease, but the hero... Dry. Abysmal. Boring. No one would fall for the bore, and she'd never make her deadline.

Between the news of Mother's surgery, the damage to her cottage, and the dreadful Sam intrusion, her mind drifted in vicious circles. That man. He was at the center of her frustration. The smug smile and those blue eyes. Deep cerulean in the center with dark indigo circles around the edge. Her hero came to mind.

No. Halt.

Sam what's-his-name was not and never would be her muse.

Grabbing her computer, Elinor headed to the main house. At the door, her mother collided with her, a handbag dangling from her wrist.

"Are you leaving, Mother? I thought maybe we could go visit Miss Zula at Memory Oaks."

"Oh, hon, I'd love to, but I have to go down to the Krewe's den to gather decorations, then I'm supposed to have lunch with the other ladies. I'd skip, but with Emma reigning as queen this year, I'm expected to go." Lines crinkled her forehead, and she gave Elinor's arm a gentle touch. "How about you come with me? Then we can go see Miss Zula
~~~

afterward?"

A million times no. Society life had never been for her. "Thanks, but I'll go on to Memory Oaks. I need a quick break, but then it's back to work." No sense making Mother feel guilty about having plans.

"I'm sorry. I didn't know you'd want to do something together."

So much for not making her feel guilty. "It's fine. I go there by myself every week."

The lines loosened. "Okay, but that reminds me. You're so involved volunteering there, you should take my place on the steering committee that's heading up the renovation plan. You'd be great with the interior design piece. If you could make the time, that is."

The idea elevated Elinor's spirits, lifting a bit of the fog from her brain. Redecorating the nursing home for the residents she loved so much could be just the thing to spark her creative juices. "That sounds nice. Inspiring even. I may ask for an extension on this book. It's not going well, anyway." Plus she'd have to take time off because of the surgery.

"Wonderful." Mother's lips lifted in a tender smile. "I'll let the Krewe know."

Chapter 6

Wrinkled fingers curled around Elinor's hand. Last Saturday, her beloved former middle school English teacher had been unresponsive, but today, Miss Zula was having a better day. "Let's move you over to the window for the warm sunshine and a nice view."

Elinor checked the footplates of the wheelchair before unlocking the brake and rolling Miss Zula across the room. The alert residents looked on, waved, and smiled. Elinor stopped to speak to each one. They were such dear people. And maybe the only friends she had.

At least twice a day, the staff led the residents to the living room for socialization and activities, whether the patient could respond or not. Not all the residents had Alzheimer's. Some had suffered strokes, a few experienced other forms of dementia or memory loss, and two were men who came to live with their wives who'd become incapacitated. What kind of love did that take? Incredible.

"Little lady, do you know Jesus?" A gnarled hand waved at her, bringing a smile to Elinor's lips.

"Yes, Brother Hammill. I do." She stopped beside his wheelchair and squeezed his shoulder. "How are you today?"

"Doing pretty good for a young man." The same response he gave every single time, though he was well into his nineties.

"You do look good. Is there anything I can get for you?"

He leaned forward and cupped his mouth. "This place is pretty stingy with the cookies."

The crumbs on his shirt and lap told another story. "I'll find you a treat after I visit with Miss Zula." The thin man could put away the food but stayed the same size. If his metabolism could be patented, someone would make a fortune.

Once she and Miss Zula reached the window, Elinor stopped and mashed down the brake on the wheelchair. She scooted a seat alongside and pulled a book from her handbag.

Beyond the locked windows, centuries-old oaks stood like towering umbrellas shading the grassy lawn. Farther out past the chain-link fence, a ragged rope swing dangled from one of the tree limbs, and an occasional car traveled the old country road that led to the marsh. A small creek ran along the edge of the adjoining property, and stone pavers led to a rickety wooden bridge where a lonesome snowy egret stood among blades of tall grass. The scenery whispered a story, a time when the Memory Oaks residents were young and lived full lives. A time when they loved and laughed and danced. Many had shared their stories with her, at least what they remembered, and she treasured each one. Somehow, the time she spent here filled a bit of the hollow place in her heart.

Elinor glanced at Miss Zula and held up a book. "I brought the work of one of your favorite poets." Opening the tattered pages at a section near the end, her finger slid across the words. How she loved the feel of a real hardback book. "*The Poetical Works of Elizabeth Barrett Browning, Volume 1.*"

After clearing her throat, Elinor began reading. The rhythm of poetry, the beats, and the pacing lifted the older woman's head.

Miss Zula nodded in time with the cadence. "Yes, that's right." Her aged voice trembled, barely audible.

The spark of life in the older woman jolted Elinor, but she continued reading. She hadn't heard her friend speak in weeks. Definitely a good day.

After a few more pages, Elinor stopped. They'd connected through the poems, but perhaps she should give her friend a rest. Setting the book aside, she took Miss Zula's hand. "How was that? As beautiful as you remember?"

No verbal answer, but the woman's hazel eyes met Elinor's and focused for a moment. It seemed the eyes were smiling, and maybe the head of gray, curly hair nodded an answer.

Behind her, Brother Hammill's voice rang out. "Welcome,

fellas. Come on in."

Footsteps padded across the room. "Afternoon, Brother Hammill. I brought a friend with me today."

Daddy? What was he doing here? And with a friend?

She turned as her father introduced the *friend.*

That interloper again. That's what he was. An interloper. Meddler. Intruder. Tension pricked at her scalp. The man made her want to pull her hair out one piece at a time. Why was Sam Conrad at Memory Oaks?

~~~

The elderly man took Sam's hand. Quite a firm handshake for an old guy. "Hello, sir. I'm Sam Conrad."

"I know you. We go way back. Remember? You used to call me Nubbin on account of me cutting off most of my pinky toe that time with your daddy's lawn mower."

Sam pressed his lips together, partly because no words came to mind to answer and partly to hold back laughter at the nickname. Sounded like a funny story. He should go along with the old man's delusion. "Yeah, Nubbin. It's been a long time. How are you?"

"Good. Good." He motioned to a chair. "Pull up a seat and chew the fat."

Now what? Turning toward Big Roy, Sam raised his eyebrows.

Big Roy nodded and looked to be holding back a grin himself. "Go ahead. You two catch up for a few minutes, and then we'll continue on our tour."

Sam pulled a rolling straight-back chair over and sat, one ankle resting over the other knee. "Remind me of that pinky toe story again. I love to hear that one."

"First, let me ask you a question." Nubbin leaned forward, staring Sam in the eye. "Son, do you know Jesus?"

A lump formed in Sam's throat as his equilibrium shifted. First a sunrise Bible study and now this. Not quite the conversation he'd expected.

Before he could answer, another wheelchair rolled over. He glanced up at the passenger, an older woman with wavy gray
~~~

hair. Then he followed the young hands and arms up to the driver. Blue eyes hammered him. And took his breath away a little bit, if he was honest. What was *she* doing here? The control freak cat woman.

"Daddy, why are you here?" Elinor's blue gaze became more intense as it turned his direction. "With him?"

"Hey, darlin'." Her father's arms wrapped her in an embrace as he planted a kiss on her forehead. "Good news. My buddy Sam's here for a tour, so he can head up the steering committee. He's taking my place and is handier than indoor plumbing."

Sam held in a chuckle. He wouldn't go quite that far.

The redness of Elinor's cheeks, along with her white hot glare and clenched jaw, indicated the control freak didn't take this as good news at all.

"Mother asked me to help with the project because I spend time here." Her hand swatted toward Sam as if he were a pesky mosquito. "He knows nothing about the place."

Big Roy stepped back and rubbed the whiskers on his chin for a moment. "Hmm. You do know most of the ins and outs." He snapped his fingers. "I have it. Sam's a money man and you're a knowledgeable insider. You'll make the perfect team to balance each other." He rubbed his large hands together. "Boy howdy, this place will be better than new."

Face crumpling, Elinor's lips pinched together. "We'll talk at home." With a gentle turn of the wheelchair, she walked away, then turned the corner in the hallway and disappeared from sight.

Sam's stomach sank. The last thing he wanted to do was work with Elinor Bosarge on any kind of project. And part of him felt a little sorry for her. She'd looked so…wounded. "Roy, I don't have to be involved with the committee if it's going to cause you problems."

"Nah. Elinor Elizabeth has her conniption fits, but deep down, she's a reasonable girl. Tenderhearted, too. She loves these residents like her own family." He patted Sam's shoulder. "I'll talk to her, and it'll work out. You'll see."

Sam studied his mentor. The man was nice, but he might be a little delusional, too.

Chapter 7

Elinor took her time massaging lotion onto Miss Zula's hands and forearms. The nursing home's empty hair salon served as the perfect hiding place to escape yet another disappointment. How could her father in any way conceive a world where she and that Sam Conrad could work together on an enormous project? A project so close to her heart? Daddy had a bigger imagination than most authors she knew.

A mumble came from Miss Zula, and Elinor glanced at her face. The corners of Miss Zula's mouth lifted a fraction. "That's nice." Her words came as little more than a whisper. Hazel eyes looked out from beneath deep wrinkles and met Elinor's. "I like you."

"I like you, too." Her heart squeezed. The woman hadn't remembered her name in two years, but they still connected. Elinor's career launched as a direct result of Miss Zula's passionate love for literature. In English class, the teacher had linked history and culture with the words and stories. They read aloud, acted out scenes, and produced fun modern interpretations of the older works. The teaching style brought literature to life. Not only that, Miss Zula encouraged her students to find authors they enjoyed and gave them rewards for reading outside of class.

The wooden door swung open, and a nurse entered, pushing a small cart. Her coffee-brown skin beamed next to the pale blue scrubs. "I heard you two were down here beautifying and pampering." Tara's deep, joyful voice held a hint of her father's Jamaican accent despite her mother's Southern heritage. "You wouldn't be hiding, would you now?"

"You caught us." Elinor worked up a smile for her friend. "Miss Zula said she likes me. We're having a wonderful day despite all the shenanigans my father is pulling." If only that were wholly true.

"I'm glad to see her doing better. She's had me worried, not wanting to eat or drink. But what shenanigans would Mr. Bosarge have up his sleeve? No doubt something for his daughter's own good, if I know him as well as I think I do." While she talked, she mixed the finely crushed pills into a cup of applesauce. She moved closer, eyeing Miss Zula. "Let's see, can we get this down without choking, sweetie?" One spoonful at a time, she fed her patient. "Good, girl, now."

Once the container was empty, Tara tossed the trash into a bag on her cart then faced Elinor. "What would be troubling you today? I saw your dear father upstairs."

Elinor huffed. "My dear father has taken on a new person as a project. I can't believe he'd trust someone again after last time. Not only that, he wants me to work with the beastly man on the makeover here. What am I supposed to do? I want to help, but not if I have to be around another one of Daddy's mentees."

"Your father is a good man. He would never intentionally risk hurting his girl. Perhaps he believes you both must learn to trust again. Think of all the ways we fail our Father in heaven, but He keeps pursuing us with His love. Besides, this place needs you to look out for our best interests."

The words crept into Elinor's heart, softening the hard places and barriers she'd built up. "Maybe you're right. But Sam Conrad is the most annoying man I've ever met. I'd rather throw my trust elsewhere."

One side of Tara's mouth lifted, along with one dark eyebrow. "A smiling man who tickles your ears with what you want to hear is not always better than an annoyingly truthful one." She let out a soft giggle and rolled her eyes. "I should know. I married one who drives me out of my mind, but I love him something fierce."

An enormous disparity lay between Tara's funny emergency-room-doctor husband and the sarcastic wealth manager staying in the boathouse. "But your Grayson is wonderful. He's different—a real hero saving lives."

Still, Tara's comments nailed a minuscule hole in Elinor's image of the perfect man. Especially after the silver-tongued Craig.

But not all women were gluttons for punishment. She'd rather be alone than around an irksome man like Sam Conrad.

~~~

Beads, creepy masks, and flamboyant costumes dangled on the walls of the Krewe of Hope's warehouse, or "den" as Big Roy called it. Crates overflowed with purple, gold, and green shiny things. In the center of the room, the Mardi Gras float took up most of the space. A large area filled with boxes of colorful coins labeled doubloons lined one wall along with a stack of clear crates holding hundreds of Moon Pies.

Sam tapped the lid. "Does someone have an obsession for these things or what?"

Big Roy belly laughed. "I reckon it's a mighty big tradition to throw those at the parades. Hurts a lot less than Cracker Jack boxes, too." His hands went to his stomach. "It's not banana puddin', but it'd taste pretty good right about now. Let's break a couple out." He lifted the lid, offering one to Sam and taking one for himself. "You've tasted a Moon Pie, haven't ya?"

"It's been a long time." Like since he was a three-year-old. The wrapper crinkled as Sam peeled it away. He'd need another run tonight. Maybe even chance a swim with the control freak. The layers of chocolate, graham cookie, and sweet marshmallow melted in his mouth. Not bad. Maybe he should bring one back to sweeten up Roscoe on his next run. Or he could try it with Elinor.

Nah. Wouldn't work. And why would he want to anyway?

Roy wiped his whiskers then pulled another snack cake from the box and unwrapped it. "So, Sam, tell me what you dreamt of doin' when you grew up—if no one had turned your steps in another direction."

The ragged pieces of Sam's heart shifted. It had been a long time since he'd laid his dreams to rest. "Sports medicine,
~~~

physical therapy. I majored in biochemistry and was accepted into PT school, but my ex-fiancée and my father shot it down. Insisted I finish my MBA and work at the bank. Since I was red-shirted my first year on the football team, I had an extra year to keep taking classes. Living in a college town, I actually ended up with a good many academic hours." He shrugged. "Taking classes was something to do when I got bored." That and a few less healthy activities.

"Huh." Roy nodded. "An educated man has choices. Near as I recollect, there's a physical therapy school around about these parts." He laughed strong and loud. "For that matter, apply to medical school if you feel like studying another decade."

Sam licked the sticky mess from his fingers. "Not sure I want to go back to school for that long. PT with athletes is more what I'd originally envisioned." His head dipped. "When I had a vision."

"Don't get to feelin' puny." A big hand squeezed Sam's shoulder. "Do what God created you to do. And do it with love. After supper, you fetch that computer of yours and look up where those PT schools are and what it'll take to get accepted again. It may be too late for a spot in the fall, but I'm willing to bet you're good to go for the next year. You'll see."

Sam's mood lifted, along with the pieces of his heart. Big Roy gave him courage, but did he dare dream?

Chapter 8

Sam found his pace. The sound of his feet pounding the asphalt soothed him. There was nothing like the part of the run when his legs got their groove and his mind roamed free. Filling his lungs with the thick warm morning air, he returned to the questions he'd pondered all night. He and Roy had found a PT school nearby. Needing only a handful of good references, he'd be eligible. With Roy's encouragement, he'd applied and worked on getting those references. It would probably help to start observation in a couple of clinics. If he could get a spot, his bank account held enough for three years of tuition and living expenses as long as he managed it well. He could sell his house in Oxford, too.

All he had to do now was make a decision. Easy, right? He puffed out a breath. Funny, now that his dream could become a reality, his mind came up with a thousand reasons to tuck tail and haul it back to the bank. At least he'd been successful as a wealth manager. Made plenty of money. Would he even be good at physical therapy? After all, he wasn't really a touchy-feely kind of guy.

He circled the end of the cul-de-sac, then headed back toward the boathouse. His first meeting with the committee to renovate Memory Oaks started in two hours. He'd prepared his research, and he was ready to deal with the ice queen. Maybe.

But she couldn't be *all* ice. Though he'd steered clear of her to preserve the peace, he'd noticed her interacting with the elderly residents before he'd left the facility. The way she'd held their hands and showered them with kindness. The woman might possess more substance and angles than he'd suspected. He'd only been on the pointy end of her substance and angles so far, though.

The tinkling of wind chimes floated across the muggy breeze as he neared the house. He rounded a massive cyprus tree whose knees sprawled out in wrinkled forms like gothic statues along the road. Splashing and frolicking just beyond, Elinor swam to one side of the pool then flipped over and pushed off to glide back to the other. Her long red hair floated in the water like a moving work of art. Sam's feet halted. He couldn't seem to pull his gaze away from the red, hypnotizing waves.

Stop. He clamped his teeth together. *Snap out of it.*

Were her eyes closed under her shades?

Her feet hit the bottom of the pool, she stood, and lifted the glasses. "Do you think you're at liberty to skulk around, sir?"

Again—who talked like that? "Um. Not skulking. I was going to ask if you wanted to ride to the committee meeting together." He wasn't skulking, was he? "I mean, we're both going." He stepped inside the fence and moved to the edge of the pool.

Elinor ripped the sunglasses from her face. "I think not." Her blue eyes reflected the water and sky as they embedded daggers into his.

"Fine." Sam tipped his forehead. "I get your message loud and clear, missy." Definitely an ice queen. And a control freak. No doubt worse than Tiffany.

Once out of earshot, he stomped around the boat-house, his insides churning. Why did he let that woman irritate him so? He picked up a throw pillow and paced the room.

He stopped and hit himself over the head with the pillow. More than once.

Stay. Away. From. Women.

The safest course in life.

Alone.

~~~

Elinor chewed her lip as she stood at the boathouse door, wrapped in her towel but still dripping. She'd been rude.
~~~

Mostly because he'd caught her off-guard. And maybe another reason she couldn't pin down right at this moment.

She should apologize, though. But she still wasn't riding with him anywhere. Her hand hovered near the door, preparing to knock. Through the window, motion caught her eye. She craned her neck to peek past the open blinds. What was he doing? Hitting himself with a pillow? Now that was weird. Too weird. She'd apologize at the meeting.

An hour later, she entered the boardroom next to her father's office. She smiled at memories of their special lunch dates. He had always made time for each daughter, and he'd allowed them to play school in the boardroom on occasion when their mother was busy. Her throat itched a little as she took a breath, and she cleared it. Three sneezes squeezed out. Probably the carpet holding dust.

Since she arrived first, Elinor moved toward the head of the table by the entry. She paused at the huge binder and laptop that sat in the rolling leather chair and took in a slight scent of crisp linen and woods.

"Don't touch that."

Elinor's head snapped toward the voice entering the double doors. That Sam fellow lurking around again. And bossing. "I didn't see your things until I pulled the chair out." Her chin rose a bit. "You shouldn't put your laptop there. It could get broken."

"The receptionist was clearing the table after an earlier meeting. Thanks for caring, though." His tone and pointed stare effectively shushed her.

Oh, that man. Why'd he have to show such a lack of decorum? She couldn't force out the apology she'd planned, so she dragged her feet toward the window at the other end of the long table. Like an anchor around her neck, Sam Conrad sunk her mood. His attitude confirmed her luck with men. None.

Committee members filtered in. Strangers so far. Good. She hadn't shut herself off in a cottage on a quiet section of beach just because of her allergies and her writing.

Sam hurried to greet each new arrival, hobnobbing as if he

owned the place. She'd mostly seen him in running shorts until this meeting. Not that he looked bad in the shorts, but his dark pinstriped suit fit nicely over his broad shoulders. The sleeves ended at the perfect place on his wrists, and the trousers just touched his loafers. Obviously tailored well. The navy brought out glints of gold in his hair and made his cerulean eyes pop.

Oh my. She'd been staring, and now he crossed the room toward her.

His arm brushed hers as he neared. One side of his mouth raised into that smirk he did so well. "Take a picture if you want."

Of all the nerve. "Each day confirms my opinion of you further."

"Hate to break it to you, missy, but I didn't come to Mobile to get your opinion." He passed her and powered on the interactive whiteboard adjacent to the window.

Elinor flopped into her chair and let her chin rest on her palms. The man would be her undoing.

~~~

The filter just didn't work around that woman. "Let's get this meeting started." Sam checked his watch. Looked like most everyone was here. If they weren't, too bad. Nothing annoyed him more than tardiness. It wasn't professional. If they didn't care enough to show up on time, he didn't need their input. He opened the three-ringed binder of Alzheimer's and dementia studies and other ideas he'd found in his online research. "First, let's go around the table and introduce ourselves quickly. Tell us your field of expertise. I'm Sam Conrad, a financial consultant for Mr. Bosarge."

Elinor's gaze nailed him as if he'd made that up. His muscles flinched. Essentially that was his job. For now. Why'd she have to get under his skin?

Each attendee gave a brief introduction. The architect and commercial construction guys had made it. With only six others in the group, the decision-making should be a breeze.

But at the other end of the table, Elinor sat, her chin on her hand, lips pouty as usual.
~~~

"Your turn."

"I'm Elinor Bosarge—"

"Oh, Elinor Elizabeth Bosarge." From the door, a woman called as she entered. "You've graced Mobile with your presence." Another woman trailed the first, and they took brisk steps to the end of the table and sat. "You probably know her better as author Liz Hart, her pen name. She tries to keep it under wraps, though."

Both women wore outfits that made them look as though they were headed to Rodeo Drive instead of a business meeting. The one speaking had squeezed into a silk top, short skirt, and red heels. Her brown bangs topped a face covered with makeup that more rivaled the eighties styles than anything in this decade. She was attractive, though, in a Tiffany sort of way.

Sam's stomach churned at the thought. He turned his attention to Elinor. Her cheeks sagged as the women scooted in close beside her. He'd heard of the author Liz Hart. Maybe seen a movie made from one of her books? Could the ice-queen-control-freak really be a romance writer?

Earlier, he'd been too annoyed to notice Elinor's appearance. Okay, other than her red hair and blue eyes. She wore a white long sleeve blouse. Maybe he'd noticed a black skirt and matching low heels, after all. An appropriate outfit for business. And muscular calves.

"I'm Lexi Downing. I graduated high school with Elinor, and this is my friend Keely Tisdale." The Rodeo Drive chick pointed at the woman next to her. "Keely and I went to Auburn together. She's just married a Krewe member and was dying to get involved, so here we are."

Keely stood and held up a laminated picture of what looked like a fancy resort. "I'd like to move that we sell the current property of Memory Oaks and relocate it to another piece of real estate. I have an interested buyer who thinks the current location would be perfect for a resort on the bay and bring a ton of money in for the nursing home. Of course, I have plenty of alternate locations to suggest for the facility for the elderly."

~~~

No, no, no. This couldn't be happening. Elinor twisted her neck to the side and kneaded the muscles in an attempt to release the tension forming there. That Lexi Downing and her friend. What was it? Keely? It was bad enough that Lexi had announced her pen name in front of everyone. And Sam. In the five years since her first bestseller, she'd managed her dual identity pretty well. And in three seconds, Lexi had ruined that. And now she and Keely thought they'd move Memory Oaks away from the bay. They'd have to run over her body with a bulldozer before that happened. "I don't think—"

"I hate to interrupt all you ladies." Sam laced his fingers in front of him and cleared his throat. He directed his gaze to Keely. "May I ask if either of you are real estate agents?"

The sign in Keely's hands lowered. "I am."

"Were you original members of this committee? I don't have your names listed."

"I just joined. Like Lexi said, I'm trying to get involved."

Sam stood and opened the door to the conference room. Wide. "I appreciate your eagerness, but it appears you have a conflict of interest. Perhaps Lexi does, too? The Krewe of Hope is presenting and funding a plan for upgrading the facility. Not selling or taking over management. The final recommendation will be ap-proved by the nonprofit board that runs Memory Oaks." He motioned toward the door with his head. "Thanks for your charitable interest, though. Try getting involved on another committee."

Inside, Elinor both giggled and screamed for joy as the women huffed and left. For once, the man's rudeness worked in her favor. If only the rest of the meeting would go this well.

After Lexi and friend left, Sam loaded a slide from his computer onto the interactive whiteboard and stood to the left of it. "As I said, the goal is to offer a plan to the Memory Oaks board for approval. We'll start with a list of requests from the facility, vet those, and establish priorities. Once we take a look at the requests, you can throw out an idea or concern." He clicked through each item. When he finished the talking points,
~~~

he took a seat.

"Questions? Concerns? Ideas?"

An older gentleman Elinor recognized as a friend of her father's smiled. "Thank you, Mr. Conrad. I'm glad you put a lid on those two." His thumb pointed toward the door. "My father moved to Memory Oaks two months ago. Personally, I'd like to see the physical therapy room enlarged and new equipment purchased. Maybe fund another therapist or assistant, depending on the numbers."

Sam's eyes widened, and his mouth hung half open for a second. Finally, he nodded. "Good."

Each person spoke. Of course, he asked Elinor's opinion last. She took her time before speaking. "All lovely suggestions. I'd add that I'd like to see cosmetic improvements. A good coat of paint. Maybe yellow to brighten the place. New light fixtures. Artwork hung at eye level from a wheelchair. More stimulating activities."

Sam raised one finger. "The art will have to be planned specifically for dementia patients, as well as the activities and lighting. Not terrible ideas, but they'd need to be tweaked. No yellow paint."

Unnerving. Of course, he wouldn't be agreeable to any of her suggestions. "And why not?"

Instead of answering, Sam passed out packets of information in folders. "Study these articles before the next meeting, and we'll discuss each topic further."

Chapter 9

Blasting through the door of her parents' house, Elinor muffled a scream. The ones in the car had been much louder. Maybe she should start writing horror literature instead of romance. Stories that centered on torturing wealth managers. A variety of scenarios came to mind.

Her mother stuck her head out from the kitchen. "The meeting went that bad?"

"Worse than bad. Dreadful. Abysmal. Horrendous." Elinor pressed her fingers to her temples as a headache began. "Between Lexi Downing and her friend wanting to relocate Memory Oaks and that Sam rejecting my ideas, I don't know what was worse."

"Relocating?" Mother's eyes widened. "She wasn't even on the committee."

"Fortunately, Sam thwarted her plans, too." The one tolerable act since he'd arrived. "I'm going to gather my beach attire and drive out to the cottage. I want to check in on the repairs and take a walk on the shore. Maybe swim in the surf."

"You've got time. Your sisters won't be in until really late, and I had dinner catered. Except Emma's favorite bread pudding, and I've got it ready to bake when she gets here."

A landslide of pain shot through the nerve endings in Elinor's forehead. "That's tonight? Emma gets here tonight?" Oh, please, no. She struggled to keep her expression more surprised than mutilated.

Her mother wrapped her arms around Elinor's shoulders. "It's okay you forgot, but let's be supportive of your sister while she's queen of the court. What if I go to the beach and walk with you?"

"You don't have to." Besides, time alone might help her

throbbing head.

A wistful smile curled Mother's lips. "Everything's about done, and I may not get to walk in the sand for a while after the surgery. We could even take the Dauphin Island Ferry over."

Guilt stabbed her. How could she say no to that? Of course, she wanted to spend time with her mother. It was just a few bad days getting under her skin. "You should come. We'll have a nice stroll and play in the waves." But where was the ibuprofen?

Two hours later, seagulls scattered as Elinor left the boardwalk. The state of the cottage repairs did little to ease her headache. Wires dangling, hammers pounding, and the mess… *Enough.* Water, shore, and sunshine lay before her. A favorite picture framed for her by God. Her place of refuge and peace. Feet sinking into the sand, she walked beside her mother. The nice thing about her mother was she never felt the need to fill every moment with conversation.

Once they reached the edge of the water, Elinor stretched up and down on her toes. Her calves missed the workout of beach walking. Just a few feet out on the surf, a pelican torpedoed beneath the water to capture a fish.

"I love it here." Her mother offered a tender look. "I know you've missed the beach and your writing these past few days. I feel bad now that I got you onto that committee. Those meetings can be torturous when you're not used to them."

"It's a good thing you asked me. You know I'll fight for what's best for Memory Oaks, and I'd be furious and helpless if I weren't involved." She shot Mother a smile. "This way I'm just furious."

Laughing, her mother turned toward the end of the peninsula. "I won't be able to walk as far as you normally do, but let's have at it."

The ocean breeze pushed against them, blowing its fingers through Elinor's hair. There was nothing like the beach. Her headache dissolved, her emotions calmed. She would protect Memory Oaks and take care of her mother after the surgery.

And be nice to her baby sister, Emma. Somehow.

A good bit more sensible, her older sister, Cassie, had been easy to get along with. The only downside to Cassie visiting would be watching her with the new husband. The two were such love birds. Always kissing and holding hands. Cassie deserved happiness, but it served to reinforce her own bleak love life.

Low gray clouds hovered on the distant horizon with hints of blinding silver radiating around the edges. If only her heart could find that place above the gray.

~~~

"Let's blow this pop stand and go out to the docks." Big Roy clapped his hands, then rubbed them together. "I'll show you how I came up."

Blinking, Sam shrugged and closed his laptop. "Okay." A load of work waited, and temperatures soared into the upper nineties outside. Plus, he really wanted to start digging into the personal investments. Stocks, bonds, mutual funds. Not to nose around, but because he actually knew what he was doing. Roy was the boss, though.

Within half an hour, they were on the cement port staring at a massive cargo ship. Every man they passed knew Roy and stopped to share some tall tale they'd heard on one of the ships. Equipment hummed and rumbled, transferring loads or supplies. Rows of massive containers and drums lined the river.

Sam wiped his brow. If only he'd been able to change out of his good suit before he came here. What was the point of this visit anyway? He wasn't looking to be a deckhand. The only boats he'd spent time on were ski boats and fishing boats, many times listening to his father schmooze the next big client.

Moving farther, Roy pointed as he walked. "I spent a lot of years on these docks. Our trailer was outside of Mobile in a little place called Wilmer. My father was a no-account. He'd get a job, make enough money to give my mother a bit, then go get drunker than Cooter Brown and wake up in Biloxi or Pensacola. Momma and me would go haul him home. Then
~~~

he'd start over." His feet stopped, and his eyes met Sam's. "Momma got sick, and you might find this hard to believe, but I was a bit of a rascal as a young boy. So, my great uncle Dale Bosarge and his wife took me in."

Sam studied the big man. Not the kind of life story he'd expected, but it explained a lot. "That had to be rough."

Roy's lips pressed down as his gaze went out to the water. "Never saw my daddy again after one of his trips. And he wasn't dead. Just an ol' polecat. Momma got well, married a new husband, and moved to Nevada. I saw her a few times over the years." He turned and leveled his gaze back on Sam. "I was blessed. The best things that ever happened to me came through those hard times. I met Jesus and my Ruby."

So this was a lesson. Sam bobbed his head. "I get it. Someone helped you, and now you help others."

"And?"

A lesson and a test. "Your hard times made you stronger."

"And?"

Quickly becoming an annoying test. Sam threw his hands up. "I don't know."

"It led me to Jesus and the other love of my life."

Did Roy want to take him to church, or fix him up with a nice girl, or both? Because that wasn't why he'd come. "I'm glad for you."

Based on the cloudy look on Roy's face, that had been the wrong answer. But that was all he had to say.

A flock of seagulls took sudden flight off a pier, squawking and screeching above them. A second later, something splatted on Sam's head and shoulder. A wet, sickening something. Not the suit. Again.

Of all the rotten timing. He had to be standing under them when…

Roy chuckled and slapped Sam's back. "Occupational hazard. Let's get out of this heat." He glanced at the mess on Sam's suit. "We better go to the house instead of the office, because you're a sight. The girls are coming home tonight, anyway. Plan to have supper with us. After you change."

Sam cringed. Would his timing be any better at dinner, or would he be dumped on again, this time by Elinor Elizabeth Bosarge?

Chapter 10

"Daddy!" A shrill voice echoed through the living room.

Mashing a finger to his ringing ear, Sam stood. The voice didn't belong to Elinor, who'd just come down the stairs, or Cassie, so it must've been the younger sister, Emma.

Roy rushed to meet the tall blue-eyed blonde as she entered, then lifted her off the ground. "Here's my baby girl about to be the queen of the ball." He kissed the top of her head as he set her on her feet. "Where's Cassie? I swanny, I'm like a pig eatin' slop, I'm tickled pink to have all three of my girls in the same house this week."

The girl looked familiar. He'd probably seen her with Cassie at some point. Sam stepped forward. "I'm Sam Conrad. Nice to meet you."

A grin lit up the boisterous blonde's face. "Hey, Sam Conrad, but we've met in Oxford. Everyone calls me Em now. You can, too. I'm still trying to train the family." She locked his elbow in hers. "You look nice and strong. Come help me unload my things. Being the queen demands a lot of suitcases."

Chuckling, Sam allowed her to lead him. How did these three sisters come from the same parents and turn out so differently?

The door opened, and petite Cassie clattered in rolling the largest suitcase Sam had ever seen. He extended his hand to take the handle. "Let me get that, and I'll carry it upstairs."

"Thanks. It's Em's."

Roy poked his head out the door. "Where are the men folk?"

Cassie stretched, smothering a yawn. "Dylan will be here in a day or so. I wanted to come on with Em to help get things ready and go to the luncheon. Oh, and Benjamin has ballgames and is staying with a friend."

After releasing Sam's arm, Em patted her father. "My date had to work, but he'll be along tomorrow night." She squealed. "I couldn't wait to get down here and get this party started."

As Elinor and her mother exited the kitchen to greet them, Em's head turned in the direction of Mr. Darcy's painting leaning against the wall. Her lips quirked in a dramatic downturn. "What? No." She pointed. "We can't have that hideous cat painting in the house where my friends might see it."

The dejected drop to Elinor's shoulders pulled at Sam's gut. He'd obviously upset her earlier at the committee meeting, and he felt bad enough about that. "You can put it in the boathouse by the fireplace. There's room." Had he really offered to put that freak of nature's picture where he had to see it before bed every night? He swallowed back a gag. Until her sky blue eyes caught his and brightened. A pleasurable warmth replaced the heaving sensation.

Roy put Em in a teasing headlock and rumpled her hair with his knuckles. "Don't start aggravating your sister." When he let her go, he flexed one arm. "And I may be three days older than dirt, but I can still tote the suitcases for you girls. No need troubling our guest. Y'all sit down to supper, and I'll be along in a jiffy."

Crossing the room, Elinor lifted the picture as if it were a basket of eggs. "I'll carry this over so it doesn't get banged up."

Of course she didn't trust him to do anything. Sam couldn't stop the smirk. The least she could do is thank him.

As she passed him, she slowed and lifted those blue eyes to meet his. "Your offer is honorable and appreciated. I know how you detest my pet." With that, she lifted her chin and continued out the door.

Her words both pleased and stung. In all reality, he didn't know the cat well enough to detest it. And he'd seen hurt in her eyes that ripped at him both this morning and just now. Maybe Roy was right. Elinor Bosarge was a sensitive soul.

Way too sensitive for him.

~~~

How would she endure her little sister and Sam? Plus, Lexi and friends attending the ball? Elinor sighed as she trudged to the boathouse. It was only this week for Em and Lexi. Sam—another story. How long would the man impose on her family?

She leaned the portrait against the fireplace and looked around. The place held the slight scent of men's cologne. Woodsy with a bit of linen. Same scent she'd noticed in the conference room. Not unpleasant. At least the obnoxious man smelled nice. And he'd kept the place tidy. Too bad she couldn't stay here where it was quiet, but she'd better get to the house for dinner.

Back inside, the others had seated themselves at the long dining room table. Of course the only place left at the table was next to Sam.

"I'm back." Not as though they'd missed her.

Her father held out his hands. "Take a seat, and we'll say a blessing, then."

Oh great. She settled herself next to Sam. Now she had to hold hands with the man, whose eyes slid toward her. His arm still close to him, he extended his hand. Not far though. Obviously not in his comfort zone either. She lay her hand on his. Barely. His fingers folded over hers. Not too much pressure, just nice. If that were possible.

"Amen," her father ended.

Somehow she'd missed the whole prayer.

"I can't wait to dig into that mess of greens you bought. And cornbread." Her father smiled at his wife as he spooned the food onto his plate, passed the bowl, and then turned to Sam. "This caterer is the best. Aside from my Ruby's cooking, that is."

"So, Nora, how's the new book?" Em took a serving of black-eyed peas.

Nora? Not that ridiculous nickname. "It's Elinor, and I put this manuscript on hold for a bit."

"That's not like you. You're usually writing like your hair's on fire. Barely stopping to notice anyone else. Except that thief
~~~

Craig."

Elinor's stomach catapulted to her throat. How could she? One minute into dinner.

Her father laid his fork on his plate with a clang. "Bridle that tongue, little miss."

"Yes, sir." Pretending to be sorry, Em addressed Sam. "Did you know Nora's a famous author under a secret name? She writes historical novels set in the 1800s, which explains why she talks so weird half the time. Like she lives back with Jane Austen or something."

Cassie elbowed Em, shaking her head.

That was what Em thought bridling her tongue meant? Elinor squeezed her eyes shut.

"I heard about the books." Sam's voice. "I think I've seen a movie based on one of them. Very impressive."

What? Sam saying something nice? Opening her eyes, Elinor gawked. "I'd prefer to write literary fiction, but it doesn't pay the bills. I'd once hoped to be a literary master."

"Does explain a few of your verbal idiosyncrasies." He paused and scraped his fork around his plate. "And I almost married what one might call a swindler myself. Happens to the best of us."

A lump formed in Elinor's throat. A barb, then a heart-wrenching confession. What should she say? "I'm impressed at your correct usage of the word idiosyncrasies, sir."

He gave her the smirk again.

~~~

Why did he even try to be nice to this woman? Much less bring up the most humiliating point in his life? Maybe because the little sister seemed set on embarrassing Elinor. No wonder she had the middle child complex. Cassie was smart, professional, and controlled. A hard act to follow. Then to have the needling blond beauty for a baby sister. He had sisters and knew how they fought.

A laugh erupted from Roy. "Y'all would've split a gut today down at the docks. Sam-man is handier than a coat pocket to have around, but you should've seen his face when a flock of
~~~

gulls christened him and his fancy suit."

A sound came from Elinor. A high-pitched giggle which sounded like it should've come from a baby dolphin. She held her hand over her mouth, but the giggle became more pronounced until she bent over in an all-out laugh.

Sam frowned. "It wasn't that funny." The baby dolphin sound came harder, until he couldn't help laughing himself. "Well, it did happen right after your dad tried to church me and maybe offer to find me a woman. I don't know. I blew him off, and then I got bombed. Felt like a big egg cracked on my head and oozed."

Tears ran down Elinor's cheeks. Hearing her laugh opened up a long-forgotten place in his heart. Even if she was laughing at his expense.

"Good grief, Nora." Em pounded the table. "I don't think I've seen you laugh in two years, since—"

"Uh-uh, little miss." Roy shot her a hard look.

Why wouldn't Em give it a rest? Let the woman laugh.

A lamp crashed to the ground as Dashwood chased Mr. Darcy around the living room. The whole group turned to stare.

Elinor jumped to her feet. "No. Dashwood! Bad dog! Leave him alone."

The dog stopped, and the cat turned to face his attacker head-on. Spitting, Mr. Darcy stood on his hind legs like an angry bear and stared down the dog. The cat's paws went crazy, pelting poor Dashwood. The dog winced and took off down the hall, the cat chasing after him.

"Oh, no. I hope Mr. Darcy is okay." Elinor rounded the table.

Sam cleared his throat. "I'd say Mr. Darcy just gave the dog a butt-whooping. I'm impressed."

A small curl lifted the pout from Elinor's lips. A real smile. Wow. "I'll go check on them both, just the same."

Once she left, Em took over. "You know the last man Daddy helped asked Elinor to marry him, then stole our cash and Momma's jewelry and pawned it right about time for the

Krewe ball that year. Took off to gamble."

Cassie nodded. "Broke her heart."

"I didn't realize what a pole cat he was until too late." Roy's mouth turned down. "A gambling addict. His daddy had died on a rig, and his momma asked me to try to get him back straight, but—" he shook his head—"he was a slippery one."

Poor Elinor. "Did you get anything back?" He knew the harsh reality of betrayal.

"We recovered some of the jewelry from pawn shops here to Biloxi. The money, no. You can't get blood from a turnip."

Em rolled her eyes. "Daddy talks like a redneck with all his sayings, but he's as smart as can be."

Ruby gazed at Roy. "Part of his charm. He doesn't put on airs. I call them Royisms. They're cute, like my Roy."

Royisms. That fit. Sam imagined what it would be like growing up in this house. Not perfect, but obviously Ruby and Roy adored each other and tried their best to keep the peace. Not so much like his house. His moody, controlling father kept his mother a nervous wreck. A tiny bit of chaos, like here, would've been better than the festering tension any day.

Elinor reentered. "They're fine. I put Mr. Darcy back in my room for a while. They don't usually fight, but normally we're in the boathouse."

Another little dig.

"So, Nora. Tell Sam some of your terrible first date stories."

Elinor's cheeks dropped, and the pout formed back over those lips. "I'm not very hungry. If y'all don't mind, I'll excuse myself to go write. I have an idea pressing."

Ruby nodded. "Of course, hon. Leave your plate. I'll save it for later in case you get hungry."

So much for the smiling, dolphin-giggling Elinor. Sam's heart squeezed. He'd enjoyed seeing another side of her. Even when she was laughing at him.

Chapter 11

Curled in a ball on Elinor's lap, Mr. Darcy purred. Elinor scratched under his chin. "You're a brave kitty, aren't you?" Like a replaying song, Sam's words bounced in her mind. He'd probably only been nice to her so he could be rude to Em. The same as earlier in that meeting. Bossing and rudeness were his way.

But still. It had been pleasant to have someone on her side. She rubbed Mr. Darcy's bald head and attempted to open her laptop with her other hand. Working for a few minutes would be a welcome distraction from the stressful day. New ideas thrummed in her imagination for her hero. Tall and cynical, but deep down, he had a good heart. Maybe blue eyes. Perhaps she could save this novel after all.

One knock on the door, and it swung open. Em's head popped around the frame. "Can I come in?"

Why not? She would anyway. So much for hero ideas. Plucking at a loose string on the covers, Elinor nodded.

With rapid steps, Em crossed the room and threw herself onto the bed. Mr. Darcy flinched at the movement, digging his claws into Elinor's leg.

"Ouch." Elinor nabbed the cat's paws. "Em, you're scaring Mr. Darcy."

"I'm sorry." Blue eyes batted and looked up at her like a big puppy. "Mom said I upset you downstairs and should apologize."

"Mom said?" Was that the only reason Em had troubled herself? "Forget about it."

"No. I'm really sorry." Em rolled up on one elbow. "I was trying to be funny, I guess, and didn't think it would bother you so much."

Tearing at the wreckage of past mistakes? Funny? Steam piped to Elinor's ears. "What if I'd started blabbing about when your boyfriend cheated on you with your best friend? Or the time you drove your car into that fraternity house?"

"I wouldn't like it." Moisture filled Em's big eyes. "I don't know why I say such crazy stuff. It just blurts out." She sniffed and squeezed Elinor's hand. "I'm really sorry. Forgive me?"

Pinching her lips together, Elinor bobbed her head. She'd never been able to stay mad at her little sister, no matter how unbearable her behavior. "Sometimes I blurt out completely idiotic words, too. Maybe it's hereditary."

Em laughed and rubbed Mr. Darcy's head. "It skipped Cassie, and I got a double dose."

"I won't dispute that." Elinor chuckled. "Want to find Cassie and watch *Sense and Sensibility*?"

"Always." After hopping to her feet, Em rushed to the door. "I'll get her and bring you a dish of bread pudding. You missed dessert."

Warmth for her sister filled Elinor's chest. "That would be nice."

Before she disappeared, Em poked her head back in one more time. "You think Sam's hot, don't you?"

"Of course not." She huffed. "Go. Before I change my mind."

"Change your mind about him being hot?" A giggle echoed down the hall.

"Insufferable little sisters." Elinor's head fell back against the wooden bed frame with a thud. Sam wasn't hideous or anything, but she didn't think he was *hot*.

Did she?

~~~

Sighing, Sam shut the door to the boathouse and fell onto the couch. His belly filled with all that country cooking and his brain exhausted from the long day, he stretched his legs and grabbed the remote. In front of him loomed the huge painting of the hairless cat. A shiver ran across his shoulders. It was like the thing was staring at him no matter where he moved.
~~~

Why had he felt sorry for Elinor? Of course, he'd rather have a painting of her than that ugly cat beside the fireplace. The image flashed of long red hair cascading around those blue eyes. Impossibly blue.

He shook his head. Maybe he'd go sit on the bed and work. After pushing to his feet, he turned his back to the skulking portrait and fought the urge to run to the bedroom. All the reading he normally did waited on his computer. Reviewing the markets around the world, studying the previous days' effects on mutual funds, checking news on companies where he had major holdings.

At least a thousand emails sat in his inbox when he opened it. Didn't his father have another manager taking care of his clients? He ought to check the important ones first. The monthly financial statements should've gone out, and his clients may be wondering why he left. Should he compose a letter to each one? A blanket email to all?

As he glanced through, message after message appeared from his father, each more angry than the last, insisting he return at once.

He looked to his phone. He'd kept his phone on silent all week for that very reason, but it looked like his father had tried a dual attack through email and phone. The voicemail storage had finally filled. Tiffany's name was among the callers, too. Sam lifted the cracked screen and scrolled through. He really needed to get this thing repaired. His finger hesitated over her number. What in the world did his ex-fiancé think she could say to get him to come back and manage her new inheritance? He pressed delete over her name and over all the calls from his father. Left the list a lot more manageable. He did the same on his laptop.

The least he could do was explain his departure to his customers. Better to get this over with because he was starting a new life. Wasn't he?

Staying here might not be the best idea with all the Bosarge family had going on. And one of them really hoped he'd leave. He paused and let his head fall back.

The name Liz Hart came to mind. Elinor's pen name. Maybe he'd download one of her books. For a laugh. He could put off contacting clients a little longer. His fingers flew across the keyboard of his laptop. A minute later, Sam lost himself in the 1800's.

~~~

The trill song of a mockingbird outside the window opened Elinor's eyes. Sunlight streamed across the room. Beside her on the bed lay Em and Cassie. She twisted her neck to release stiff muscles. The new hypoallergenic mattress was too firm, but her parents had been kind to try to help with her allergies.

Em woke with the movement. "Oh, shoot, we have nail appointments this morning before the luncheon." She nudged Cassie. "When do you ever sleep this late?"

Blinking, Cassie rolled off the edge of the bed. "When my sisters keep me up all night." She smiled. "I'll get ready as soon as I have a quick cup of coffee."

Em turned her attention to Elinor. "You're going, too, right?" The big eyes again.

With a groan, Elinor folded her arms. "You know the smell at the nail salon irritates my lungs." And the women at the luncheon would irritate the rest of her.

"Pretty please? I want you with me."

"I'll do my best. Even if it kills me." Not like Em would accept asthma or even death as an excuse anyway.

Hours later, Elinor dove into the pool. Her eyes and nose still burned from the smell of acetone and nail polish, but at least the luncheon hadn't been so bad. Floating in the water, she allowed her head to relax. Tonight, more guests would arrive for a Krewe seafood boil. How much more socializing could she take?

Long shadows fell over her, and she lifted her head to find her father and Sam. "Yes?"

"Don't just lay there like a bump on a log, sugar. Come on out with me and Sam to check the crab traps." Her father held out a towel. "It won't take but an hour, maybe two."

"What? Why?" She kept her gaze locked on her father.
~~~

"You don't need me to go."

"Your momma said you'd probably rather get out on the boat than help set up in the yard." Shaking the towel, he grinned. "You can show Sam a thing or two. He's never been."

Crabbing would be easier on her allergies than setting up for company on the grass. It had been a long time since she'd made so many concessions. Had her own reign as queen been such a bother for the family? Hopefully not. "If you need me, I guess I'll help. But no going up the river. Only out toward the bay." She kicked her feet to swim to the ladder.

Laughter belted from her father. "Okay. Just toward the bay. Get your snake boots, but leave the pistol. I like my new boat."

One of Sam's brows rose. "Sounds like a story behind that one."

Her father's index finger flew to his mouth. "Ruby's banned us from telling stories about Elinor."

Blinking against the searing heat both from the sun and the thought of Sam hearing her stories, Elinor took the towel. She dried off and plodded over to her boots. Mentioning a story without telling the story equaled to the same thing, and Sam stood waiting. She turned the tall shoes upside-down and pounded them on the concrete. One never knew what could get in when no one was looking. After slipping on the boots, she pulled her white cover-up dress over her wet swimsuit. "I'm ready if you are."

"Atta, girl." Her father led them around the boathouse to the slips where two boats waited. One was a smaller skiff, the other a much larger vessel made to fish offshore. He stepped into the smaller one, his weight shifting the boat as he moved around. "I'll check under the seats and all for you. No sense you being as nervous as a long-tailed cat in a room full of rocking chairs."

The corners of Sam's lips turned down, and his eyes shifted to watch her from the side. Smug again.

Of course Daddy had to make a big production of looking around. She may as well spill the story and get it over with. She flung her hand out. "A few years ago, up river, a water moccasin dropped from a tree into our boat. Beside me. It was gargantuan, and its white mouth hissed at me, so I grabbed a pistol and shot it. A few times." Her chest tightened at the memory. "In the bottom of the boat."

A sound barked from Sam's throat.

What was that? "Are you laughing?"

His lips turned up, and the sound continued. Sam pressed his fist to his mouth and nodded.

"You sound like a seal with a cough," she said.

Another bark, and his head whipped toward her. "That coming from a woman who laughs like a baby dolphin." He mimicked the sound.

She laughed like a dolphin? Why was everyone set on humiliating her?

The smirk appeared on Sam's face. "How soon did the boat sink after you blasted holes in the hull?"

"Daddy got us to the shore before the boat sank…all the way."

"You can get in now. It's clear." Her father held out a hand to her, and she took a cautious step into the boat. "We'll check the traps near the bridge pilings and come back."

Elinor took a seat at the front, avoiding Sam's stare. What was the man gawking at?

~~~

The image of Elinor blasting bullets into the bottom of a boat shook Sam's chest. He hadn't laughed that hard in a long time. Of course, it was pretty cool that she knew how to shoot a gun. As they left the pier, he took in her red hair falling down along her shoulders in damp strands. The white cotton dress she wore over her bathing suit only served to further bring out the deep fiery color. He should tear his gaze away, but the woman captured his attention like a slow train wreck. She was a fragile enigma. Perplexing and strange. And a tiny bit beautiful.

She cast a glance at him over her shoulder and caught him staring. Her brows knitted together. Above the hum of the
~~~

motor, she yelled, "What?" Her unflinching gaze stabbed him.

How long had he been staring? "I didn't say anything." Breathing in a lungful of Gulf air, Sam willed his pulse to calm. So he'd been looking. She was right there, after all. Not like he could help it. "I'm sitting here taking in the view."

"The view?" She scoffed.

Not at all what he'd meant to say. "The water and the birds." With his head, he motioned toward a heron by the shore. "See? A bird."

Down the waterway, the motor quieted as Roy stopped at a buoy, seemingly oblivious to the discussion. "Here's the first trap. Let's check this play-pretty and see what we got." Leaning over the edge, he caught the floater in his hands and pulled the line.

Carrying a large bucket, Elinor moved to join her father.

"No one steals from you?" Sam watched on as they worked.

Hand over hand, Roy tugged the basket closer. "Every now and then, some rascal will poach a crab trap, but not often. Most of us know each other round here."

The container came up, dripping and crawling with crabs. Elinor stood ready with a net. As Roy shook the basket, she bucketed the wiggling catch. Three pelicans floated over to inspect the action. Likely hoping for a treat.

One large crab escaped and scrambled toward Sam. On instinct, he hopped up, grabbed the crustacean, and tossed it toward the container, but not before a small pincher sliced his skin. "Ouch, he nipped me." He squeezed the bleeding finger with his other hand.

Elinor's blue eyes widened. "Oh, I need to disinfect that. You might get an infection." She turned to Roy. "Are you okay for me to help him, Daddy?"

"I reckon I'll manage. Don't want Sam to get to feeling puny." A smile played on Roy's lips, and he reloaded the cage with bait. "Looks like we'll have a few dozen or so."

After digging through a plastic first-aid kit she'd found under the seat, Elinor approached and seized the injured finger. "This will sting a bit."

"What is—?"

She squirted a clear gel on his cut.

"Oww." He jerked his hand away. "That's hand sanitizer."

"That's the point. I'm sanitizing the wound." She held her palm toward him. "Now if you'll quit behaving like a child, I'll bandage the cut."

Sam's hand stayed in place by his side.

"Do you not understand my request?" Her chin jutted up as she reached out.

"I'll be okay without your bandaging."

"Hordes of germs and flesh-eating bacteria live in these brackish waters. I need to cover that wound."

"Fine." He allowed her to wrap a waterproof bandage over the small cut. Her soft hands cradled his as she examined her work.

"We have time to check at least one or two more." Roy patted the side of the boat. "Everything hunky dory now, sailors? Feeling good?"

The soft fingers released his, but warmth remained where they'd touched. Sam took a seat. "Feeling good." Better than he wanted to feel.

Two hours later, they'd docked with a nice catch and without further incident. After a shower, Sam joined Roy and friends in the yard where fryers and boilers blasted heat into the already warm air. The spicy scent of crab boil combined with fried oysters in the heavy humidity sent a rumble through Sam's stomach. These people knew how to eat.

Cassie and her movie star husband, Dylan Conner, approached. Sam extended his hand. "Good to see you again."

Returning the handshake, Dylan grinned. "Surviving the Big Roy adventure?"

"So far." Sam held up his bandaged finger. "Only a cut, and Elinor's lecture on bacteria. She scalded it with sanitizer and wrapped it up."

Cassie laughed. "Elinor reads too much, researching ailments for her novels. All the stories in the news scare her to death."

"Speaking of scared, her snake phobia cracks me up. Plodding around in those big boots."

The smile faded from Cassie's lips. "I feel responsible for that." She looked away. "One Mother's Day when Elinor was little, I took her out to pick flowers. I wasn't watching, and she went near a culvert. The next thing I know, she's screaming." Cassie's eyes met Sam's. "A copperhead bit her little chubby hand. The wound got so swollen, it had to be lanced, and she was sick for days. Poor baby."

Sam's stomach lurched and his heart ached as he pictured a young, sweet Elinor being scared out of her wits and in pain. He pressed his eyes shut. No wonder the woman was afraid. "How old was she?"

"About four."

What could he say? Now he felt like a jerk for laughing at her. "That would throw anyone for a loop, I guess."

"Elinor's always seemed to have a bit of bad luck and weird health issues." Cassie pointed across the yard. "I better be quiet. Here she comes."

A sleeveless, flowered dress flowed down past Elinor's knees as she walked toward them. Floated, even. Soft rays of the setting sun glistened against her hair, lighting it to the color of fire. Sam's breath hitched at the vision.

Without warning, Elinor hopped up and down on one foot and flung her sandals off. "Oh, oh, stupid fire ants." She ran a ways and swiped her feet, then hopped again. "Ow, ow. I detest these prickly sweet gumballs of torture all over the place." She sneezed three times. A second later, she stopped at a water spigot to rinse her feet. She sneezed a few more times.

Sam eyed Cassie. "I see what you mean about bad luck."

A shriek pierced the air, and Elinor sprinted back toward the house.

Had another snake bitten the poor girl? Sam's heart accelerated, and he ran to catch up. At the back door, he grasped at her shoulder. "What happened? Are you hurt?"

"Yellow jacket sting." Her blue eyes watered as she held out her arm.

A man near a big fryer hollered and stuck his finger in his mouth. "I have some chewing tobacco you can put on it."

Sam shook his head. "I'll find something else, thanks." He held the door for her and took her elbow. "Let's go in the kitchen. I know just the thing. My secret cure."

"What is it? Will it burn?"

"Not like the sanitizer you put on me." He gave her a smile. "It should take the sting out. Where's the spice cabinet?"

"By the stove." Her feet stopped. "I can probably just wash it. You don't need to put some strange concoction on me."

"Come on." He nudged her forward. "Just a little meat tenderizer. A sure cure." Opening the cabinet, he searched through the various containers until he hit the right one. "Jackpot. Let me see the sting."

Slowly, she held out the arm with the red and swollen skin. Sam shook a pile of the powdery granules into his hand and splashed a few drops of water from the sink on it to form a paste. With cautious moves, he rubbed the angry spot, checking her expression for any sign he was hurting her.

She released a long breath. "That does seem to be helping." Her eyes met his for a moment. "Thank you."

Warmth flooded his insides, sending his heart to his throat. Helping this woman did strange things to him. "No problem." He glanced down at her speckled feet. "Never used it on fire ant bites, but it might be worth a try."

She didn't respond, so he bent down and pressed the mixture over a few of the bites on her feet, gently massaging. His fingers tingled. Why was he enjoying rubbing this woman's feet? Maybe it was boredom or the sea air intoxicating his brain. He was turning to mush.

"Okay. That's good." She stepped away from his reach. "I can put more on myself later." Now her face blotched with pink.

He stood and examined her. "Did something sting your cheeks? They're changing—"

"Nothing stung my face." Grabbing the container from his hands, she spun on her heels. "It must be sun from while we were on the boat. You run along, and I'll be out later."

Almost in a sprint, she hit the staircase and disappeared.

Run along? He could punch himself for being so sad to see her go.

Chapter 12

The day of the ball, Elinor organized the supplies and decorations in the room of the convention center designated for the queen's reception. Sheer fabric of purple, gold, and green already hung across the ceiling and down the walls, and the elaborate thrones and backdrop stood at the far end of the large space.

Being away from the rest of the pack solved a few of her problems. Em's date, Bryan, had arrived. Em claimed the boy was only a friend, but her sister's eyes told another story. And she'd insisted the poor guy sing and play song after song with his guitar. He sounded great, but the scene became awkward after a while.

Then there was Cassie and Dylan, still newlyweds. The two stayed so close together all the time, they were practically spooning. Also awkward.

Elinor sighed. Other than Mr. Darcy, no one had snuggled up to her in a couple of years. And she'd spent too many nights trying to forget that Craig disaster.

At least she'd managed to avoid Sam for one day by staying on her mother's heels. But today, decorating the tables in the queen room was her responsibility before the ball. For some reason beyond comprehension, her mother assigned Sam to help. Did her parents not get that she didn't want to be around another one of their protégées? So far she'd kept him busy unloading plastic containers. She scanned the room. Now which one held the tablecloths? The long banquet tables had been placed along one wall, and the extravagant floral arrangements on the other. Was that the way the Krewe had set up in the past? Her nose already itched and her chest tightened just being in the same room with the plants. The quicker they finished the better.

Sam entered with a huff. "Here." He dropped the box by the door. "That's the last of the ones marked queen room." Wiping the sweat from his brow, he motioned toward the serving tables. "Why are they all on one wall? We should slide a few on the two adjoining walls for flow."

What did a man know about flow? "I don't know. I need to see a picture from last year." She pulled out her phone. "Maybe there's one on the Krewe website."

"Why do we have to do what's always been done before?" Approaching a table on one end, he slid it diagonally across the room.

"Wait." Elinor held up her hand like a stop sign. "I haven't found a picture yet." Of all the nerve. "I dare say you know nothing about culture in Mobile." Moving to the table, she braced her hands to scoot it back.

"The definition of insanity is doing the same thing over and over and expecting a different result." He pushed the table flush to the wall and headed toward another on the other end.

Racing over, Elinor blocked his way. "You aren't from here."

The smirk curled his lips. "And you're the queen?"

Her fists punched her hips. "Not this year, but I was."

"How were the tables set up that year?" His gaze leveled on her.

Avoiding his eyes, she wracked her brain. How did it look when she was queen? She really hadn't noticed or cared.

"Um, we need to get cracking, your highness." Sam tapped his watch.

"Fine." She stamped toward the decorations. "Place the tables all wrong. Doesn't matter to me."

A second later, he'd aligned another table against the opposite wall.

After opening a few lids, Elinor grabbed three gold tablecloths and two purple ones, then the centerpieces. She placed one gold cloth in the middle of the main tables. Maybe scrunching it around the centerpiece would look better.

"What are you doing? That looks terrible." Sam unfolded the purple cloths and laid them flat on the adjacent tables, then added the centerpieces. "Clearly, this is the intended design."

Elinor scoffed. "You're the one who said we didn't have to do what had always been done."

Lines creased Sam's brow. "Unless it looks tacky."

"Tacky?" Pressure built in Elinor's ears. "You're saying I'm tacky?"

A vein popped up in his forehead. "I'm not saying you're tacky. I'm talking about your decorating skills. I mean, take that crazy cat portrait for one."

Surely a vessel exploded in her brain. Elinor pressed her fingers to her temples. "Says the martyr who saved everyone from enduring my ugly cat painting." Without warning, her vision blurred with moisture. She turned away. No way she'd cry in front of the man. "You, sir, are mistaken about a great many things."

In an instant, he moved to her side. "You're not tacky. I shouldn't have said that." He nudged her with his elbow and bent his neck to meet her eyes. "You're different. Unusual. That's a good thing."

"Now you're calling me weird?"

"No. I think if we put one purple tablecloth on flat and use another gold one circling the centerpiece…it could work."

"Why do you think you know so much?"

His lips turned down as he shrugged. "Being forced to serve on hundreds of philanthropy committees for my job."

Elinor's stomach churned. "How dreadful. No wonder you're so grumpy."

The bark she'd heard days before erupted from his throat. "You could be right. Let's try to finish."

She followed his lead, and they set out all the decorations and serving dishes.

Her father walked in just as they finished. "Looks about right, sugar, but fix that, will you?" His big voice boomed as he pointed.

"Fix what, Daddy?" Elinor stared in the direction his finger indicated.

"Those gold tablecloths are all catawampus around the centerpieces and need to be straightened out."

~~~

Near sunset, two limousines arrived at the main house to carry the family and a few friends downtown to the convention center. After stretching his arms through his coat, Sam stepped out of the boathouse to wait for instructions. The bulk of his tuxedo combined with the moist air heated his neck. He straightened the white vest once more and moved under the shade of an ancient moss-covered oak.

The back door opened, and Roy came out dressed in his own black tux. He waved, and pointed at one of the limos. "You ride in the second car with Cassie, Dylan, and Elinor." Grinning, he nodded his head toward Em and Ruby who followed him. "Aren't they a sight, all gussied up? I got my two queens up here in the number one."

Lingering sunlight danced on Em's elaborate white evening gown studded with glittering gold stones that matched her golden hair. A huge smile filled her youthful face. She practically glowed when she took her date's hand. Sam nodded and gave them a thumbs up. "Beautiful, ladies."

Next Cassie and Dylan joined them, laughing and walking closer together than Sam thought possible. The urge to put his finger down his throat passed through his mind. Good grief.

Once they'd taken a seat, Sam stood with the car door partway open. Should he get in or wait for Elinor? It wasn't like she was his date or anything. Thank you. Knock on wood and all that.

The door to the house slammed shut, and he turned. Her back was to him, and the pale blue ball gown dipped at her shoulders, cascaded down from her waist to touch the ground, reminding him of another era. Perhaps from one of her books. Her red hair curved up into a sort of twisted ball with a few wisps touching her long neck. Almost like a princess.

More brain muddling. He needed to stop.

Then she turned to face him, blue eyes shimmering in the
~~~

twilight.

Sam swallowed. Twice. His heart rammed against his ribs. Elinor was stunning. His feet moved toward her of their own accord. Without thinking, he extended his elbow to escort her to the limo.

Her gaze flitted to him for a moment as she accepted. "Thank you." With the last syllable, her voice rose as if she'd asked a question.

No words came to mind, so he simply walked straight ahead with her arm in his, swallowing hard at least two more times. Brain dead. He was brain dead. Like a zombie. Maybe he'd eaten a bad oyster and had botulism.

Dylan and Cassie chatted, but he couldn't focus on the words. The ride passed in a fuzzy blur until the car stopped to let them out downtown. He vaguely remembered nodding on the way and the slight scent of roses. Near the sidewalk, a group of gulls squawked. That snapped his attention. "Let's hurry before those birds bomb me again."

Elinor squeaked, maybe a laugh, and picked up her pace. Inside, she turned to face him. "Are you okay?"

"I think so." Was he? He did feel strange.

She motioned down the carpeted hall. "Let's go check the queen room once more and maybe pick up a mask."

"I'm not wearing a mask." Sam shook his head. "Those things freak me out. That and clowns."

A baby dolphin sound came from her way. "Something that scares the mighty Sam?"

They stepped into the room to observe their finished product once more. With the overhead lighting dimmed and candles flickering, the room took on new life. Elinor spun around in each direction, her dress swirling. "Not bad." Her eyes met his. "What do you think?"

His brain froze as he stared at her swaying there. "About what?"

"Have you been imbibing?" Her brow cocked as she neared and sniffed him.

"Imbibing?"

"Indulging in alcohol."

"No. And who says 'imbibing?'" Her books he'd been reading came to mind. "In this century, no one says 'imbibing.' Anyway, I must be tired from all your bossing me around. Carry this. Move that."

A pang of guilt hit him as soon as the words left his mouth. Filter blown to oblivion.

"You poor, abused creature." She stepped away and picked up a glittering red mask. "I'm headed to the big room for the coronation. Do as you please." And she disappeared out the door.

Why? Why did he say things like that?

~~~

Why? Why did she let that man get under her skin? Elinor's eyes stung as she joined the crowd waiting for Em to make her entrance. For a brief shining moment, she'd imagined Sam was a nice guy—that maybe if they stood together tonight, the ball wouldn't be so miserable. An idiotic supposition. She'd even allowed him to escort her to the car like some high school homecoming date. One might think *she'd* been imbibing. Believing she could enjoy Sam Conrad's company for a few hours competed with her stupidity in trusting Craig when he'd claimed to love her.

She scanned the room until she spotted her mother and then wound her way through the crowd to stand at her side. Cassie and Dylan stood a few feet away. The Krewe leaders had asked Dylan to be an honorary captain and had given him a gold crown. Ladies swarmed to greet the movie star. Thank goodness the attention landed on the other side of her mother.

The band struck a few notes, and then the lead singer stepped up to the microphone while the lights lowered. "Ladies and gentlemen of the Krewe of Hope, prepare to meet this year's reigning queen. Emma Catherine Bosarge."

A spotlight shone on the right of the stage, and Em stepped forward, arm-in-arm with their father. The crowd cheered and applauded. Last year's queen presented her with a giant bouquet of fresh flowers. Her baby sister looked radiant under
~~~

her crown, and a huge grin filled her father's face. Memories of her own coronation at her father's side returned. Though she'd only carried on the pretense of enjoying the social event for her parents' sake, she'd treasured walking on her father's arm. Perhaps the only aisle he'd ever escort her down.

Younger girls held Em's train as she made a circle, waving to all the Krewe. Once they'd completed the loop, the band played the traditional jazz tune. Her father held out his hand to Em, and they took the first dance.

"She looks great, and your father looks happier than a pig in mud," a deep voice whispered against her ear.

Elinor whipped her head to find Sam way too close for comfort. What was he saying? Pig in mud? She stared at him, standing tall and regal in his tuxedo, his gaze shining down at her. With the mirrored ball glittering from the ceiling, the light danced in his blue eyes like constellations on a clear summer night.

"Sorry about earlier." He dipped his chin lower. "I didn't mean to say…you weren't…" Clearing his throat, he pressed his face close to her ear, cinnamon breath warming her cheekbone. "You looked so pretty, I felt like I couldn't punch my way out of a wet paper bag."

Stunned, Elinor's heart fluttered. Why would he speak to her this way? And with those words? Was he ridiculing her and her father, too?

His elbow nudged hers. "I'm trying to apologize, and I threw in a few Royisms to lighten the mood." He shook his head. "Not working, huh?"

"Apologize? Truly?" Her mouth hung open.

One side of his mouth lifted, and his eyes brightened. "Truly."

"Okay." No other words came as her mind went blank.

"Okay." Sam tucked his hands in his pockets, his blue eyes slow to leave hers before he turned to watch the dance.

Maybe the man would go stand somewhere else now that he'd expressed contrition for his discourtesy. As if she could ever believe him anyway. Her stomach twisted. She should give

Sam a Royism… She'd sooner eat a handful of wiggling green snakes than entrust a man with her heart again.

Chapter 13

As the first song ended, Elinor watched her father escort Em to her waiting date, the singing guy, Bryan. Once they'd cleared, other Krewe members took to the dance floor. The ladies' jeweled dresses shimmered in the lights.

Father came and held out his hand to her. "May I have this dance, princess?"

How she treasured him. "Of course, Father." At least she was a princess in someone's eyes. And not the evil queen.

She followed his lead into the crowd until he chose a spot with room to move about. When he bowed, she curtsied like she'd learned to do as a little girl in ballroom dance classes.

With the agility of a twenty-year-old, Father led with dapper steps. Wrinkles creased the corners of his eyes as if he'd been smiling his whole life. How did he always stay so joyful? If only she'd inherited that trait.

"I know all this fanfare isn't your favorite, but are you having a good enough time?" He studied her face as if hoping for a positive answer.

Lifting one shoulder, she gave a nod, trying for a pleasant expression. "It's fine. Em looks beautiful, and she's in her element."

"Emma Catherine's always in her element." He chuckled and then grew serious. "You know, sometimes you have to let the old wounds of the past be what they may and grab onto hope. Let hope sustain and heal."

"I'm trying, Daddy."

Judging from the sudden slump in his shoulders, he didn't believe her. "Like weeds in a garden, bitterness can take root and choke out the flowers."

He was right of course, but how could she heal? Or get rid

of the bitterness after Craig? "You should be a writer. That was a lovely metaphor."

"Only lovely if it makes a difference."

"Pray that I can let go of the past. I want to. It's just so difficult for me to trust again."

As the song ended, he squeezed her tight. "I pray for my girls day and night." Releasing her, he tipped her chin. "You're talking to Him, too, aren't you?" He pointed toward the ceiling. "You haven't given up on the Lord, right?"

"Never." Emotion choked her. "Besides you and Mother, sometimes it seems the Lord's all I have." She managed a small smile. "And Mr. Darcy, of course."

"Good girl." He pressed a kiss on the top of her head before he led her off the dance floor. "It'll all work out for good. You'll see."

~~~

His apology had sunk like an anchor. Sam stifled a groan. Forcing the words I'm sorry from his lips zapped his strength as though he'd just swum across the bay. He'd really tried, and all he'd gotten in return was an okay. Was nothing ever good enough for this woman? Or any woman for that matter?

When would the night be over?

He watched as Elinor danced with Roy. Didn't she know how lucky she was to have such great parents? Visions of her as a little red-headed girl flitted through his mind. Learning to fish, crab, to ballroom dance with her father. A smile lifted Sam's lips. On the minuscule chance he ever became a father, he'd want to be one like Roy.

He should force his gaze away, but it seemed to be glued to her as she swayed to the music. At last the song ended, and he dropped his gaze to the floor.

Roy returned her to the spot right next to him and headed over to ask Cassie for a dance.

Sam offered a smile as Cassie and her father passed. Purple and green balloons escaped from a nearby vase and floated upward, their gold ribbons dangling. His eyes followed them as they drifted to the ceiling, then he took a quick glance at
~~~

Elinor. She stood, stoically staring forward, obviously still annoyed with him.

As the night wore on, the band switched from jazz to top forty. Across the room, a woman lifted her jeweled hand and waved. Sam cringed. The Rodeo-Drive-chick from the committee meeting threaded through the crowd, aimed at them. Great. As she neared, a bearded man fell into step alongside her, also walking and waving their way.

With one finger, Sam touched Elinor's shoulder. "Your fan club's coming."

"Who?" Small lines crinkled her forehead as she looked up at him.

Those blue eyes. Sam pointed toward the approaching duo. "They're almost here."

By the time her gaze traveled over, the two arrived.

"Elinor," they spoke in unison, then turned to each other in surprise.

"Lexi." The man nodded. "I didn't notice you there."

Fists punched on hips, Lexi rolled her eyes. "Probably, Miller Lowery, because you were gaping at my old high school friend." Scanning both Sam and Elinor, she lifted her chin. "Elinor, are you playing with another one of your father's pets?"

Heat crawled up Sam's neck, and his jaw clamped shut. Pet? He wasn't anyone's pet.

Miller stepped in front of Lexi and held out a hand. "Want to dance, Elinor?"

And who was this Miller? The man looked twice Elinor's age.

Elinor laced one arm through Sam's and fiddled with his bow tie with the other hand. Her chin made that defiant tilt he'd seen so many times. "Sam is my father's wealth manager and my date. He's no one's pet." She tugged his elbow, brushed past Lexi and Miller, and led him to the dance floor.

Sam followed, more than a little dazed by her sudden attention. What was she doing? They wove through the couples until Elinor turned to him and moved closer. She didn't quite meet his gaze, but she wrapped her arms around his neck and stepped in time with the music.

Sam's head tingled, his arms and neck joining in. Intoxicating. And he hadn't even imbibed. He forced his feet to move in time.

"Grin like a mule eating briars and laugh really loud." She stared into his eyes, a big smile pressed on her face, almost every tooth visible.

"Mule what?" When her words registered, he laughed hard. Mule eating briars. Was she defending him or herself? Or both? He breathed in the scent of her hair. Roses. Didn't matter why she was holding him.

Her breath tickled his ear, and she leaned close. "That woman never got over me being Azalea Trail Maid and Krewe Queen when she didn't get picked."

He pulled back. "Am I supposed to know what an Azalea Trail Maid is?"

"Not unless you have a daughter in high school here."

"Doubtful. What's the story with Miller?" His gaze wandered to her mouth. He hadn't looked at those pouty lips in a while.

"One of my many bad first dates Em wanted to tell you about."

"Oh, I can top your bad date stories any day."

"I think not." Her chin tilted again, allowing a stray tendril of red hair to escape. "How about your date picking you up wearing driving gloves and a racing jacket to ride to a restaurant only five miles down the road in a four-door sedan? I nicknamed him NASCAR after that. In my mind only, of course."

Sam's fingers itched to brush the strand of hair from her cheek. Or maybe just touch it. "What about picking up your date for a bank awards ceremony, and she's so drunk she throws up in your car on the way there?"

"That is impressive." She nodded, her eyes softening. "How about when on a first date, the man informs you he has a room in the motel next door to the restaurant for dessert?"

Sam's eyes widened. "No. He. Did. Not."

"Indeed." Her gaze challenged him.

"Okay." The game was on. He worried his lip as he looked around, searching the vault in his brain for a prize disaster. "Food Nazi. Took a woman out, and she tried to stop me from eating meat and even banana pudding. Some kind of a tyrannical vegan."

"Good one." She clucked her tongue. "But what about when your date takes you to the most expensive restaurant in town, but all four of his credit cards are declined."

"Okay. I took a girl to hear a band at a club, but she couldn't get in. She'd lied to me about her age. Luckily, she was at least twenty."

"So dreadful." This time she let out a bit of the dolphin giggle. "I shouldn't tell this. It's not even funny."

"What?" Sam couldn't stop the laugh from escaping his throat for no reason other than that she was laughing.

"This guy…" She swiped at her eye with one hand. Her feet slowed as she laughed harder. "It's really not funny."

"Come on. I have to know now."

"On a blind date, the guy stops by his grandmother's visitation at the funeral home on the way to take me to a concert." Her shoulders lifted as she giggled. "It was sad, but I didn't know a soul and had to walk by to view her body in a coffin with him. So mortifying."

A huge bark came from Sam's throat. "That's creepy wrong." He laughed again. "And I do sound like a walrus."

"No." She let her head fall against his shoulder. "A seal with a cough…says the dolphin."

The music sped up, but they stayed close in each other's arms. Warmth spread through Sam. Not an uncomfortable heat or a fiery desire, but a tenderness for this fragile, beautiful soul who fit so nicely against him. His heart thrummed a happy tune in his chest. For once in his life, all seemed right with the world.

It was bound to end soon.

~~~
~~~

Head spinning, Elinor breathed in the man that was Sam. A mixture of the woodsy, crisp linen scent of his shirt and his cinnamon breath against her neck. Like swimming against a riptide, Lexi's rude words, along with the prospect of a night spent talking to Miller Lowery, had propelled her on course to the dance floor and into Sam's arms. Oddly, the progression felt right. As though floating under water with the ability to breathe. Natural and a bit tingly.

What was happening? Was it sympathy? The poor guy may've had as many bad dates as she'd had. Not likely, but maybe. Enough to understand the disappointing prospect of continuing the unsavory process. A seemingly tender place in his prickly personality.

Song after song, they danced, sometimes chatting, other times quiet. She nestled against him, eyes closed to the world around her.

A tap on her shoulder interrupted her dreamy state. "Darlin'?"

Blinking, she gazed up into her father's jovial face. "Yes?"

"Glad y'all are enjoying the festivities, but the band went on break. Want to take a walk down to the queen's reception room for some refreshments?"

Elinor's head spun. The band went on break? Only one other couple stood swaying on the dance floor, and from the looks of them, they'd definitely imbibed. "Oh my." What had she been thinking? Or not thinking? "How long since the band left?" The tips of her ears burned. She couldn't look at Sam. So embarrassing.

"Only a minute or five, nothing to get out of kilter about. Come on, y'all." Her father guided them out, rambling about something she couldn't quite focus on.

Once they reached the queen room, Elinor made straight for the punch. Perhaps her ears would cool. Were they red?

The smell of the floral arrangements made her nose tickle. Her chest tightened.

"Thirsty after all that dancing?"

Elinor turned to find Lexi, who seemed to be battling to

keep her smile in place. "And what's the scoop with you and the rude but good-looking money guy?"

Whatever Lexi's reason for making conversation, it couldn't be good. Since their days as kids in private school, the girl was always devising schemes, usually for no one's benefit but her own. One by one, Elinor shuffled through possible motivations for the woman to be talking to her now. All seemed poised to come back and haunt her.

"Nora, I need your help." Em's shrill voice cut across the room.

For once, the childhood nickname came as a relief. After slugging back the fruity punch, Elinor patted Lexi's shoulder. "I'm so sorry we haven't had the chance to catch up, but duty calls."

Lexi's fake smile faded. "Of course. But I wouldn't know. Having never been queen of the ball."

The wrong thing to say. Lexi would never let go of that one. With quick steps, Elinor escaped toward Em. It wasn't as if she'd been responsible for keeping Lexi from being an Azalea Trail Maid or queen at the Krewe of Hope or any other Mardi Gras club.

Once Elinor reached the other side of the room, Em grabbed her elbow with one hand while still gripping the bouquet in the other. "I need you to see if you can get a microphone in this room."

"A microphone? What for?" Elinor sneezed. The sweet scent of the flowers so close had her throat itching now.

Em motioned with her head toward her date. "For Bryan. I want everyone to hear him sing, silly." A look of rapture filled Em's face. "His voice is so beautiful, and his music brings you closer to God."

Those words kicked Elinor in the stomach. Em talking about God? If it meant that much to her sister, she'd do her best. "I'll try. I'm just not sure where to start."

"What are you looking for?" Sam's voice heated her ears again.

"Look at you, Sam." Em nudged Elinor to Sam's side. "I

may be queen, but you are most definitely a handsome prince, and look at the princess next to you. Isn't she beautiful?"

Sam's gaze met Elinor's. "She is. Can't say I've ever been called a prince, though."

"I don't believe that for a second." Grin growing larger, Em nudged Elinor again. "Doesn't he look like a handsome prince, Nora?"

So much for escaping drama and enjoying the nickname. She examined Sam, avoiding his eyes. He stood tall and stately. The suit did fit well. "His tuxedo gives him an air of distinction." Elinor's chest tightened as she spoke.

"She means you look hot." Em giggled. "I wanted her to find a microphone so Bryan could sing a few songs."

"I'll handle it. Be back in a few."

Elinor blew out a long breath as Sam walked away, partly in relief, partly because he did look like a handsome prince. Just a little.

~~~

A couple of twenty dollar bills sped the process of commandeering a microphone from a convention center worker. Sam carried the equipment back to the reception room. As he entered, his gaze fell on Elinor. A bulky man with short, cropped brown hair stood close to her. Really close. Black ink ran up the man's neck to his ear. What was that tattoo?

Sam crossed the room as fast as he could. Was the man bothering her? Bryan and Em stood near but faced the other way. Elinor nodded as the man spoke, but her lips pinched together.

After setting the equipment down by an outlet, he tapped Em. "The microphone you requested, your majesty."

Em squealed. "Yay, thank you." She turned and pushed her bouquet toward Elinor. "Hold these, please."

The wide-eyed expression on Elinor's face as she took the flowers gave Sam all the nudge he needed. She didn't want to be in a conversation with the guy. And that was the top of a snake tattoo peeking out of his collar. She definitely didn't like snakes. "I'm back, princess." Sam stepped up and planted a
~~~

kiss on Elinor's cheek.

She froze, as did the man.

Snake man's beady eyes squinted as he extended his hand. "I don't think we've met. Dante Dye."

"Sam Conrad." He gave Dante's hand an extra firm squeeze. "Thanks for entertaining my Ellie while I was off on an errand for her sister."

An arrogant smile covered Dante's face. "I'll entertain *Ellie* anytime." He turned his gaze to her. "In fact, my band plays in Gulf Shores next week if you wanna be a groupie."

The combination of the alcohol on Dante's breath and the way his eyes travelled over Elinor released a torrent of fire in Sam's gut. Waves of adrenaline roared in his ears, and his muscles flinched. He felt like slugging the guy.

Elinor covered her nose with one hand and held the flowers out. She sneezed four times. Dainty little sneezes. Her eyes shut as she coughed, and a wheeze came from her throat.

"Oh no." Sam took the flowers and set them on a table. "You need to step outside?"

She nodded, sneezed again, and started across the room.

Sam grabbed a pile of napkins and followed Elinor as she sneezed and coughed all the way down the large hall, out of the building, and onto a terrace overlooking the Mobile River. "Here." He held out the napkins. "Can I get you something else? Water?"

Shaking her head, she took his offering and leaned over the rail. She took slow breaths. Her chest rose and fell, but the breaths seemed shallow. Was she okay?

What should he do? He couldn't let something happen to her. Hesitantly, he placed his hand on her back. "Do you have asthma?"

She nodded. "I'm okay now." Her voice was quiet. A breeze came up from across the water.

"Do you have an inhaler?"

"Father has it, but really, I'm good."

"Allergies?"

"Terrible allergies."

"What about shots?" His forehead scrunched together as he tried to ascertain if her breathing sounded normal.

"I took allergy shots twice a week until I had an anaphylactic reaction not long ago. Needed two shots of epinephrine to save me."

The vision sent a shiver through Sam's core. "You are a disaster waiting to happen, aren't you?" A beautiful disaster.

"I guess." She chuckled and turned to face him. "The flowers must've set me off." Her lips quirked up as her eyes met his. "Or Dante Dye."

A deep spring of contentment seeped through him. Elinor was okay now, and he'd been right to step in. Even as her smile soothed him, his pulse raced. "I hope I didn't run off your suitor and bust up your next bad date, but I saw that snake tattoo…"

Laughing, she let her head fall back. Lights reflected and glittered off the dark surface beyond her. The perfect backdrop for the beautiful picture before him. "That was the least scary thing about Dante. Em dragged me down to one of his shows a year or so ago. Every single song he plays has his last name in the lyrics."

"Dye?"

Her hands flitted about. "Do or Dye. Never Say Dye. Dye in My Arms."

Sam smiled. "Dye of Boredom?"

More laughter. He loved that sound.

Then she pressed her lips together and quieted. "Thank you for your assistance."

"Couldn't have you going on another bad date and beating my record."

Her posture straightening, she tilted her chin. "I won the contest."

"I don't think we finished all the stories. If we did, I'd school you."

She let out a long sigh. "I've delved into enough bad memories for one day. We'll have to call it a tie and continue the competition at a later date."

"Deal." He couldn't stop his smile. "You know, in Bible study with your dad, we talked about Joseph. That guy went through a ton of bad junk, but things worked out for good in the end. There's hope for us, I guess."

"But not everyone gets a happy ending in real life. And romance isn't necessary for a complete life. God's love is enough." She looked away and rubbed one hand at the back of her neck as if working out a kink.

A million stars pricked the dark sky while frogs chirped in synchronized rounds with a chorus of crickets. Water slapped against the edge of the outdoor terrace overlooking the river. They stood in silence. Had she given up on love? A lump formed in his throat.

Had he?

"So, you and my father have Bible study together?" She spoke without looking at him.

"Every morning. Not really my thing. I haven't been to church in a while, but he makes it apply to leadership. And life. You're lucky to have such good parents." He shrugged. "Blessed, I guess you'd say."

"Not every aspect of my life is a disaster." She faced him. "You don't have good parents?"

A bitter chuckle escaped. "If you like having someone control and criticize every minutiae of your life."

She let that sink in. "Sorry."

"It could've been a lot worse, really." And it could. Plus, looking back, at some point, he'd allowed the control. He should have stood up to his father years before.

"Not to change the subject, but did you say the word *suitor* earlier?" Her curious gaze snared him.

Sam's abs tightened. She'd caught his slip. "I may've read one of your books the other night."

Her blue eyes widened. "You did?"

"I was bored. I looked up your pen name online." He lifted one shoulder. "You're welcome to search me back if you want."

"Maybe I will."

Moonlight streamed across her face, accentuating her features and creating a maze of confusing feelings. Protectiveness, compassion, and a few more he shoved away. "How do you create the men in your novels after all the…unfortunate experiences? Are they based on someone?"

A vigorous shake of her head. "Purely made up."

Good. But why did he care? "What are you writing now?"

"Really?" Her cute nose scrunched up. "You want to know?"

"Unless it's some big secret."

"No." She shrugged. "This novel's about a landowner's son in an arranged engagement." All manner of gesturing began as she spoke. "He's cynical and gruff because he's been hurt before, and he can't inherit unless he marries. Deep down he's good, but the girl doesn't want to marry him. She's smitten with a man who seems perfect, but really he's a scoundrel. In the end she'll figure it out before it's too late."

"I hope so, or your book will be really depressing."

"We couldn't have that. My readers want happy endings. Maybe because so few of us have them in real life."

The breeze blew red hair across her face, leaving a piece on her cheek. Sam moved to gently capture the strand. His fingers lingered on soft skin. His breathing slowed. He was in dangerous, uncharted waters.

~~~

Elinor's cheek tingled under Sam's fingers. They still lingered though he'd brushed the hair away. Gaze falling to his lips, her breath hitched. Didn't she want him to move his hand? She pressed her lips together and tried to form words. "Think you'll stay here?" Heat flooded her face. That made no sense at all. "In Mobile, I mean?"

"I…I like it here." His chest rose and fell as he paused. "This place, the river, the bay drips with life."

"It does. You should see my backyard in Fort Morgan."

"I'd like that."

His eyes sucked her in like a whirlpool. Who knew it could feel so good to drown? "I'm on the beach. The water, the
~~~

waves, the sun…" The sky as blue as his eyes.

His other hand touched her shoulder as his lips moved closer. "Ellie, I…"

She should move, but her body protested against her will. She inched closer to him and closed her eyes.

"Sam? Elinor? You kids out here?" Her father's voice broke through the currents sweeping her away.

"We're here, Daddy." She forced her feet to step back and turned toward the building. "My allergies were bothering me."

"You okay, darlin'? Need your inhaler?"

"I'm fine now."

"The party's wrapping up, and luckily, we're not on the cleanup committee. Thought we'd call it a night if y'all don't mind."

"Of course." Disappointment saturated her. In a weird sort of way, despite Lexi Downing, Miller Lowery, Dante Dye, and her allergies, the night had been a good one.

Back inside, Father gave her a hug. "Sorry to be a party pooper, but my knee is all kinda tight tonight. Must be one doozy of a rainstorm on the way."

Sam pulled out his phone to check the weather. "Says the first hurricane of the season is brewing in the Caribbean."

Roy's brows raised. "Kind of early for much to come of a hurricane, but you never know when the next big storm will hit."

Chapter 14

In the limo, only Roy and Ruby rode along with Elinor and Sam. The others had left while they'd been outside. Still, Elinor sat close to him, and Sam soaked up her warmth. Her hand rested on her knee, mesmerizing him with a debate on whether to take her fingers into his. Or not. Why was this such a deliberation? They'd danced. They'd almost shared a kiss, hadn't they? His mind traveled back to the moment. Yes. They'd been close. But Roy would say close only counted in horseshoes and hand grenades.

What would Roy think about him making a move on his daughter?

It was just a hand, though.

Roy talked on and on about this and that, but those fingers obliterated Sam's concentration. *Do it, for goodness' sake.* In one swift, clumsy move, Sam put his hand over hers without looking at her. Like he was in junior high or something. *Oh, man.*

Elinor stiffened for a second, but then her fingers curled around the tips of his. The simple movement washed a river of emotion over him. She seemed to understand him and what he'd gone through in the past. And her weirdness was reasonable…lovable. He never meant to get in this deep. He'd lost control of his heart, but he'd ride out this torrent and see where he landed.

The rest of the trip passed in a giddy daze. No doubt his face held a goofy smile. Near the last curve, his thoughts turned to what he should do when they exited the car. Should he walk her to the door? Ask her if she wanted to sit by the pool? Give her a peck on the cheek?

Good grief. No more thinking.

As they pulled into the circular driveway, a beat-up truck came into view. Was another friend visiting? Like a vulture, a raven-haired man stood waiting. The limo came to a halt, and Sam pointed. "Who's that?"

They all turned to see.

"No." Elinor's hand slipped from his as she gasped. "It can't be. Why would Craig dare show his face here, Daddy?"

Roy hurried to exit the car. "I'll get to the bottom of it, darling." He helped Ruby out. "Sam, would you mind taking care of the driver?"

"Got it."

In a few long steps, Roy towered over Craig.

After pulling some cash from his wallet, Sam sent the limo on its way. The magic of the moment broken, Sam stayed close to Elinor, who clung to her mother's arm. Craig's dark eyes flashed, a look incongruent with the pleasant expression on his face. The impulse to drag the man off the property shouted in Sam's head.

Sam studied Elinor's expression. In the past, his own heart had been slashed with a dull knife by Tiffany. But seeing the shattered look in those impossibly blue eyes completely gutted him. Worse than any pain he'd endured before. Right then and there, he made the decision. He'd fight to protect Elinor Bosarge from more pain. Or go down trying.

~~~

Crashing like a tidal wave against the shore, Craig's smile and ebony eyes seized the remaining tattered shards of Elinor's heart and smashed them into tiny pieces. Again. She hadn't seen Craig's face since he'd disappeared with the jewelry and cash right before the charity ball two years ago. His presence tonight of all nights uprooted the depths of anger and pain she'd thought long buried. Why was he here now?

She took a step away from her mother and towards Craig. "How dare you…?" Her faltering voice betrayed her. All the hurt she'd locked inside a tiny compartment of her soul spilled out. "You must know we don't want you here after what you've done to our family."
~~~

"I know, Elinor." Craig craned his neck to see her beyond Roy. "I want to do the honorable thing and heal the pain —"

"What do you know of honor, or of my pain?" Her shaky voice rose. "You're quite wrong if you think you can ever repair the gashes you've gouged in my trust." She punched her index finger toward him. "I doubt this was your first time to swindle people who've shown you kindness, nor will it be your last."

"Elinor." Roy rotated to face her, his voice gentle. "You go inside with your mother. I'll handle this."

"I'm really sorry, Elinor." Craig removed a knapsack from his shoulder. "I came to repay your family for everything."

"Repay us?" The bitterness swept out as a huff while her whole body shuddered. "If you had any regard for my family or my feelings, you'd never have shown your face here again."

Taking a step toward her, Roy held up both hands. "Princess, if you've said your piece now…"

Sam touched her arm. "I'll come inside with you, if you want."

She couldn't meet Sam's eyes. Couldn't let those eyes mean anything. Couldn't go through pain this deep ever again. "No. I want to be alone."

~~~

Sam's chest squeezed as Elinor turned without looking at him and strode toward the house. Would she block him out now? Secure the walls that guarded her heart? His fingers formed fists. He should throttle this man. Once she disappeared inside, Sam pivoted and moved to Roy's side. "You've got a lot of nerve coming here."

"Who are you?" Craig bowed up his chest. "This isn't your business, so stay out of it, if you know what's good for you."

Roy placed a hand on Craig's shoulder. "Don't go looking for trouble, boy. Even Elinor could whup you as mad as she is right now. But that's what she's got a daddy for." His eyebrows rose and his chin lifted as he looked down at the man. "Lucky for you, I'm just gonna bless you out."

The bravado left Craig's posture. "Yes, sir. That's fair."

Releasing Craig's shoulder, Roy took a small step back.
~~~

"Where have you been all this time?"

"On a rig, sir. Making money to pay you back."

"I know every little pig path and pond in these parts." Roy squinted his eyes and scratched at the whiskers on his chin. "Not a rig around here, or I would've heard."

"Further down the Gulf."

Rolling his eyes, Sam bit his tongue. Further down the Gulf? Could the guy be more ambiguous? What a liar.

Sweat beaded on Craig's face. "Then I went in a program for gamblers. Found a higher power."

Sam smirked. "Court-ordered no doubt."

"Shut up. I'll—"

"Uh, uh, Craig," Roy's deep voice held a firm command. "You're on my turf."

Craig pulled down the zipper of the knapsack, reached inside, and pulled out a pile of cash. "I have your money, times two. Like in the Bible."

Sam mumbled under his breath. "I think it was three or seven, not two." He'd been to Sunday school as a small boy, after all.

This time, Craig shot a dirty look his way without speaking.

"I don't want your money." Roy nudged the offering away. "You give it to your momma. She's been dragged through the mud on account of you." He raised one finger. "And I *will* verify that you do give it to her. But Craig…" His voice took a more sober tone. "You stole something that can never be repaid. I can forgive you, but the damage done to my sweet Elinor can't be traded for any amount of money or jewelry. For her sake, I'm gonna have to ask you to leave and not to come back."

The words sent Craig to one knee. "I was protecting you all. I owed money on a loan to some heavy-hitters. They threatened to hurt anyone I cared about if I didn't pay up."

Sam's stomach churned. The man was probably lying through his teeth to save his own skin and get back in Roy's good graces. But the thought the thief might've put Elinor and her family in danger boiled under Sam's skin. "That's even more despicable."

Roy eyed Sam and shook his head before turning back to Craig. "If you knew me at all, you'd have known I'd help. People know Big Roy around these parts, and I could've protected you. I'd have given you the money and more if you'd been honest." He let out a long sigh. "What's done is done now."

Craig rose, his pleading expression disappearing. A more conniving look took its place. "I'd take this to my mother, but if there's a warrant out for my arrest, I don't want to get caught at home. You give it to her."

Sam swallowed the bile in his throat. He knew a shark when he saw one. The man was trawling for information. Not sorry. Otherwise Craig wouldn't have slithered in this late at night. Had he been casing the place for another theft?

"No warrant for your arrest." Roy shrugged. "At least not from what went on here. Once I looked at the video from the pawn shop and saw your face, I was madder than a hornet, but I wouldn't press charges on account of your momma." A slump weighed Roy's shoulders down as though he'd really cared about this bilker at one time. "What I saw on that video was a man who looked nice on the outside, but on the inside, he'd fallen out of the ugly tree and hit every limb on the way down." He shot Craig a pointed look. "You get my drift."

"Yes, sir. Thank you for not filing charges, sir."

Roy's lips turned down. "Don't thank me. Get yourself right with your momma and the good Lord. But somewhere a far piece down the road from here." His firm gaze left no doubt Roy meant what he said.

Pressing his lips in a hard line, Craig took the knapsack and left.

Unsure of what to say, Sam stood with Roy as the truck disappeared.

The big man sniffled and ran his fingers through his graying red hair. "I need to have a word of prayer for that boy tonight."

"What?" Sam's jaw flinched. "Why? Unless it's a prayer that he runs his truck into the river."

"None of us is perfect, Sam-man. It'd be a sad day if we all got what we deserved." Moisture filled Roy's eyes as he turned to meet Sam's gaze. "As long as he's breathing, there's a chance he'll turn from his evil ways. God's full of mercy, and He longs for His children to come back to Him. No sin's too big for His love to cover if we truly repent. When we give our loving Father the reins of our life, we aren't guaranteed a smooth course, but at least we're in His merciful hands."

Shame slid down Sam's back as the words pricked at his heart. His own sins came to mind. What if he got what he deserved? He'd never swindled anyone, but he wasn't perfect by any means. "Okay. Maybe I don't want him to drive into the river." Just a creek. "But he'd better stay away from Elinor." That sounded weird. Sam cleared his throat. "And the rest of your family."

Roy wrapped an arm around Sam's shoulder. "I appreciate your loyalty. It was hard to trust after Craig, but Cassie says you're legit. A good place to start again." Roy released him and stepped away. His lips lifted in a small smile. "The Lord sent me a good friend this time."

"Me, too, sir."

"I'll see you bright-eyed and bushy-tailed for church. We'll go to early service so we can have brunch with Cassandra Jane and Emma Catherine before they get back on the road to Oxford. It starts at eight. We'll leave about twenty minutes ahead of time."

Church? Early service? Sam stifled a groan. "Okay." Not what he'd planned, but Elinor might need him.

Eyeing the house, Roy motioned. "There's another battle ahead that'll need prayer."

"Sir?"

"Seeing that rascal may sink Elinor into a dark place again. She'll shut herself off like she's tuckered out on the human race."

Sam's gut tightened. He couldn't let that happen.

~~~

She'd heard enough. Elinor shut her upstairs window as
~~~

Craig vanished down the drive. No doubt the same as he'd done two years ago, carrying their money and jewelry. And her heart. She pressed a palm to her stomach to fight the threatening sobs. No more crying over that swindler.

Fumbling around the room, she found her computer case. She'd go home until Mother's surgery. No matter if the roof leaked or workers hammered. The beach gave her sanity, and she needed that now.

A quiet knock on the door interrupted her packing. Would they go away if she pretended not to hear?

The door cracked open. "Hon, can Daddy and I come in?" Her mother stood in lounge pants and a cotton shirt while her father still wore his tuxedo.

Elinor shrugged, her bottom lip trembling too hard to speak.

They took slow steps into the room. Mother sat on the bed, smoothing imaginary wrinkles from the cotton spread, while Father moved to Elinor's side.

"He's gone, darlin', and he won't be back." Father tried to assure her with a gentle touch to her shoulder.

The contact released a torrent of tears. "Why can't I find love like you and Mother?" Eyes burning, her throat tightened as she sobbed.

Father's big arms pulled her close to his chest. "You will."

"No." She buried her head into his shoulder. "I won't. And I'm finished trying." She sniffed and wiped her eyes. "It hurts too much."

"Everyone goes through heartbreak."

"You and Mother didn't. Maybe you used up all the good fortune in the family." Her stomach shook as she hiccupped. "Cassie's first husband betrayed her, Craig stole from us, and even Em's first boyfriend cheated. All liars."

Her mother stood and crossed the room to join them. "Cassie went through a hard time, but she came out on the other side. You and Emma are still young. There's plenty of time to find the right person." She hugged Elinor from the other side.

"No." Elinor gave a slow shake of her head. "I'm terrible at relationships and dating. You know that." She pressed her nose against Father's coat. "The ones I like don't like me and vice versa." Wiping her eyes, she lifted her head and took a deep breath. "It's okay. I'm used to being alone. I have God. And Mr. Darcy."

They all looked around the room for the cat.

"Where is he?" Elinor pulled away and bent down to the floor. "I want to go home until your surgery."

"Not tonight." Her father's mouth twisted. "We're going to church and brunch as a family to see your sisters off."

"They won't care if I'm there or not." Elinor crawled across the floor, peeking under each piece of furniture. "Mr. Darcy?"

Mother touched her shoulder. "Please stay through brunch. You can go home after that. It would mean so much to me to have all my girls together at church."

How could she say no? "I'll stay as long as you want." She plopped down on the floor, tears flowing. "Now I can't even find Mr. Darcy."

Chapter 15

Of all the nights.

Fuming and still in his tuxedo, Sam stomped down the wooden planks of the dock that jutted into the river. Clouds drifted overhead, filtering the moonlight and shadowing the water. Why couldn't that slime bucket, Craig, have shown up on one of the other three hundred and sixty-four days of the year?

At the end of the pier, Sam plopped down and let his legs dangle. Heat and anger pulsed through his torso. The thought of Elinor's teary eyes and crumbled expression pinched his insides. Terrible timing. They'd had fun, for goodness sake. And he'd felt something between them. Something much stronger than anything he'd felt with Tiffany. Hands down—no comparison.

His arms slid across the boards supporting him, and a pebble rolled under his fingers. He picked it up and propelled it across the surface of the river. It skipped twice before it sank in the murky darkness. Timing. For most of his life, he'd had terrible timing in relationships. Probably a bit of bad judgment too, if the truth be told.

Hoot owls exchanged haunted calls on nearby trees, adding to the gloom of the cloudy night. Sam released a frustrated groan. How could he make Elinor believe he was different than Craig and all the other losers she'd dated? How could he make her forget the pain? He *was* different, wasn't he?

His phone vibrated in his pocket. Who'd call in the middle of the night? After slipping it out, he checked the number. Mom? Guilt gripped his stomach, joined by a little panic. "Mom? Is something wrong?"

A curse responded to his question. His father's voice.

"Yeah, something's wrong. You don't answer my calls. You've got a week to get yourself back to work, two tops, to end this childish foolishness, but it's coming out of your vacation time." He grunted. "I've told everyone you're training and vacationing in Europe. Managing your clients myself—"

"Dad, I want to go to PT school." Most likely.

"I vetoed that nonsense when you were in college. No one in their right mind takes an intentional pay cut. If this is about Tiffany, and you can't get past your juvenile emotions, I'll find another broker to manage her account."

"No, Dad. I have to make my own decisions. Be my own man."

A bitter laugh came through the line. "Then quit acting like a spoiled brat. If it weren't for me, you'd never have been so successful. You think you'd have the client list you manage without my connections?"

The hurtful words embedded deep in Sam's confidence. Was he making a mistake?

"You've got two weeks. Do you hear me, Sam? Do you understand what I'm saying?"

He understood. Bile hit the back of his throat. "I'm hanging up now."

"You better not…"

Sam ended the call. This was why he'd left. The constant belittling and controlling. He lay back on the wooden pier and stared into the overcast sky. Working on the docks of Mobile sounded more appealing than going back to work for his father. Even with the seagulls.

~~~

A scurrying sound pulled Sam from a light sleep. He flinched and sat up. Foggy light met his blurry vision. Where was he? Something landed on his face and pricked his cheek. He swatted at the insect, eyes blinking. Was he outside?

The horrible ending of what could've been a great night came back full force. Elinor. Craig. His father. He cringed. He must've nodded off. Thank God he hadn't rolled into the river. Especially in his favorite tux.
~~~

Movement drummed the boards of the pier. He turned and scanned the row leading back toward his temporary home. Between the boathouse and himself, a pointed nose lifted, teeth bared, and a low growl rumbled from the animal. Sam sucked in a breath and forced his eyes wide. A possum with at least six babies on her back stared him down. This time it hissed.

A nice way to start the morning. A showdown.

With quick moves, Sam stood, clapped his hands, and stomped, giving his own loud growl at the animal.

No action from his opposition. What now? Sam growled louder, clapped, and jumped up and down.

A voice called from the back yard of the big house. "Sam-man, you okay?" Big Roy stood beside Elinor under a large moss-covered oak that hosted a wooden swing at the end of two ropes. They both held a hand over their brow and stared at him.

The varmint fled underneath the dock. No doubt before either of the Bosarges noticed the dilemma.

More bad timing, as usual. "I'm fine."

While Elinor turned back toward the house, her sleeveless turquoise dress flowing around her knees, Roy walked closer. "You don't have to wear a tuxedo to church. We're pretty casual these days. Jeans are even okay."

"Yes, sir. I'll change." No sense trying to explain. His head throbbed anyway. Sleeping on a dock had left a kink in his neck, too. A long shower and a couple of ibuprofen were in order. And coffee.

"Okay, see ya in fifteen minutes. Early service today, remember?"

Fifteen minutes? "Right."

~~~

How strange. What was Sam doing out there? Elinor rubbed her swollen eyes as she entered the back door of the house. She sank into a leather recliner in the living room, and Mr. Darcy jumped onto the arm of the chair. The little stinker had been hiding in one of Em's suitcases.
~~~

Her father continued trying to console her, but his words did little to mend the shreds of her heart. She needed time. And the beach.

Seeing Sam only made things worse. She'd carelessly danced and laughed with the man when no doubt getting close to him would end in some other equally dreadful disaster. And what was he doing jumping around out there in his tuxedo? Had he imbibed after they'd gotten home? Sure, she'd tossed and turned and drenched her pillow, but why would any of last night's drama trouble him? If she weren't so forlorn, she'd have laughed at the sight.

Never mind. As soon as church and brunch ended, she'd go to the cottage, dive into her story, and put reality aside.

The back door opened and closed, and her father took a seat on the couch across from her. He fumbled with a newspaper. "Hope the others come down soon or we'll be late."

"I'm sure Cassie and Dylan are ready. I saw her carrying two coffees up a good while ago, and Mother woke Em."

A second later, her mother came out of the kitchen about the same time a giggle echoed from the top of the stairs, then clomping high heels. Em led Cassie, Dylan, and Bryan down, and then stopped. "I'm mad at all y'all. You, Momma, Daddy, and Sam."

Elinor squinted. "What? Why?"

"You missed my grand exit from the ball. Where were you?"

The river, the moon, the terrace came to mind. Sam's lips. Elinor's ribs squeezed as the air caught in her lungs. They'd almost…

"Elinor had an allergy attack." With a yawn, Father rose and stretched his arms in front of him.

"It figures. Let's go." Em threw her purse over her shoulder and locked her arm through Bryan's. "We'll be late. I can't wait for you to hear Bryan sing in church." Her blue eyes glazed, lashes batting at her friend.

"We've all heard him sing." She didn't mean to say that, especially in a sharp tone. "And he's incredibly talented."

Elinor coughed, her throat still itchy from the night before. Probably a good thing because she should just be quiet.

After a tap on the back door, Sam entered. Red blotches spotted his face, and dark circles carved under his eyes.

Elinor gasped.

"What happened to your face?" Tugging Bryan along, Em walked over to inspect.

Sam ran his hand across his left cheek, scratching. "Mosquitoes. I sat out on the dock last night a little too long."

"Do you want to borrow my cover stick? I have a good one." Em released Bryan and rummaged in her handbag.

"I'm fine."

Worry tugged at Elinor. "You should wear repellent. You might catch West Nile Virus."

Sam's eyes met hers, wide and tender. "Thank you. I'll try to remember that."

Was he being sarcastic? If so, his voice didn't give him away. She dropped her gaze to the floor. "We should go."

Cassie jangled her keys. "I can take seven in my van, but there are eight of us."

"I'll take my car and follow." Sam slipped his own keys out. "I'll be in the red Mazda."

In no time, Em was at Elinor's side, nudging her. "You need to ride with him, Elinor. In case he gets lost."

"They make phones with GPS now. I'm sure he can keep up with a minivan in his little sports car." The last thing she wanted was to carry on a conversation with him today.

"He's our guest." Em kept at it, as if manners and decorum were suddenly at the top of her list. "And the van will be too crowded with seven."

Sam sucked in a deep breath and shrugged. "I wouldn't mind the company. And sometimes the GPS takes you all around the world."

There seemed to be no winning. "Of course. Where's your car?"

He motioned with his head. "I parked off in the side yard under a shade tree, so everyone could get in and out last night."

He pointed to her father. "Roy said it was okay."

"I'm sure it's fine." The sooner they got going, the sooner the morning would end and she could go home.

Outside, they crossed the drive, heat smothering the early morning already. Elinor followed a step behind Sam without speaking. Could they go the whole ride in silence? It would make things less awkward. Or would it? When the sports car came into view, they both stopped. Splashes of white covered the red car, and dozens of White Ibises roosted in the tree's branches overhead.

"No. No. No." Sam groaned. "What's with wildlife here? They hate me. First the dog chase, then seagulls, then that possum, now this."

"Possum?"

Their voices spooked the flock. The birds honked and grunted, shook their wings, and took flight.

Glancing up, Elinor covered her head with her purse. "I hope your misfortune isn't contagious. I've enough trouble of my own." She waved him forward, and they ran toward the house. "Let's take my car."

~~~

Hands over his head, Sam tailed Elinor, not stopping until they reached her car. The locks clicked, and they both jumped in. "Of all the foul luck." He slammed the door. Attack a man, but not his car. "I hope there's a good carwash nearby. If I can even see to drive through the mess on the windshield."

"I wouldn't know." Elinor cranked her Lexus and backed out the drive. "I clean my car myself."

Why was she being so snooty? It wasn't like she drove a bargain vehicle. He glanced around at the pristine, dust-free leather. "Hard to believe your car stays this clean without a detailer."

"And why is that?" Her chin lifted as she pulled onto the flat road surrounded by sand and green foliage.

"It's spotless, and if you can afford to buy one of these, you can afford to get it cleaned."

"I bought this car for the reliability rating. I am a woman
~~~

alone, who'll no doubt stay alone, and I want a reliable vehicle."

Stay alone? A throbbing ache gnawed in his chest. Were they both doomed to be lonely? "Ellie, just because Craig was a slime bucket doesn't mean you—"

"Halt." Her voice and her chin trembled. "I cannot talk about that man or last night or anything else right now."

"But—"

"Please." Tears welled up in her eyes. She kept her gaze straight ahead.

"Okay." Frustrated, Sam worked his jaw. Somehow he needed to get through to her. But how?

There's another battle that'll need prayer.

Roy's words came back to him. Praying? He'd give it a try. Nothing else had worked in his life, and Roy sure believed in God's love.

He mashed his eyes shut. *Lord, please help Elinor believe in love again. For that matter, help me believe and figure out what I'm supposed to do with my life. In Jesus' precious name, amen.*

Roy often ended his prayers with those words. Seemed fitting.

"We're here. Are you asleep?" Elinor's voice broke through, and Sam opened his eyes to find hers searching his face.

He held her gaze until she turned away to open her door.

"Come on. You can nap later. I hope you don't fall asleep in church. Unless one is over seventy or under ten, it's considered rude."

"I wasn't sleeping." Sam shook his head. She'd gone back to the snippy, bossy Elinor. The one with the high walls and maybe even a deep moat sealing off her heart. How would he ever breach her defenses?

Chapter 16

Inside the large, contemporary church, Sam followed Elinor as she joined her family. Roy and the others stood visiting with friends in the rows around them. When the director began a song, a momentary hush fell over the group, and they took their seats.

Elinor squeezed past knees to plonk down on the other end of the line of cushioned chairs, leaving Sam beside Cassie. The action speared his chest and allowed little doubt that Elinor wanted to be as far away from him as possible. Somehow he had to prove that all men weren't jerks. Okay, maybe he'd been a jerk a few times, but nothing nearing criminal. And he'd been wronged by a woman just as badly.

A deep sigh ran through him at the thought of Tiffany and their almost-wedding day. Standing at the altar in the Oxford church wearing a tuxedo, waiting like an idiot in front of friends and family. That romance crashed and burned. Likely, nothing good would come of this romance either. He'd traveled to Mobile to regroup and start a new career, not find a girlfriend. If Elinor shut him out, there'd be little hope of changing the stubborn woman's mind. Why bother?

Sam squirmed as those around him sang. It'd been a while since he'd been to a church service. Although his mother took them through elementary school, by junior high, Select Soccer and Baseball tournaments filled most of their weekends. And the only reason Dad ever went was to talk to clients.

Sam's focus pulled back to the voices around him. Bryan really did sound fantastic during the three or four songs he led, which seemed to be focused on faith. And hope.

As if God were bolstering his resolve.

Then the minister stepped onto the platform. He asked the

assembly to follow along in their Bibles, so Sam opened the app Roy suggested he download on his phone. Hebrews 11 and 12. The church must plan these things because the reading also spoke of faith, of things hoped for. The first chapter listed and commended men and women of the Old Testament. Sam glanced at Roy. They'd talked about many of the historical figures in their daily Bible studies on leadership. The passage referred to them as pilgrims seeking a homeland. Believers who'd suffered severe trials.

Many verses applied to the place he found himself, while others brought home the fact that he'd really enjoyed an easy life overall. Sure, he'd suffered a heartache and humiliation from Tiffany and harshness from his father, but never persecution. One verse spoke of running the course with endurance. A fire lit in Sam's heart. He had nothing if not endurance. With God's help, he'd run harder, try harder, and not give up, no matter where his path led him. He would not be shaken off course this time.

The sermon ended with the rereading of one of the beginning verses. "But without faith it is impossible to please God, because anyone who comes to God must believe He exists and that He rewards those who earnestly seek Him."

Could he have that kind of faith? He wasn't sure, but maybe he wanted to try.

~~~

Ridiculous allergies. Elinor searched for a corner of the tissue she hadn't filled with the moisture collecting in her eyes. When her mother squeezed her knee, more liquid dripped to her cheeks. Not tears. She wasn't crying. Even though the songs and the sermon unnerved her a tad. But why?

Faith and hope. She'd always had faith in the Lord, and she worked hard to weave in a clean, virtuous message for the readers of her books. She had hope in God. Maybe not in mankind, but there was nothing wrong with keeping her personal life between her and the Lord. Still, her stomach churned, once rolling so loudly that Em looked down the row at her and giggled. Such a little brat.
~~~

After the benediction, Elinor grabbed Mother's arm. "Will you ride with me? We can reserve a table at the restaurant. Sam can take your place in the van." She gave her a beseeching look. "Please?"

Mother pressed her lips together and nodded. "Okay. Let everyone know the plan so Sam doesn't get left at church."

Exhaling a long sigh, Elinor searched for her keys. "I will." Did her mother think she'd leave the man? Although the idea held appeal, they were at church, after all. She'd tried to soak in the lesson. Some. Now, which family member to tell? She glanced down the row. The obvious choice was Cassie. Her older sister would make sure Sam didn't get left behind and wouldn't barrage her with questions.

After notifying Cassie, she approached Sam. The least she could do. And Mother said she had to. Elinor tapped his shoulder once with a quick touch.

Sam turned, cerulean and indigo eyes exploring her face. "Great service. I like this church. I hadn't been in years, so…" He chewed the corner of his lip for a second and shrugged. "Let's say I wasn't looking forward to attending, but I'm glad I did. You?"

Words tangled in Elinor's throat, forming a chokehold. The unexpected question delivered a harsh blow to her plan. Here the man stood, wanting to discuss the worship service while she'd come to rid herself of him. "Yes." Perhaps the simple answer covered her distress.

Still staring at her, he waited for more words. Why was he hounding her about the service? Elinor searched her mind for an insightful comment that might end the discourse. "The heroes of the faith chapter in Hebrews is one of my favorites."

Sam waited as if she'd say more. When she didn't, he bobbed his head. "Heroes of the faith chapter. Good name for it. Figures you'd like the heroes. But I also related with the next chapter when the writer talked about endurance."

Heat blazed to Elinor's ears. "What? Why would I like the heroes?"

"You're a writer. Writers love the heroes, right?"

The man presumed to know her deep emotions now? "Would you allow me the courtesy to ruminate my own thoughts?"

Sam's brows converged in deep furrows above his nose. "What?"

Mother moved around the end of the row to join them. "Ready?"

"Absolutely." Elinor pointed at the rest of the family, who stood a few feet away. "Sam, you'll ride with Cassie while Mother and I go on to the restaurant."

His face contorted further, forcing Elinor's stomach to twist into a tighter knot inside. She wouldn't let him get to her, though. After all, Craig had attended church with her family. And none of Craig's words had meant a thing.

~~~

Sam unfolded his legs in an attempt to exit the backseat of the van. His foot slipped on a children's book and projected him forward, bonking his head.

"Are you okay?" Em waited and checked on him but seemed to be holding in a giggle.

"Fine."

The giggle broke out. "Good, but now you have a big red spot on your forehead. At least it matches your mosquito bites."

"I'm lucky like that."

"Come on, then. Let's see if Mom and Nora got us a table."

He followed the family inside, going last through the door. If he'd had his own car, he would've bowed out. Obviously, Elinor didn't want him around.

In the entrance, she stood beside her mother, annoyance written all over her face.

Em groaned. "No table yet?"

"Yes. We just prefer to dawdle around by the hostess desk rather than sit and eat." Elinor's thin shoulders hunched as though she carried a weight on her back.

"Um…*somebody's* especially cranky today." Em's hands went to her hips. "What's got your—"
~~~

"If it isn't my beloved Elinor Elizabeth Bosarge." A man dressed in a black suit slipped between patrons to stretch out both arms toward Elinor. "Mon bella chéri." He grabbed her shoulders and kissed both her cheeks. "Your eyes still twinkle like the stars in the sky. So blue like the sea and heavens on high."

A look of horror widened Elinor's eyes. They were blue like sea and sky, but not currently twinkling. "Bo? What are you doing here? I thought you moved to New Orleans." Her jaw tightened and twitched. Like she hoped he still lived in The Big Easy.

Sam stifled a laugh that ended up coming through his nose as a snort. The man's accent almost sounded French—but not. And the rhyming…

"Ahhh, my fleur, alas, like the tender morning shoots, I have come home to my roots." Bo's arms gave a dramatic wave around. "I'm the new proprietor here." He tucked his head down and lowered his voice. "And I go by Beauregard now."

"Beauregard?" Em belted out the name like a cheer at a pep rally.

"Oui. Beauregard Wylie at your beck and call, come one, come all." He bowed. "For the lovely Elinor Elizabeth, time will not waste. I'll make haste and procure the best table in the house. For I will give no cause for her to think me a louse." He shook each of their hands and then shuffled off.

If Em's voice sounded like a cheerleader last time, her cackle couldn't have reverberated through the room any louder if she'd held a microphone. "Nora, what's the scoop with that one? Or should I say, keep me in the loop, what's the scoop, don't make me jump through a hoop?"

Sam pinched his mouth and nose closed with his hand to stop any words or chuckles from escaping. The crazed look on Elinor's face told him she was close to losing it.

"Is he the poetry guy, Elinor?" Cassie's voice stayed low as she leaned in.

A slight nod was the only answer.

"Ooooh, that's him?" Em's eyes grew round as her

eyelashes lifted. "I forgot that one. You weren't exaggerating at all."

The poetry guy? Sam studied Elinor's mangled expression. "Bad date?"

"If you must know. Yes."

"Where's he from? I can't place the accent?"

"Alabama, but he spent a semester abroad. Ever since, well, he tries—key word tries—to act European." Her eyes rolled back as she shook her head. "I hope he doesn't start harassing me with poetry again through the mail."

"Harassed by poetry." He shot her his kindest look. "You win."

Her lips quirked for a second as if she might smile.

Until Bo reappeared.

Holding menus, Beauregard led them to a table overlooking the bay. "My quest is only the best for you, mademoiselle." His eyebrows raised and lowered as he pulled out a chair for her.

Before taking a seat, Sam bent near Elinor's ear. "You're welcome to use me as an excuse again. Pretend I'm your date."

Her gaze stayed focused straight ahead. "Your assistance is not required."

Chapter 17

A nap might help. Sam used one foot to push off a leather loafer, did the same on the other side, and then swung his feet up on the couch. Between the late night, his father's phone call, and the early church service, his energy had crashed during brunch. Elinor's snub didn't help, zapping a large part of the hope he'd mustered.

Not all, though. She was still reeling from Craig's surprise appearance. She needed time, and she'd gone for it, abandoning them all as soon as the last fork hit the plate. Off to her beach cottage.

Back to his nap plan. Sam closed his eyes, and images appeared in his mind. Red hair and blue eyes set against the white sand and the Gulf's clear waters. What did her cottage look like?

He sat up. No lying around pining for a woman. The hairless cat in the portrait by the fireplace stared back at him, almost a pitiful stare, really. Elinor had taken off from the restaurant, leaving the rest of them to squeeze into the van. Had she left Mr. Darcy behind, too?

Why did he care? Ugly cat.

He pushed his feet to the floor and bounced up and down on his toes a few times. A run always cleared his head, but one step out the door into the midday summer heat stifled that idea. Swimming? He shook his head. Reminded him of her.

Work. He'd do something productive. At a makeshift desk on the kitchen table, he rifled through files, turned on the laptop, and checked the to-do list on his phone. With the charity ball over, the remodeling of Memory Oaks took priority. Even though Elinor served on the committee, he'd have to get moving on the plans. A drive over to the retirement home this afternoon might start his gears to turning.

Sam shut his computer, slipped his feet back into his loafers, and headed out. When he neared his desecrated car, he groaned. He'd wash this baby first, then on to Memory Oaks.

~~~

Waves tumbled over Elinor's back and legs as she sat, the warm salty spray misting up in her face, washing away all the memories. Only sun, wind, and tide. The sand slipped from beneath her as the waves pulled back the other way, taking small shells and hopefully her cares back out to sea. The constant rhythmic motion set her at ease.

A few feet away, a toddler and her parents played in the small surf lapping the shore. Their laughter and squeals of delight both warmed and pinched Elinor's heart. She'd never be a wife and mother. Not that a single woman couldn't have a good life. In fact, she had a great life—writing in her little cottage…dining on fresh seafood most nights with Mr. Darcy, and watching God's sunset paint a brilliant canvas. It all gave her contentment. All that plus a publishing contract, good health, and wonderful parents.

Wind caught the little girl's pink beach hat and sailed it over to drop near Elinor's toes which peeked out of the water. On instinct, she snatched the hat before another gust or the surf carried it farther away. Elinor struggled to stand and waded over. "Here you go, hon."

Only a few yellow curls grew from the smiling toddler's head, making her blue eyes stand out. Good thing she'd caught the hat, or the girl's head would burn in the midday sun. Her parents still gripped the toddler's hands on either side and made no move to take the hat, as if they were afraid to let go of her. Elinor gently replaced it.

"Thank you." Both parents spoke at once and then exchanged smiles with each other.

"You're welcome. She's a doll."

"She is. We're so blessed." The mother spoke with intensity.

What a deep, powerful love. "Has she been to the beach before? A lot of kids don't like the sand."
~~~

"Never." The father shook his head. "But she's been a trouper. We're in youth ministry, and this is our first vacation as a family since we had her. A member of our congregation loaned us a cottage down here this week."

"How sweet. I'm a local and live in the yellow cottage behind you." Elinor pointed at her home. "If you need directions or restaurant recommendations, come by. Oh, except I'm helping my mother in Mobile some." Why was she telling strangers she'd be gone?

The man squinted. "The cottage with the blue tarp?"

"That's the one." After offering a forced smile, Elinor returned to her spot in the sand. She plopped down. If it weren't for the crazy storm damage, maybe she wouldn't have seen Craig. Or met Sam. No. She shook her head. The surgery. The ball. The Memory Oaks committee. There'd been no way around meeting…him.

An urgent feeling overtook her, like a nudge from above. She needed to go to Memory Oaks. *Perhaps something is wrong. Is that you, Lord?*

"I need to go see Miss Zula."

A jogger stared at Elinor as he ran by. Had she been talking to herself out loud again? Living alone, or rather with a pet, and writing imaginary characters bred a bad habit. Talking to and answering oneself.

She glanced at the family again. The little girl was so adorable. What would her own children look like if she had any? A blue-eyed girl? Or boy?

Sam's face came to mind.

Elinor groaned. Seeing Miss Zula was a good idea. She'd go now, and come back to the beach when fewer people would be out.

Chapter 18

The pungent smell of antiseptic and pine hit Sam's nose as soon as he entered the front hall of Memory Oaks. Could be worse. But he'd look up the latest research on odor management later. He showed his ID and signed in at the front desk, and then made a note on his phone to find out what other security measures were taken. Cameras? Alarms?

Being Sunday, family members visited in little groups here and there. Sam made another note. *Check on forming small visiting areas.* A nurse met him as he entered the common area where residents milled around.

"Mr. Conrad. Hello. Mr. Bosarge here?" The nurse's big smile pulled him from business mode.

"Just me." He lifted one shoulder. "With the charity ball over, the numbers will be in soon, so we'll need to be ready to give a proposal to your board for approval."

"So wonderful." The grin widened, revealing straight, white teeth. "I'm thrilled for the residents and can't wait to see the recommendations."

"Hmm." Sam scratched his chin.

Dark eyebrows lifted. "Aside from my dear husband, these people are my heart."

"I'm sorry." After pocketing his phone, Sam extended his hand. "I forgot your name."

"No worries." With a strong grip, the brown hand took his. "It's Tara."

"Would you be willing to look through the ideas and give feedback? An honest opinion? You know this place better than I do."

"It'd be an honor."

"Maybe you have suggestions, too?"

A deep, rich laugh followed. "Sam Conrad, a woman always has a few notions, don't you know?"

"I'm a slow learner sometimes." He fished a card from his wallet. "Email your suggestions, and I'll send you what I have."

"Will do." She slipped his card into a bag and turned to continue on her way.

"Wait."

"Yes?"

"Where's Nubbin? Um, the preacher?"

"Ah. Mr. Hammill." Her smile faltered. "He fell while trying to get up, and his back's hurting. You can visit him in Room 203."

A pang of compassion mixed with worry tightened Sam's stomach. "Any breaks or fractures? They had him examined, right?"

"Yes." Tara nodded. "An MRI, even. No breaks. He has some good bones, just muscle strain."

"What's the plan for recovery? Physical therapy?"

"Starts tomorrow."

Sam clucked his tongue. "I'm doing PT observation hours. Maybe I could observe here part of the time?"

One side of her mouth lifted. "With Mr. Bosarge as your recommendation, I have a good feeling you'll receive a green light."

"Great. I'll see you soon, Tara."

Once he'd navigated the stark white halls to Room 203, Sam hesitated. What would he say to the man? Doubt trickled in. What did he know of bedside manner?

Faith.

Hope.

Run with endurance.

Sam knocked then pushed open the door. "Mr. Hammill?"

"Hey, stranger." The old man waved him in. The movement caused Mr. Hammill's jaw to flinch, but the smile never left his face. "Come sit awhile. And call me Nubbin."

"Sure you're up to it, Nubbin? I heard you took a spill."

"You know better than most, takes more than a little fall to get old Nubbin down."

Chuckling, Sam pulled up a chair and crossed one ankle over the other knee. "They feeding you good?"

"I could use a cookie in a minute." Through the layers of aged and wrinkled skin, Nubbin's expression became serious. "First, tell me, son, do you know Jesus?"

"Sir, I'm getting to know Him."

~~~

What was *he* doing here? Elinor groaned as she passed the freshly-washed red Mazda in the parking lot. There seemed to be no escaping the man, but since she was already here, she may as well go in.

In the entrance hall, she looked left then right. No sign of Sam. Quick strides carried her as fast as possible toward the nurses' station. She greeted and smiled at residents along the way. Seeing Tara's pink scrubs and dark hair at the desk relieved a bit of the tautness in Elinor's forehead.

"Thank goodness you're here." Elinor kept her voice just above a whisper and leaned beside the chair where Tara worked. "Where's that…that…*pesky* man?"

"Hello to you, too." Cocking her chin, Tara tapped her fingers one at a time on the desk. "I've seen a lot of men today."

"You know who I'm talking about."

"I do and I don't." Tara's eyebrows lifted as she gave her a sidelong glance. "Mr. Conrad is here. Last I heard, he was visiting with Mr. Hammill, and there's nothing pesky about that."

"Okay." That was a bit nice, but he probably had some ulterior motive. Like Craig had. "Where's Miss Zula? I want to see her, but can't deal with running into—"

"I didn't want to call you with the charity ball going on yesterday." Tara placed a hand on Elinor's.

A whirlpool of emotions sucked the breath from Elinor's lungs. Her chest tightened. "What's wrong? She's not…?"

"Hospice came yesterday." Tara squeezed Elinor's shoulder. "She's slipping away. Her time is close."
~~~

"But she seemed better a few days ago. Spoke even."

"Many times they rally just before the end. She hadn't wanted to eat or drink in a while."

No. Not yet. Moisture filled her vision. "Is she in her room?"

"Yes."

"Has her son been notified?"

"On his way. He'll be here tomorrow. I hope she lasts until…"

"It happened so quickly."

"Sometimes the disease accelerates, with others they linger on years and years."

Perhaps quicker was better, but she'd miss her so. "I have to go to her." Gathering strength and determination, Elinor took a step. It didn't matter if Craig himself stood between them, she'd be with her dear friend and teacher.

"Want me to go with you?"

"No. I… No."

Fingers of grief clawed her insides on the way down the lengthy, carpeted hall. So many lovely memories of Miss Zula. Hours spent chatting about their favorite heroes and heroines. Miss Zula's encouraging and helpful comments on rough drafts of novels. Her bright smile and wit.

Elinor steeled herself. The end was inevitable, and in some ways welcomed after a battle with Alzheimer's, but it still hurt. Why hadn't she thought to bring a book to read to Miss Zula?

Inside the dimly lit room, soft hymns played. A small woman in her late sixties, gray hair in a bun, sat at Miss Zula's side. She stood when Elinor entered. "Are you her daughter?"

"Not a biological one." The weight of her feet increased exponentially with each step closer to the drawn-up body in the bed.

"The best kind of daughter sometimes. A daughter of the heart." The woman smiled. "Take my seat. I'll pull a chair outside the door and give you privacy."

A nod was all she could muster as Elinor searched the sallow face amid a pile of pillows. A slow, raspy breath lifted Miss Zula's thin chest a fraction.

"You can talk to her. The hearing is the last thing to go, they say. I don't think she has much longer." After pushing out the chair a little, the hospice worker disappeared, leaving Elinor alone with Miss Zula.

"Hello. It's me. Elinor." She took one of the wrinkled hands and flinched at the coolness of the bony fingers. A pale, bluish hue tinted the skin. Reality choked Elinor's thoughts, and her eyes burned. She had to keep her composure. It wouldn't do to fall apart blathering. Why hadn't she picked up a book? A sigh rushed through her lips. "I'll see how much poetry I can quote. You made us memorize all those lines way back when."

Come on brain. Remember something. "I know." She took a deep breath. "She walks in beauty, like the night."

Elinor continued until Miss Zula gave a long exhale and then breathed no more.

~~~

"See you later, Nubbin." Sam shook the old preacher's hand. He'd stayed longer than he'd expected, talking and watching the Braves game. At least he'd made a few notes on his phone while they hung out.

Nubbin held tight to Sam's hand, a powerful grip for any age. "Before you go, would you mind getting me a cookie? Or three?"

The ladies in the kitchen had given Sam some strange looks the last two times Nubbin had sent him on a dessert run, so going again would be a delicate undertaking. "I'll do my best."

"That's all I ask." A grin lifted the wrinkled lips.

A quick but quiet pace took Sam to the hall by the kitchen, where he waited until the workers handed out juice to residents in the living area. The cookie jar, though hidden on a top shelf, was accessible if one were crafty. He slipped in, lifted the lid slightly, and grabbed. With a light touch, he closed the cabinet and tiptoed away.

Halfway down the hall, he glanced backward to make sure he had gotten away clean.

"Watch out!" An all too familiar voice punched him. He stopped just in time to avoid a head-on collision with Elinor.
~~~

Her face held a fierce look, and he offered a sheepish smile. "Sorry. I was on a secret cookie mission that required stealth." Would humor ease the anger in her voice?

"You could seriously injure someone here if you aren't careful. This isn't a football field." Her fierce gaze sliced with the precision of a scalpel.

One would think he'd killed someone the way she looked at him. "You must've been going fast yourself. I only glanced back for a second."

Her chin tilted then lowered with her gaze. "Please, just move."

Sam took a step to the left. "Have you had a chance to study the information I gave you?"

Bracing herself on a doorframe with one hand, she pressed her fingers over her eyes and the bridge of her nose. No answer.

"For the committee, I mean. Since the funds will be tallied this week, I thought we'd need to make some decisions." Why wasn't she talking? "I spoke to Tara, and she's going to chime in on everything." Should he blunder on or shut up now? "Seeing how she works here and seems to love the residents, I thought—"

"For once—since you arrived in Mobile—can you leave me alone?"

The words hit like a slap in the face. He stepped back, swallowed the hurt. "Yep." The last thing he needed was more verbal abuse. He worked his jaw as he took off to Nubbin's room. Cookies delivered, he hightailed it to the parking lot, slammed the car door, and slapped the steering wheel. That woman exasperated him to no end. Left him feeling just as incompetent as his father always had.

Chapter 19

Throngs of pupils spanning forty years filled the church to celebrate the life of their favorite teacher. The minister read an encouraging letter Miss Zula had written and addressed to all her former students while she still had her wits about her. Many went forward and shared stories, poems, memories—some poignant, others humorous. Elinor brushed back the third onslaught of tears since breakfast. Mother took her hand and squeezed. At least the funeral had all been arranged in advance.

The memorial service ended, and Miss Zula's son, Rob, caught Elinor in the parking lot. "I know I said it at the visitation, but I'm glad you were with her at the end. She told me many times you were like the daughter she never had."

"I loved her." Elinor's throat felt as if pierced with thorns. No more words found their way to her tongue.

"She knew. And she left something for you." Rob held up his hand. "Wait right here." His pained expression and brisk stride reminded her she wasn't the only one hurting. No doubt Miss Zula's only son wished he could have made it in time to say goodbye.

Elinor hugged her arms around her waist and swayed, soothing herself as a child would. In about two minutes, Rob strode back carrying a package as big as two shoeboxes.

"Here." Rob held it out. "She wanted you to have this. Packed it when we got the diagnosis."

The package pulled Elinor's arms down as she took it. "Oh."

"Heavy." One side of Rob's mouth lifted. "Maybe it's bricks. Or some old antique books you two were so crazy about."

Elinor's breath caught. "Rob, I can't. Sell them for your ministry."

"She gave me plenty to sell for the ministry. These few are for you to keep." His hazel eyes locked on hers, the same color and steel gaze she'd seen so many times from his mother. "I mean business, young lady."

A soft chuckle found its way out at Rob's impression of his mother. "Yes, ma'am. I mean, sir." Elinor's arms hugged the gift while her fingers caressed the brown packaging. "She was proud of you and your ministry. She told everyone about the orphanage in Texas back when she…remembered."

"I know." He gave a slow nod. "I wish she'd been willing to move closer to us, but she planned out everything with Memory Oaks. Mobile was home. Maybe I should've moved her once her mind got bad enough. She might not have known, and I could've been there when—"

"Don't. She wouldn't want you to carry a burden of guilt. You got here as soon as you could. It just went faster than expected."

After saying goodbye, Elinor turned her car toward Fort Morgan. She needed the beach. She needed time to think and to process this loss. How hard it must be on Rob, losing his mother. She shuddered at the thought.

Back at the cottage, the carpenters banged around. Elinor took a couple of ibuprofen, left her shoes on the back deck, and carried the package out to the beach. One piece of tape at a time, she pulled off the plain brown paper. Breath held, she lifted the lid. *Pride and Prejudice, Poems by Emily Dickinson, British Poets 7 Volumes.*

The last book in the stack brought fresh tears. *Kindred Devotion* by Liz Hart. The first book Elinor had sold under her pen name. She opened the cover.

A paper lay inside. Her fingers shook as she unfolded the stationery.

Dear Elinor,

There is power in story. Stories change thinking, change lives. There is beauty in words. Words work their way into our hearts and nuzzle us up to greater heights. Words and stories inspire leaders, change societies, and spark revolutions.

I'll never forget the first essay you wrote. I knew right away I had a writer in my class. You have a God-given gift, dear Elinor. You wield the power of story and the beauty of words. I ask you to continue to hone that gift to bless, inspire, and nurture. Transform lives for the better. Spark a revolution of love for the first Author.

You know I could write on and on, but sometimes less is more. I'll leave you with three more thoughts. Though I'm old enough to be your grandmother, you are my daughter of kindred devotion. To truly love God, you must love man made in His image. Your kitten is not your Mr. Darcy.

Love always,
Zula Mae Chastain.

Chapter 20

Why couldn't hospitals look cheerier? At least paint a few beach scenes on the walls, maybe a nice blue sky and white clouds on the ceilings. Elinor stood at her mother's side as medical personnel fastened monitors, asked the same questions five times in five different ways, and attached an IV pole. A machine beeped in another little alcove nearby. With each bleep, shivers crawled up Elinor's neck. They'd been here a couple of hours already—practically since dawn. What took so long? Didn't hospitals have a schedule to keep?

At last, the anesthesiologist came in. He asked all the questions once more, and had the nurse inject something into the tubing.

Elinor's stomach clenched as she kissed her mother's head. "I'll be waiting and praying. Love you, Momma."

"Be sweet to Roy, hon. He's nervous, too, you know."

"I will." She forced her lips to form a smile.

After all that waiting, a nurse rolled Mother away. She disappeared around a corner, taking a chunk of Elinor's heart with her.

She trudged to the waiting room and sat beside her father. "They took her and said they'll call us with updates." She pointed to a small counter with a portable phone. "That's the phone they'll call us on."

"I sure hope they take good care of my Ruby." Bent forward, elbows on knees, his palms supported his head.

"Everyone looked very professional and careful." She hesitated before resting a hand on his back. "I've been praying for her all night and this morning, too."

"Thank you, princess. I know that helps, and I sure am glad you're here." He swiveled toward her. "Your mother is, too.

You're a good daughter."

Elinor nodded. Would she be a good caregiver, though?

~~~

A few hours with his mind wrapped around Roy's financial statements allowed Sam a needed respite from the drama that was Elinor Bosarge. Sam's fingers ran across the computer keys as he reviewed each investment. Roy's financial planner seemed sound except for one recent large transfer to a mutual fund. He'd never heard of it, and the product didn't show up on any of the sites where he'd expected to find a review. Sam made a note to schedule a meeting with the broker soon. It couldn't hurt to make a call to his friend who worked for the Securities Exchange Commission.

The phone rang, vibrating on the desk. Not a number he recognized, but a local area code so he should probably answer. "Hello."

"May I speak with Mr. Samuel Theodore Conrad?" The woman's voice sounded professional.

"You've got him."

"I'm calling from the School of Physical Therapy here in Mobile."

His pulse accelerated. "Yes, ma'am."

"I wanted to speak to you in person, since you came so highly recommended, and your circumstances are a little bit unusual."

"Okay. Thank you." There was a big but coming in this conversation somewhere. He could feel it.

"Your academic qualifications are excellent. However, this late in the summer, all of our spots are filled for fall. And there's the fact that you were accepted into another premier PT school in the past, which leaves me with questions."

"I understand. Ask away."

Didn't sound promising. Obviously, she'd talked to the university in Mississippi.

"If an unexpected spot came open and we gave it to you, what's to say you wouldn't back out at the last minute again?"

"Honestly?"
~~~

"I think total openness is the best course for me to understand the whole picture."

"At the time, I was pressured by my former fiancée to take a lucrative job offer rather than go to school full time for three more years." No need to mention his father's intrusion.

"I see. Former. And you've been employed at the same place since that time?"

"Yes, ma'am. Steady, hardworking employee, but I'm ready to pursue my own life dream now."

A pause hung between them. "Hmm, what if—to show your sincerity—I asked you to find a position as a physical therapy aide until the next opening?"

"I'm listening. Calculating." The salary would be lower as an aide. He'd have to dip into his savings, not only for the tuition and living expenses during school, but also for months before. What would Elinor think about a man on a tight budget? A man who already reminded her of that slimeball Craig.

"That's important. It could be up to a year. Consider carefully and let me know. Let's say…by the end of next week?"

"I will. Thank you."

Once the call ended, he leaned back in his chair. He'd need to check rentals in the area. There was no way he'd impose on Big Roy for much longer. He wasn't the kind of man who lived off the generosity of others. He'd prove to Elinor he was different than Craig. But…he would be living poor for three or four years, then a salary, though even that would be significantly lower than what he'd come to rely on. The other alternative would be to stay in Mobile and keep working in an industry he cared nothing about, but at least he'd have money. And maybe Elinor's respect.

Why was she in the center of his decision?

The phone vibrated with a text. "What now?"

He checked the name. Mom. Probably just Dad. Again.

Your three week "vacation" is over at the end of next week. Expect to see you bright and early the following Monday morning or you can forget ever working in this town.

Yep. Not Mom. And no Father-of-the-Year award for Dad. Not that his father could keep the competition from hiring him. Other people in Oxford respected his business skills, but that would bring more friction to an already explosive family relationship.

He blew out a long breath. At least he had a solid deadline to decide his future—the end of next week.

Sam glanced at a shadow out the window. A cardinal tweeted from the sill. The sharp crimson crest and feathers stood out against the blue sky and water behind. Such a deep red. Not as pretty a color as Elinor's hair.

For all that was right in the world, why did everything have to remind him of her?

After checking his watch, he shut down the laptop and took the last swig of coffee. Ruby's surgery should be starting soon, and for some irrational reason, he felt compelled to sit with Roy. And Elinor. A glutton for torture, no doubt. Maybe that was why he'd worked for his father for so long.

Where was that hospital? Hadn't he seen the information hung from a magnet in the big house? He walked briskly over and unlocked the back door. Dashwood and Mr. Darcy rubbed circles around his legs as he made his way through. "Hello, dear fellows."

He rolled his eyes at the naked cat. "I must be losing my mind." After petting each one, he found the note and typed the address into his phone. Squinting, he read the directions through the cracks of the damaged screen. Shouldn't take more than twenty minutes with no traffic. His car stood shining in the midmorning sun. Probably hot as an oven, but no bird desecration like when he'd parked under that big shade tree.

On the interstate, only a few cars got in his way. One in particular. Why couldn't slow people drive in the slow lane? *Maddening.* He punched the gas and passed on the right. The mission to get to the hospital weighed on him for some reason. Maybe he should pray. Not his normal routine, but it seemed appropriate. *God, please help Miss Ruby come through the operation okay.*

The GPS lady's voice interrupted his prayer and directed him to the exit. A tan brick building came into view. As he parked near the back of the lot, his conviction dissipated. Was he intruding? Would his presence make things worse?

God, was I wrong to come here? The urge felt so strong.

Fingers stiff, he opened the car door and followed the path to the entrance. Cool air blasted out as the glass door slid to the right. He chewed his lower lip, stepped through, but stopped just inside.

"Can I help you?" A woman behind a cubicle stared at him.

He may as well go in and find out if he'd made a big mistake. "I'm looking to sit with the family of patient Ruby Bosarge."

The woman clicked a few keys on her computer. "They're in the next waiting room." She pointed. "Down the hall and on the left."

Onward. He was a grown man doing a nice thing. Why did his heart have to sprint?

When the door opened, blue eyes met his. Fearful blue eyes. Elinor stood by a counter, holding a phone to her ear. Probably a surgery update. Roy's large frame dwarfed a small chair, his back toward Sam.

"Roy, any word on Miss Ruby?" Sam clasped one of the big shoulders.

Roy stood, pulled Sam into a bear hug, and squeezed. Hard. "Sam, thanks for coming. You're a good man."

How long had it been since anyone had said he was a good man? The words warmed him like the Alabama sun.

Bags under Roy's eyes dampened the usual cheerful smile. "Elinor's getting the update from the doctor now."

"I wanted to check in. Can I get you anything? Snacks or a Coke?"

"Nah, sit here and keep us company. Distract me." His voice lowered. "I don't know if you've noticed, but Elinor Elizabeth can be a little intense. Kinda like a cat in a dog pound."

Had he noticed? *Really?* A nod was the most polite answer

to that question. "I'll take a seat then." But which chair? By Roy, or should he leave one between them? Either way he was stuck by…her.

A second later, Elinor placed the phone back on the counter, pushed a few stray strands of red hair from her face, and walked their way.

Her expression was unreadable.

Here comes trouble.

Roy held out a hand. "What'd the doctor say?"

A small smile, as forced as a stretched balloon, lifted the corners of her lips. "He said it's taking more time than expected." Her throat lowered and lifted with a hard swallow. "There was extensive arthritis and a bone spur, plus scar tissue from that time she tore her meniscus several years ago. They said it was rare, but not anything to worry about. Just taking longer."

Something like a boulder cannoned Sam's chest. What should he say to ease her worry? If only he could take her in his arms.

Snap out of it. She'd probably slap him clear across the room. "Um, I researched the surgery last night and the risks are extremely low for complications." Maybe that was helpful.

Her head tilted, and a crinkle formed between her brows. "You researched the surgery?"

Sam frowned. Was he in trouble for researching now?

~~~

Elinor's pulse throbbed in her ears. Why hadn't she read up on this surgery? Sam had, and he wasn't even related. What kind of daughter was she? She prided herself on research for her books. She should care more about real life events. "What else did you find out online?"

Sam's lips twisted as he hesitated. Had her tone been accusatory? She didn't mean to take her guilt out on him. Although, his unnecessary presence bordered on intrusive. She and her father were fine.

She bit back a sigh. "I mean, is there something we need to know when we take Mother home? Preparations we should've
~~~

made? Mother didn't mention any, but she was so busy with the ball."

One of his shoulders lifted, and he crossed an ankle over his other knee. "Most likely they'll send her home with a walker. But I could go out and get a few other items that might be helpful."

"Continue. Um, please."

"Ice packs are a must. If they offer to rent you the ice machine, take it. You could have optional equipment like a bedside toilet chair, a tub chair with a transfer bench, a hand-held shower sprayer, grab bars in the bathroom..." He stared at his fingers. "Once she's up to it, a stationary bike at home would be convenient."

"My word. We haven't planned for this surgery at all." The weight of the responsibility drilled away her composure, and moisture stung her eyes.

"No, no." Sam's hand rested on top of hers and squeezed. "Those are extras, and she won't be released for a couple of days. Most people get by fine without all that. Except for the ice."

"My mother will not just get by." Elinor stripped her hand from beneath his. "Father, you have contacts. While we wait, can you call and have the bars installed and the other equipment delivered?"

"I can handle it." Sam's voice buzzed in her ears worse than a worrisome horse fly.

Why was he here anyway? He barely knew her parents, really. What was in it for him? He didn't seem like the charitable type. If they dug deeper into his past, they'd probably find Sam was a swindler like Craig, maybe of a posher sort. He was probably trying to get in her family's good graces just to ask for a loan or something. "My family's lived here all their lives. I'm sure we have plenty of friends to help in the time of need." She glanced at her father, then around the waiting room. But where were all their friends?

"Darlin', Sam's here and willing." Her father's words came out hushed, but slow and measured. "Let him help."

At least running errands would keep him out of her hair. "Yes, sir."

Her father stood and pulled out his wallet. "How much do you think it'll run ya?"

"Oh, no, sir." Shaking his head, Sam rose. "I'll keep receipts. If we end up not needing the items, I'll return them. If we do, we'll square up later."

They shook hands, and then Sam turned to her. "Call me if you need anything." His eyes locked onto hers. "I mean it. Anything, day or night."

A dagger couldn't have sliced further into her determination to despise the man. That look, his words, the willingness to help. She managed a single nod before he took his leave.

His departure left an emptiness in the room she hadn't felt before. When would the doctor call again about her mother?

An hour later, the ring of the phone jerked Elinor to her feet. "Hello."

"I'm calling for the family of Ruby Bosarge."

"This is her daughter."

"The surgery's over. The doctor will be down soon to go over how the surgery went."

"So we wait here?" In this wretched prison?

"Only a little longer."

"Thank you."

Elinor's heartbeat thrummed in her ears as she hung up. She shuffled back to her father's expectant expression and sat on the straight chair of torture. With people waiting so long, they should provide recliners. "Mother's out of surgery, and they'll be here soon to talk to us."

"Did they say how the surgery went?"

She filtered back through the conversation. "Come to think of it, they did not."

Chapter 21

It made sense for the medical supply store to be two blocks from the hospital. Sam ordered everything the sales specialist recommended and hightailed it back toward Elinor and Roy. They'd need a bigger vehicle than his to pick up the items. His sports car wasn't designed for hauling much more than two people and a bit of luggage. He jogged across the parking lot, despite the intense heat. Once inside, he slowed to a brisk walk until he reached the waiting room.

"Family of Ruby Bosarge," a voice called out as he entered. Elinor and Roy stood. Debating the wisdom of joining them took a second, but then he rushed to Elinor's side. "I'm back. The order will be ready to pick up tomorrow."

A long sigh came from her lips, but no words.

Was it a sigh of relief or annoyance?

"Right this way." The nurse walked ahead of them through the electronic door and down the white corridor. They reached an area with multiple patients behind individually curtained partitions and stopped. "She's still groggy but awake."

"But how did the surgery go? I thought the surgeon was coming to talk to us. Is she okay? What took so long?" Elinor's eyes both nailed and pleaded with the nurse.

"Your surgeon and the anesthesiologist will talk with you." The look the nurse returned bordered on guilt and compassion.

Sam's ribs squeezed at his insides. What had gone wrong?

They entered the small area, and Sam stepped to the corner, out of the way.

Machines beeped, and the cuffs on Ruby's calves filled with air. Her eyes fluttered open, and she shivered.

Another nurse stood at Ruby's side and checked the IV.

"We'll get you something for those shakes in just a minute."

Elinor ran her fingers across her mother's forehead. "Momma, are you okay? Are you in pain?"

"Good." Ruby's hoarse whisper was barely audible.

A second later two doctors appeared. Sam prepared to mentally take notes of the conversation.

~~~

Elinor held her breath as she waited for the doctors to explain. They'd better not have committed some egregious error with her mother.

The young clean-cut surgeon shook her father's hand, then held up a pile of printed photos. "Mr. Bosarge, your wife had a good deal of arthritis, scar tissue, and a bone spur." He flipped through photos of the inside of Mother's knee, explaining each section.

Sam stepped closer and took each photo to examine.

Whether or not he knew what he was looking at, it gave her a small bit of comfort. She could barely look at the pictures without feeling queasy. Why did they think someone would want to examine the inside of her mother's leg?

"Then we had another unusual problem." The surgeon turned to the anesthesiologist, the fifty-something balding man.

"Sir, has your wife ever experienced difficulties with anesthesia or blood pressure?"

"Sick." The sheets slid as Mother whispered, and she leaned forward.

Elinor turned back as the nurse grabbed a plastic bowl just in time. A surge of panic flushed through her veins. She spun to face the doctor. "What exactly happened to my mother? She obviously isn't well, and she told you and everyone else who asked ten times before the surgery that she's never had a problem with anesthesia."

"Her blood pressure dropped to…a dangerous level during the surgery. Normally this would happen before the procedure even starts, so it's not typical. And as you can see, she's extremely nauseated. We'll have a team to monitor her closely
~~~

for the next day or so—maybe move her to ICU if we can't keep the pressure steady." A breath whooshed through his teeth. "I'm sorry she didn't respond well to the anesthesia this time. It's an issue that may cause her problems in the future. I do feel I provided adequate care, and we are taking every measure possible to make sure she recovers well."

"Adequate?" Elinor's hands fisted.

Her father slid his arm around her and squeezed her shoulder. "What's the bottom line on my Ruby?"

"I think she'll be fine. We'll need to monitor her more closely than expected." The surgeon motioned to the nurse beside the bed. "Someone will stay with her until she's alert with a steady pressure. She has a pump for pain, but since she's groggy, we'll help with that, too."

"All right." Father's mouth tightened, and he looked at a loss for words for the first time in his life.

Sam stepped forward. "Doctor, will you be on call tonight? We'll need someone fully aware of her condition."

"No, but I'll give you my personal cell." He pulled a pad and pen from his pocket. "Call me, no matter what time, if you're concerned. Of course, I'll give a complete account to the partner on call." After scribbling the number, he handed the note to Sam.

When had Sam become a family member? Elinor kept her lips pressed closed. At least he asked a good question. Maybe it wasn't so bad to have him stick around. For a little while.

Chapter 22

Finally, Miss Ruby had been moved to a hospital room upstairs. A good sign, though it took all day and most of the evening. Sam pushed through the hospital room door with both arms full. Chick-fil-A bags, two small pillows, a fleece Snuggie, plus his computer. The quick run for food and to retrieve his computer from the car left him stressed. He'd stopped in two other stores to find the pillows for whoever stayed the night. He could've almost driven back to the house by the time he'd gotten the supplies he thought they'd need.

Elinor's brows shot up. "What is all that? You're not planning on spending the night, are you?"

"Let me help you, Sam-man." Ignoring his daughter, Roy shot to his feet and hurried to take the bedding. "Mighty thoughtful of you, son. We've kept you busier than a one-armed ditch digger. How about we cut on some baseball, real quiet, and let you sit down." He motioned to the couch beside Elinor.

Neither the spot nor the expression looked too welcoming, so he handed her a bag of food instead. Then he passed one to her father. "Sir, I don't want to intrude. Thought you might eat and rest a bit." Of course, he'd brought his computer in case they wanted him to stay.

"You're not intruding. They say Ruby's blood pressure's better, and they gave her some more nausea medicine not long ago. Poor thing's stayed sicker than a dog eatin' grapes. She's sleeping hard right now." Roy opened his sandwich. "And I feel better having someone observant like you around."

A huff came from Elinor.

"Now, little missy, you've got to admit Sam asked good questions when you and me stood there scared to death, bobbling our lips like little babes." Half of Roy's sandwich disappeared in a couple of bites.

The man's words weren't the way Sam would have described the earlier scene. It had looked more like Elinor wanted to skewer the doctors. "Of course, you were upset and worried. Perfectly normal."

Between chews, Roy sipped his sweet tea. "Elinor Elizabeth was madder than a wet hen. Thought she was gonna tell that anesthesiologist he was dumber than a box of rocks."

"Me, too." Sam chanced a glance her way. "Maybe you should have." He gave her a small smile.

Her mouth twitched as if she wanted to smile back, but couldn't. "Sit and eat." She pointed at the couch. "You bought yourself something, didn't you?"

"Ate it in the car." Taking advantage of her temporary kindness, he sat beside her. "How's she doing?" He motioned toward her mother.

Tears drowned Elinor's blue irises, and she didn't answer.

"Fair to middling." Roy answered for her. "Couldn't do her physical therapy for throwing up so much. Elinor did a mighty good job caring for her mother, and she's gotta be tuckered out." He tilted his head toward the door. "Why don't you let Sam take you home to sleep and come back in the morning?"

"No." She shook her head. "You go home. There's no way I could sleep."

"I can stay, too." The words slipped from Sam's mouth before he could think straight. "In case we need to call the doctor or something…"

"You two sure?" Roy stretched his legs in front of him.

"I'm sure." Elinor's gaze shifted sideways. "He can stay. Or not." She lifted one shoulder. "It doesn't matter."

~~~

Why did her skull have to throb now? Between the hospital chemical smells irritating her lungs and her mother being so sick, she'd love to close her eyes for a while. Not to sleep, but to rest them.

But Sam. Was his presence beneficial or harmful? He had
~~~

been slightly helpful. And he seemed to know the right questions to ask.

Once her father left, Elinor shifted over to the chair next to the couch. At least she'd have her own space. "They said this reclines somehow." She pushed back and forth trying to get the seat to give. Nothing.

"Here. Let me help." With a quick step, Sam hovered over her, fiddling with a lever on the side of the chair.

His breath warmed her ear, and his proximity was much too close. "Not necessary." She grimaced. "Really." Her chair took a sudden jerk back, and an unexpected squeak escaped from her throat.

Mother let out a soft moan.

"Shh." Elinor scowled. "She needs rest."

Sam froze in place above her.

A second later, her mother quieted and drifted back to sleep, her eyes shifting beneath closed lids.

"Sorry." Sam lingered before he crept back to the couch.

His somber gaze disrupted her anger, and she diverted her attention to the glowing television screen. A woman pointed to a map. A red swirling symbol marked where a hurricane hovered, gaining strength as it left the Caribbean and entered the Gulf of Mexico.

A noise like a zipper jerked her head back to Sam.

"Sorry." His voice was a whisper. He pulled out his computer in slow motion and punched a button. A beep sounded as the screen brightened. His eyes rounded. "Really sorry again."

She turned back to the TV. A hurricane making landfall within the next seven days on the Gulf Coast could be dangerous. Even if they only had a deluge of rain and power outages. Two white lines extended out, projecting the expected path between Florida and Texas. Like they ever actually knew where the horrific storms would make landfall.

"Cone of uncertainty. Who thought that term up?" Her teeth clamped together, and she covered her mouth. She hadn't meant to speak out loud. Her gaze slid to Sam. Likely, he'd make some snide remark. Or at least think it.

Instead, he motioned her over and pointed at his screen. Goodness. She'd just gotten comfortable. She climbed out of her reclined position in the torturous chair and lumbered toward him with heavy feet. Why had she let him stay? What did he think she wanted to see on his computer? Probably some ridiculous video like Em always insisted she watch.

Sam shifted the blasted machine toward her. The image caused her to swallow at a lump forming in her throat and she sat on the edge of the couch. He'd pulled up three different tabs of hurricane predictions and computer models.

He offered the computer to her. She nodded and tried to comprehend what she read. Most of the models showed the hurricane coming ashore near Louisiana. Landfall could change though. No matter the predictions, they wouldn't know until the storm moved closer. If it moved closer. Maybe it would fall apart, and they'd get a few showers. One could hope.

When she handed the laptop back, Sam whispered, "You take the couch. I'm going to stay up and work awhile anyway."

"Work? I heard you quit your job."

"I'm actually going to figure out how long I can live on my savings if I go back to school. Of course, I can sell the house in Oxford and find a smaller place."

She glanced at Mother. Were they disturbing her? Her breathing still seemed deep, and her eyes were closed.

"School?"

"For physical therapy."

She squinted and studied his expression. Was he joking?

He shook his head. "Long story."

The hospital bed creaked as Mother shifted and moaned. They both jumped to their feet, peering over at her. When she quieted, Sam took a seat in the recliner, so Elinor returned to the couch. She nudged the pillow toward one end and unfolded the blanket. Time sure moved slowly in the hospital. After getting up so early, a short nap could be a good idea. She took one last look at Sam. The glow of the screen reflected in the light part of his blue eyes, inside that deep indigo circle, creating another kind of storm in her emotions. His head swiveled toward her, and she quickly mashed her own eyes closed. No sense giving him the wrong idea. The sooner Sam Conrad left for *school*, the better.

Chapter 23

What was that sound? Elinor started and jerked straight up. Her blurred vision came into focus searching for the noise.

Sam.

The hospital.

Mother! She lurched to her feet.

Sam held a small bowl in front of her mother who was gagging. How could there be anything left in her after being sick all afternoon?

"I'll buzz the nurse." She reached for the button.

"I already did." He didn't look her way. "Bring a cool wet washcloth."

Elinor's resolve to despise the man puddled. Not even Craig would go this far to swindle her family. Maybe Sam was…genuine?

The door swung open, and the nurse took in the scene. "I thought she'd gotten over the nausea. I'll be right back with more medicine."

Staring, Elinor stood in place. Her brain fizzled. What was she supposed to do? Take over with the bowl? Cassie would've been a much better choice to help. Maybe even Em. Neither of them would've slept through—

"Wet washcloth." Sam's voice interrupted her pity party.

"Oh, right." The one simple thing he'd requested.

In the bathroom, she wet a cloth, wrung it out, and steeled herself to go back. She couldn't fail now. She took her place on the other side of the bed and placed the rag on the back of Mother's neck. "Sorry, I…"

"You're just tired." Sam's voice held no condemnation.

The nurse scurried in with a syringe and added medicine into the IV line. "Hopefully, you'll rest easy until morning now." She moved to Sam's side. "Let me clean this up."

"Sure." He went to the sink and washed his hands while she worked.

Mother lay back and placed her hand over Elinor's. "Thank you. Both of you." Her damp blonde bangs stuck to her head, and her face looked pale as she glanced to Sam, who simply nodded.

"You don't have to thank me, Momma. You've always taken good care of me, so it's your turn." Even as she spoke the words, cold fear rooted in Elinor's gut and spread through her limbs. She shivered. What if something bad happened? How would she ever make it without her mother?

"Are you chilly? I'll get the Snuggie for you." Sam's fingers brushed Elinor's arm, soothing a bit of the worry. He brought the fleece and gently laid it across her shoulders as she stood there. "You can stick your arms in and snuggle up in it. Hence the name."

Not a very imaginative title, but a tad comfy and warm. She glanced at Sam, standing so close. What would it be like to be in his arms all snuggled up next to his chest?

Halt. Such an absurd thought.

She fidgeted with the soft fabric, avoiding his eyes, in case he might read her mind. She stayed beside the bed until the medicine took effect, and her mother's eyes closed. "I'll sit in the chair now so you can sleep."

"Whatever you want." Again his words and tone held sincerity, not only splintering her attempted dislike of the man, but igniting hopeful sparks in her heart.

She stole a glance his way as she sat. No smirk. A gracious smile caught her off guard. Moisture leaked from the corners of her eyes, and she turned away to stare at her hands. What would she do to occupy herself for the rest of the night?

Stories swam through Elinor's thoughts. She drifted in and out of sleep, playing with sçenes for her book. The hero, blond and tall, saving the heroine from being swept away in a flooded river. Clinging to the man who'd seemed so aloof at first.

A loud knock lifted her head with a jerk. Gray morning light filtered in between the blind slats over the window.

Sam jumped to his feet and opened the door. The back of his hair poked up like a fan in an adorable sort of way.

Warmth flooded Elinor's cheeks as she ran a hand through her own hair. She could only imagine what a rat's nest it was.

A woman entered the room and introduced herself as the physical therapist. Elinor rubbed her eyes and tried to focus. What had she said her name was? Cindy something?

"Your mother missed her session yesterday, so I wanted to get started with her first today." A huge grin lit up the pretty face as Cindy Whoever glanced at Sam.

The girl was much too chipper for this early in the day. And attractive. And flirtatious.

They could've at least been given time to brush her mother's hair and teeth if they'd known the therapist would show up so early. Elinor studied the supposed professional unwrapping the blow-up stockings from Mother's calves. Was Cindy even old enough to be in this job?

Then the bandage came off.

The long angry incision running down Mother's knee jerked Elinor's attention to the matter at hand. White Steri-Strips crossed the wound, and a small tube stuck out from one side. She hated to think how the thing would be removed.

"Okay." The girl looked at Mother. "We're going to bend and straighten. We have to get your knee moving. Did they give the pain meds?"

"Yes. Earlier."

"Wait." Elinor sat up straight. "When did someone come in?"

"Not long ago." Mother's lips lifted a fraction. "You were sleeping with such a sweet smile on your face, I hated to wake you."

She'd been smiling in her sleep? How strange. And mortifying. Had she said anything? Elinor glanced at Sam. Had she done anything else to embarrass herself?

"Ready to straighten?" The girl held Mother's leg.

"I'll try."

Breathing hard, Mother extended her knee, and she winced as it flattened.

Elinor cringed and fought the nausea that swept over her. How torturous to see her sweet mother in pain.

Then her mother had to bend and straighten the knee ten more times. Air whooshed from her mother's lungs and tears rolled down her cheeks, but she kept at it.

Sam took a few steps closer to the bed. "Her leg looks puffy to me."

"It's normal to have some swelling after surgery." The girl kept torturing Mother. "I'm going to press down about five seconds. Remember to breathe through the pain. Don't point your toes. Relax."

How miserable. Elinor stood helpless, moisture distorting her vision and her chest tight. Should she hold Mother's hand? Say something? Her parents should've picked one of the other sisters. They'd know what to do.

~~~

Something didn't look right about the incision. Sam squinted and edged closer. Sure, some swelling and redness happened after surgery. He'd seen plenty of his teammates…and his own ACL repair way back in middle school. Memories of the months of therapy caused an inward groan.

He glanced at Elinor. Pillow marks lined her cheek on one side, and her hair tangled in gentle waves. Adorable. But furrowed brows knitted over her glassy blue eyes. He'd be strong for her. Support her. And ask someone else about the swollen incision.

When the therapist left, Sam gingerly cupped Elinor's elbow. "How about we let her rest and get some breakfast? I could use some caffeine."

She didn't flinch under his touch as he'd halfway expected. Instead, she drifted closer to him. Almost leaning into his shoulder. "Coffee sounds nice, but I won't leave her alone."

"Coffee it is. I'll see if there's anything else edible."

As he exited, he bumped into what felt like a wall and
~~~

looked up. "Sorry, Roy. I wasn't paying attention. Just heading down to find breakfast. Want anything?"

Roy gripped Sam in a hug. "Morning, son."

"Good morning." The affection felt oddly comfortable. Had his own father ever hugged him like that?

"I already ate, but you're a lifesaver stayin' here with my girl. Come on back in for a second."

"Yes, sir."

Sam stepped into the room while Roy quickly went to his wife's side and kissed her on the forehead. "How are you, my Ruby?"

"Morning, hon." Miss Ruby managed to smile. "I'll make it, though the therapy was uncomfortable."

Elinor's mouth dropped. "Uncomfortable? They tortured you."

As if looking for truth, Roy glanced at Sam.

"It did seem painful. Her leg looked a bit red and swollen. Maybe ask the doctor to check." He didn't want to scare them for no reason. "Therapy is usually pretty tough from what I remember, though."

"When did you have surgery?" Elinor's blue eyes knifed him as if he'd made up some preposterous story.

So, they were back to that. Sam cleared his throat. "ACL. Sixth grade. Other ACL eighth grade. Plus a few random sports injuries."

Elinor's look softened. "Oh."

A rumbling chuckle came from Roy's throat. "No wonder you wanted to study physical therapy." He turned his attention to Elinor. "Come here, darlin', and let me hug you. You did a good job for your momma."

Complying, Elinor sank into his arms and sniffled. "I don't know about that."

"Now listen here." He patted her back. "I want you to let Sam take you home to eat and rest."

"But I need to stay and help."

"No siree. To help, you have to rest and take care of yourself." He tipped her chin and looked her in the eyes. "I'll be here. We're taking turns. Day shift. Night shift."

"Okay." She stepped away from Roy and took her mother's hand. "I'll be back tonight."

Roy turned his gaze to Sam. "Make sure she eats and sleeps."

"Yes, sir."

As if he could control one thing about this woman.

Chapter 24

Elinor's eyes fluttered open, and she struggled to find the source of the music that woke her. In her childhood bedroom, the phone on the nightstand continued to wail. *Mother.* Scrambling to answer, she knocked over a lamp and sent it crashing on the hardwood floor. Mr. Darcy spat and skidded out of the room.

"Hello. Hello." The call had ended. Who was it? She squinted to read the name. Her hammering pulse slowed. Just her handyman. Though she hoped her cottage repairs were finished so she could move back home, that issue seemed less urgent since the surgery. Better call him back though. She stood and pressed the contact.

"Hey there, I wanted to let you know we finished the roof, but that hurricane's meandering in the Gulf, and my men are all busy battening down their own hatches. Who knows for sure when and where it'll make landfall, but we better start getting prepared. Any way you and your daddy could come cover your windows and pull up all your patio furniture? My wife and son caught a stomach bug and shared it with me, or I'd do it myself."

The man's loud voice and bad news clattered around Elinor's tired mind. What choice did she have? Her cottage would have to wait. There was no way she could get it done today.

"Miss Bosarge?"

"No. I mean yes. I hear you." She paced across the room and back, then squeezed her eyes shut. "It's fine, Mike. I hope you feel better."

"Yes, ma'am. Tell your daddy I said hello."

"Take care." As she hung up, she fought to maintain her

composure. Her father couldn't help her, and both these houses would need to be prepared for the weather. How long had she slept? She glanced at her phone. An hour. She was so exhausted. Her eyes burned, and her chest refused to stop heaving. As a big ugly sob escaped, she dropped her head to her hands and let the tears flow.

"I heard something crash. Did you hurt yourself?"

Gasping, Elinor peeked between her fingers. What was Sam doing in here? "You're supposed to be in the boathouse."

He took slow steps toward her. "Couldn't sleep and wanted to borrow some milk. Didn't want to wake you." One of his hands touched the small of her back. "Are you hurt?"

Her ridiculous chest shook. "No." Another sob broke free despite her best efforts to hold it in.

"Come here." Both arms pulled her close to his chest. "Tell me."

His warmth enveloped her, soothing and strong. She let herself fall into him and planted her face into his shoulder. Bawling like a blubbering idiot.

~~~

Sam's heart puddled as Elinor's tears melted away every last bit of resolve he'd held. He was crazy about this woman. If only she would trust him. "Ellie." Nuzzling her hair with his chin, he pressed a soft kiss on top of her head. "What happened? Is it your mom?"

"Uh-uh." Her head shook. "I mean sort of, but not like you think."

"Explain then. Look at me." He stroked her back, ignoring the tingling shooting through his fingers.

Blue eyes gazed up at him, red-rimmed with tears clinging to her lashes. His throat thickened with the urge to kiss away every trace of sadness from her face.

"My handyman called. The houses need to be prepared in case the hurricane hits. Boarded up, patio furniture, plants moved in…" A deep furrow formed between her brows. "Oh and the boats."

"He can't do it for you?"
~~~

"Stomach virus."

Seemed to be going around lately. No wonder she was upset. More like overwhelmed. "Tell me how. I'll do it." Didn't matter that he had no idea what he was doing. He'd get it done for Ellie.

Her expression softened and cloudy eyes became hopeful. "You? You'd do that?"

"I…" How to explain? "I've grown to care deeply about your family. About you… You all feel like family to me. Even more than my own."

A small smile lifted her red lips. "Daddy's good at that. Mom, too."

"They are."

"So I'm kind of like your annoying, incompetent little sister?" Her gaze fell to the ground. "I've never been good with people."

"Ellie, you are not incompetent or annoying." He lifted her chin. "And nothing like a little sister in my mind."

She searched his face as if judging whether or not to believe him.

He stood motionless, lost in the moment and scared at the same time. Scared she'd search him and find him wanting.

Her gaze moved to his lips. "Nothing like a sister?"

"Nothing like that." His voice sounded husky in his own ears. "Like a beautiful, intelligent, sensitive woman."

Now she just stared.

Plain frightening. *Breathe*. Chest too tight. He forced in air. Was she waiting for him to kiss her? One hand went to her cheek, and he brushed away the tears with his thumb. "I'm crazy about you, Ellie."

Still she stared.

He bent to kiss the tracks of her tears on the other cheek. Slowly, gently, his lips made their way to hers. An ocean of emotion swept through as they connected, and he deepened his kiss, holding her loosely until she kissed him back. Then sweetness and light and salt washed over him like a new day.

Chapter 25

What was happening? Elinor's mind swirled. The scent of woodsy linen tickled her nose. Wholeness, strength, tenderness combined in Sam's kiss. Sam's kiss? She was kissing Sam. Her brain said to put an end to this recklessness. But her heart seemed to be occupied. Her lips, too.

Sam broke away, breathless. "Sorry, Ellie. I…I should get started if I'm going to do what you asked."

"What?" Her numbed mind grappled to understand. Where had his lips gone? What had she asked him to do?

"The weather. Getting ready in case." He kissed her nose, and then her forehead. Small, quick, luscious kisses that left residual warmth like the sun on the sand.

"The weather?" She opened her eyes, and it all came back. "Oh, right." Her spine straightened. "Let's get started. Here first, then my cottage."

"We're doing it together?" A grin lit up his blue eyes. His entire face.

She found herself grinning back. "Unless you prefer to do all the work alone while I nap."

"If you're tired…"

"Splendid." She plopped down on the bed. "I'll email the instructions."

Air whooshed through his mouth as he nodded, and his cheek muscles flinched to hold up his smile. "Okay."

A laugh burst from deep within her. A loud dolphin laugh. "Just kidding."

"You." He pulled her up and back into his arms. "I take back what I said earlier. You are annoying."

Another kiss plunged her back into a happy fog.

~~~
~~~

He really had to stop kissing the woman if they were going to get anything done. Using every ounce of athletic and academic and business discipline that had driven him most of his life…had been drilled into him since he was a child, he pulled his lips from hers and forced out words. "Let's get started."

Elinor's lashes batted, and her mouth hung open a little.

He chuckled as he took in the dazed look on her cute face. At least the goofiness was mutual.

Maybe.

He hoped.

"Um…" She ran her fingers through her hair and turned toward the dresser. "The patio furniture… Wait. What happened to my hair?" She grabbed a brush, pulled the long red waves into a bundle, and tied it up with an elastic band.

"Looked fine to me all stirred up."

"Probably your fault." One of her eyebrows rose, and a smile teased her mouth.

"You can blame me for whatever you like if I get to kiss you. So put the patio furniture inside where?"

"Normally the boathouse, but…"

"I'll arrange things in there so I can still walk through to the bedroom. What about the boats?"

"You start with the furniture while I get the shutters for the windows. Then we can pull out the boats."

"Sounds like a very competent plan, ma'am." He saluted and made his way downstairs, practically skipping. *Stop grinning like a twelve-year old.* But why would he want to stop? This was a great feeling.

One by one, Sam carried the lawn chairs and tables inside, lining them against the interior wall. He pushed the couch and chairs aside to make room for the plants. Sweat dripped from his forehead into his eyes, and he brushed his face across his shoulder. The sky sure didn't show any signs of a storm brewing today.

A glint caught his eye, and he turned. Elinor hauled metal panels from the garage toward the back windows.

"Hey, you." Sam put the plant just inside the foyer and shut the door. "Let me help. Those things are huge."

She groaned. "Plenty more where these came from."

A truck rattled into the drive as she handed him the storm shutters.

"Looks like our neighbor down the street. Mr. Nelson."

Sam nodded. "I met him at the crab boil. Roscoe's owner." He craned his neck trying to see past the reflection on the vehicle's windows. "Hope he didn't bring the beast."

"Hey, folks." The man exited his car and neared. "How's Miss Ruby?"

"She's okay." Elinor shrugged. "Hope this storm plays out."

"Just finished my house and came to help you." He snapped his fingers. "Oh, and my wife sent supper. Almost forgot." After opening the back door, he lifted an enormous picnic basket toward Elinor. "Ham, stuffed eggs, pecan pie, greens, black-eyed peas. Wife's a good cook."

"Thank you, Mr. Nelson. Daddy will be so pleased."

"There's enough for you and your boyfriend, too." He nodded toward Sam. "Roy's real fond of this one. Talks all kind of good about him. Must be a keeper."

A blush reddened Elinor's already perspiring pink cheeks, and she glanced at Sam.

The man thought they were…well, maybe… What would she say?

Sam's brows raised, waiting for her response.

"Yes. Sam's a keeper." She spun on her heels toward the house. "I'll put this food inside."

He was a keeper. Hope swirled through Sam lighting up the dark corners of his heart. How long had it been since he'd felt this good? Never.

Mr. Nelson kept talking after Elinor left. Bits and pieces made it into Sam's consciousness while they carried the rest of the panels to cover the windows. Move boats on trailers inland. Weigh them down. Let air out of trailer tires.

His mind wandered back to Elinor's lips. Soft and warm. A keeper. He should focus so they could finish this job and move on to Elinor's cottage.

What was the man saying? Something about panels slipping into an upper track and fastening to a lower track. And wing nuts?

"You got that, Sam?" Mr. Nelson gave him an expectant look.

"Sorry. Can you repeat what you were saying?"

"What part?"

The man wouldn't think he was a keeper long if he didn't pay attention. "The part about the windows. And the boat."

Mr. Nelson's chest shook with a hearty laugh. "You are whooped, aren't you, boy?"

"I think I am."

~~~

The salty aroma of ham soaked the kitchen. Mr. Darcy and Dashwood swished around Elinor's legs, begging. "This is not for you, gentlemen. I'll find you a treat before I leave." This would make a delicious dinner when her mother came home tomorrow. Just the thing to cheer her up, knowing her friends cared.

Outside, Sam and Mr. Nelson made great strides covering the windows. Much faster than she'd have been able to accomplish the task. Good thing because her throat and eyes itched from pollen in the air. They did need a good rain, but not a hurricane. She finished storing the food in the refrigerator and placed a treat in both animal's bowls. "Time for me to go back outside." A knock on the door came before she made it.

"Hello, Elinor?" Another neighbor poked her head in. "I brought food, and the menfolk said to bring it on in." Two huge baskets hung from the plump woman's arms.

"Oh, Mrs. Roberts, thank you. Let me help." Elinor heaved one and led her to the kitchen.

"My lasagna and Caesar salad, only I didn't put the dressing on yet because the lettuce will wilt. Oh, and my special Italian cream cake." A smile lifted her dimpled cheeks. "Garlic bread, too, of course."
~~~

A whiff of the garlic sent a rumble through Elinor's stomach.

"Sounds like you need to eat. Fix you a plate, honey."

"I should help the guys get the house ready first."

"Aww pshaw. My hubby's out there with them." Mrs. Roberts lifted the foil covering the lasagna. "Your mother told me how sweet you've been, and a world of help with the ball and the fundraising committee, even putting off your next book to be here for this surgery."

"She did?"

"Of course. Now sit down and eat to keep your strength up."

Maybe she should eat, because after all this work, she'd go back to the hospital and relieve Daddy. Then they'd find out how truly helpful she was.

"Knock-knock." Another female voice sang from the back door. "Anybody home? I brought a poppy seed chicken casserole. Your mother's favorite."

This one would go in the freezer. Even her father couldn't eat this much food.

An hour of sweat later, with the neighbors' and Sam's help, Elinor had the boats out of the water and set, the windows covered, and two refrigerators and a freezer filled with casseroles. Their friends brought a flashlight, extra batteries, and water, too. They set up the generator for the refrigerator and freezer just in case the storm took out the power.

Elinor waved as the last one drove away. "Wow. They were spectacular."

"Sure were." Sam grinned. "No wonder you were crying. If I'd had to face all that work by myself, I'd have shed a few tears, too."

"Thank you for saying that, but I can't see you throwing pity parties the way I do."

"Then you have to get to know me better. I can throw a pretty mean one." He cut his eyes toward her with a smirk. "Guess that's how I ended up here."

What had sent him running from his hometown…his job?

Elinor swatted at a mosquito buzzing near her arm. Maybe she should know more about this man she'd called a keeper. A man she'd kissed. "So tell me about yourself. I really don't know much, now that I think about it."

Sam's shoulders slumped and his smile fell away as he nodded toward her car. "On the drive to your house?"

"Okay." He looked so forlorn. How bad was his past? Maybe she'd made a mistake.

Chapter 26

Tightness squeezed at Sam's throat. He was navigating uncharted waters with Elinor as it was. He'd really rather not tell anyone about his humiliating personal life. His Dad's unnatural iron grip on him, the humiliation of Tiffany ditching him on their wedding day… Being a loser in relationships was bad enough without having to blab the sorry details about it.

Elinor eased the car out of the drive and onto the main road with hands at ten and two. "We have a ride ahead of us, if you want to start talking. I think Em enlightened you on most of my disastrous past." Her focus stayed on the road.

At least she wasn't staring at him. *Here goes nothing.* "My father is a driven man, to say it nicely. He tends to badger those around him until they bend to his will. I'm the youngest child and the only son, so he started on me at an early age. Birth." He shrugged. "Soccer, baseball, football. That was our life. Sports. And he was that parent on the sidelines that everyone talks about—yelling and arguing with refs."

At a red light, Elinor glanced at him. "Did you hate sports?"

"I liked them. I tried to be the best I could, but my efforts were never enough to please Dad. When I tore my ACL, he went ballistic. The second time, he was even worse. As if I could help it."

"That's ridiculous."

"Yeah, but I had a great physical therapist. Former athlete. The reason I wanted to pursue sports medicine."

"I thought you worked for a bank."

This was it, he'd spill it all. Sam sucked in a cleansing breath. "My father said no when I told him my plan, but I had a scholarship to play football at Ole Miss as a backup quarter-back. My tuition was paid for, so I majored in biochemistry and applied to PT school. Then I started dating a girl. Tiffany."

"And that's where it all went bad?"

"Something like that." A harsh chuckle escaped Sam's throat. "My father got to her. Had her convince me to come work at the bank and get my MBA at night."

"Why was he so against PT school? That's an admirable career."

"All about control."

Elinor's brows gathered as she checked the rearview mirror for traffic. "But why would Tiffany go along with it?"

"Tiffany's family went broke after some bad business deal, but she was accustomed to the high life." Sam balled his fists as the urge to slap the dashboard ran through his arms. "Then Tiffany's great aunt Hattie offered to leave her rather large estate in a trust for Tiffany if she settled down and married. Unfortunately, Aunt Hattie and my grandmother had some old feud, and Hattie withdrew her offer when she found out I was a Conrad."

"You're kidding? Sounds like something I'd put in a book. Can someone make those kind of requirements in the present day?"

"Didn't matter. After my bride was a no-show on the day of our wedding, I had a clear picture of her feelings for me."

Abruptly, Elinor wheeled into the gravel parking lot of a warehouse. Her blue eyes turned to him—waded through his humiliating past, no doubt, and saw what a loser he was. Under her scrutiny he turned his gaze to the window. He couldn't face her.

~~~

And now she knew. Elinor battled the urge to cry. She should've guessed there was a back story, for goodness sakes. She was a writer. Everyone had wounds that molded them into who they were. Scars hid beneath Sam's confident and sometimes rude façade. He'd endured discouragement and heartbreak. "What did you do? I mean when Tiffany…?"

"At the wedding?" Sam stared out his window, seemingly at nothing.
~~~

"You don't have to answer. I shouldn't have asked."

"It's fine." One of his shoulders lifted. "I sent the guests home. Took my best man on a nice trip to the Caribbean." He shook his head. "I'd go on a few horrendous dates and then swear off women for a while. I took classes, trained for marathons, hunted or water skied…went out for too many beers. Tried dating again. Kind of a vicious cycle."

He still hadn't looked at her. Was there more?

"Did you have a drinking problem?"

"More like a boredom problem." A bitter laugh slipped through his lips. "And my father got what he wanted. I threw myself into my work. Became really good at what I did. Not that he ever acknowledged my success."

"Is that why you left?"

"Should've been, but no. Tiffany inherited when her aunt died not long ago, and my father insisted I manage her new-found wealth."

Indignation ignited within her, and something else. Compassion. A longing to take away Sam's pain. And a bit more of the fury. "How dare he?"

"Yeah. The last straw."

"I'd love to give him a lecture on how family is supposed to work." She scoffed. "My father should mentor him—give him parenting lessons."

A small smile lifted Sam's lips as he glanced at her. "I might pay money to see that play out."

The sun glinted off Sam's blond hair. Her eyes followed the rays down his forehead, across strong cheekbones, and then crossed to his mouth. Without analyzing the situation further, she caught his hand and brought it to her lips.

"From one damaged person to another, I'm sorry you were treated with disrespect." She placed a kiss on his hand and offered a sympathetic smile.

"Thanks." His warm hand covered hers. "Being damaged makes it difficult to really let anyone in."

She understood that all too well. Was she really ready to let someone in? Let Sam Conrad in?

She slipped her hand to the gear shift. “We should get going.”

Chapter 27

Maybe he should've kept his stupid mouth shut. Sam's knee bounced with nervous energy as the miles passed in sobering silence. All he'd had to say was he'd had a broken engagement, not go into all the pathetic details. He fought the urge to ask Elinor what she was thinking. Probably didn't want to know anyway.

They reached Fort Morgan Road. Gradually the landscape became more secluded, and scrubby trees blocked the view of what lay at the end of the driveways. Then the scenery opened for a moment, revealing the glittering bay to the right and the ocean to the left. Sunlight sparkled off the rippling waves.

A bit farther down the road, the foliage took over again until they turned onto a street paved with broken shells. Houses of varying sizes and levels of care stood next to each other. Some were upscale and pricey-looking with pristine lawns. They loomed over smaller and obviously older houses.

"Weird neighborhood." Sam coughed. That didn't come out right. "I mean, diverse in architectural style."

"It's an older development. As people sell out, new owners tear down and rebuild. The lots are outrageously priced these days. Luckily, I bought my parents' old beach house. It's small and definitely not new, but I love it."

"I thought you were a rich author."

"Um, most writers don't get rich these days. I had an editing business on the side for several years, and if my parents hadn't given me a really good deal on the place, plus a trust fund, I couldn't have bought on the beach."

"Hmm, I read a few industry reports that some publishing companies were folding or merging."

"I'm fortunate I found an agent and a publisher when I did.

It's tough to break into the business. My manuscript was in the right place at the right time."

"But your books are really good." Oh man, he'd let that slip. He checked his email on his phone in an attempt to look busy.

"Books? You read more than one?" They pulled into the gravel drive of a yellow cottage raised on wooden stilts.

She hadn't missed it.

"I might've stayed up late a few nights reading." He closed his email and tossed the phone on the console.

She parked under a cream-colored arch that covered the carport. Her cheeks flushed a light pink. "How embarrassing."

"Why are you embarrassed? I'm the one reading chick books."

"I use a pen name because I feel awkward when people learn I'm writing romance." She opened the car door and stepped out.

Sam followed her to the white metal door. "You don't like romance?"

"Well…yes. I love the classic romance literature."

"So what's the problem?"

The deadbolt clacked as she turned the key. "As you've learned, I'm not much of a romance expert in real life."

Sam belly-laughed. "That's it?"

"What's so funny?" Her footsteps clomped up the covered wooden staircase to the main floor where she entered a code into the security system. The alarm beeped once as she opened that door.

Focused on the red hair in front of him, he followed her inside. "I didn't have to possess a fortune to become a financial advisor. I just had to understand the process and have the skills. Most jobs are like that."

"I guess." Her posture relaxed, and she swept an arm around the room. "Here's what's left of my place. Home sweet home."

Windows walled the back of the cottage. The smell of fresh paint permeated the air. Pale yellow interior almost mirrored the color of the paint outside. "You like yellow."

"It's a happy color. Like the sun." Her voice suddenly seemed more childlike than her usual excessively proper tone.

"Can't argue with that." Empty built-in book shelves lined the rest of the walls. Obviously the home to the *first editions*. A few framed beach scenes painted in watercolors still hung in the dining area. Much nicer than the bizarre portrait of Mr. Darcy, but apparently not to Elinor since she left them. Mostly light-colored furniture. Two leather club chairs and distressed white tables topped with cobalt blue glass lamps. Not overly frou-frou. Classy. Sam took it all in. He could live here.

"Earth to Sam?"

"Huh?"

"I was talking. What were you thinking about?"

Definitely filter. "I like the place. You aren't bad at decorating after all." He checked for the empty wall where the portrait of Mr. Darcy had been.

"Thanks. I think." Her forehead crinkled. "At least the workers are finished."

She opened the back door. The wind rushed in, bringing a blast of salty air. A few strands of Elinor's hair lifted and danced in the gusts, hypnotizing him. "We can start with the patio furniture." She moved out on to the decking.

Sam followed as if pulled by a magnetic force. His eyes stayed with her waving hair until his knee plowed into a heavy wooden Adirondack chair. "Ouch."

"Are you hurt?"

"Fine. Just klutzing around." And staring.

A strip of blue underneath the decking caught his eye. "What's down there in that fencing?"

"A small lap pool where I exercise when there's a rip current. We'll have to cover it, too."

"You swim in the ocean? Isn't that dangerous? I mean sharks and all. Tides."

"I check the currents every morning, and I don't go far out." She shrugged and pushed the last chair inside. "I've never seen a shark during my swims, but I don't go where people are fishing or at night."

"Weird for a girl who's so fearful of snakes." Sam brushed at a drop of perspiration on his forehead. "Another intriguing idiosyncrasy of Elinor Elizabeth Bosarge."

Her chin tilted before she took a step down the stairs. "Are you making fun of me?"

"Absolutely not. I find you fascinating."

She ducked a tad, but he thought he caught a smile. What was going on in her head? She'd seemed shy this afternoon. Had he blown it already?

~~~

After they covered the windows and pool, Elinor faced the ocean. The tall stems of the sea oats swayed, and the breeze bent their golden heads. Her feet itched for a quick walk in the surf and a bit of the warm sun and wind on her back. She turned to Sam, whose gaze seemed to be locked on her. Again. Did she have some stray lasagna on her face? She swiped a hand across her mouth and chin. "Mind if we take a quick walk before we leave?"

"I'd love to."

Her feet sank into the sand at the end of her boardwalk. The warmth spread between her toes, and she made the short walk to the edge of the water. Her lungs filled with the blessed air. The scents of brine and wind and something sweet like coconut pushed against her face. Had to be sunscreen.

A couple of teens played paddle ball, and a family sat with two young girls building a sandcastle, their floating toys resting nearby. All along the shoreline, people walked and played at the water's edge. Why were so many tourists still on the beach? She prayed they'd leave if the storm turned this way, or they'd be trapped on the peninsula.

The tide was higher and rougher than she'd seen in years. It churned trash from who knew where and laid it in zigzagging piles. Small translucent crabs ran across the clutter. They always reminded her of tiny skeletons for some reason. Gulls circled and squawked nearby, as if mocking her. She'd been such a fool in the past. Was Sam duping her like Craig had?

A deep wave smacked up from the sea, knocking her off
~~~

balance. Warm, salty water splattered all the way to her shoulders.

Sam gripped her elbow and held on to her. Anchored her. "Got ya." His whisper caressed her cheek.

She couldn't tear her gaze away. Or the amazing contradiction of her feelings since she'd met this man. Their fingers entwined, and she looked toward her cottage. "Sorry. You might be regretting this now. The wind is pushing the water so hard. Maybe we should go back."

"A little stormy water won't hurt me."

She didn't want to hurt him either. *Lord, can I trust this man with my heart?* Life would be so much easier if God could wave a big sign to direct her.

~~~

Ahead, a gathering of beachgoers crowded the sand. Sam still held Elinor's hand in his, relishing the feel of her soft fingers. Together they altered their path deeper into the water to avoid bumping into the kids playing at the edge.

She nodded toward the tourists. "I don't understand those parents up on the deck having cocktails while their children are in an enormous body of water. And there's a rip current today. Normally I'd fly a warning flag, but with this wind, I doubt it would stay put."

"Maybe they're watching from up there."

"Maybe."

"Do you want kids?" *Oh no.* What would she think of that question?

Her head whipped toward him, slapping wet strands of hair across her cheek.

"Someday?" He tried to sound casual.

"I prefer to remain rooted in the present."

What kind of answer was that? "Rooted in the present? You're an author, so I find that hard to believe. You must have a vivid imagination."

Her fingers tensed in his hand. "I don't plan on not having children, and I've enjoyed being around my nephews."

"My sisters used to pick out names for their future kids, play
~~~

dolls and house, and constantly try to rope me into playing either the dad or the kid."

A light chuckle lifted her lips, and her eyes found his. Twin pools of sky and sea, but outshining them both in his mind. "I would like to have seen that."

Warmth filled him as he smiled back down at her. "I can be bribed." His eyes fell to her mouth, and he bent toward her.

Her eyes widened, and she leaned back.

Looked like a no. Sam froze. "I think you'd be a good mother."

"I…" She seemed to fumble for words. "You…"

Over the surf's raucous voice, a cry rang out. "Dad! Help!"

A young boy clung to a boogie board, but a current swept him farther out.

Before Sam could react, Elinor dove into a crashing wave. She swam toward the boy at an angle diagonal to the shoreline. Sam's heart rammed his ribs. Should he dive in or keep in line with them or the beach? He sprinted along, holding them in his sights. He passed a group of tourists. "Call 911, they're caught in a current!" He grabbed a pink floating ring and plunged into the water.

~~~

Elinor gasped for air between the swells. At times, she sunk under a wave to pop up what seemed like minutes later, though it had been no doubt only seconds. She'd done this before, dragged tourists in from the treacherous pull that hid beneath the Gulf's water, but not in an approaching hurricane. The strength of the majestic water both amazed and horrified her.

The yellow board came into her sight as a swell lifted her up. She was almost there. "Hold on. I'm coming." She wished she'd brought a life preserver.

The boy cried as she neared. "We're so far."

"Just hang on. We'll get back." She swam up and caught the slippery edge in her fingers. Mustering all her might, she kicked at an angle toward the shore. Within long minutes, they neared shallower water, and she gave a hard thrust forward with her legs. A wave caught them, and the boogie board slipped from
~~~

her grasp, but they were probably close enough. She let her feet try for the bottom.

Another current gripped her, sucking her down, slamming her world into darkness.

Faster and farther than she'd ever been from the shore. Where was the kid? Had he made it? She sunk beneath the surface, and a silent scream ripped from her lips as icy terror squeezed around her chest. The temperature dropped dramatically. Deep water. Her throat and lungs craved air. Her legs and arms ached from trying to keep afloat, and she bent her neck back, straining to find the surface. Low light filtered through the greenish brown haze and bubbles above.

She had to relax. Drift with the current. And stay conscious.

Chapter 28

Waves pushed and pulled against Sam, but he kept his course set on the last place he'd seen Elinor. He popped his head up to check again. The boy trudged out of the waves and onto the beach with another adult holding onto him, but where was Elinor? Terror seeped into his limbs, sending a shiver through him. He stroked harder to reach deeper water then stopped. He needed to save his strength for when he found her. Swimming around with no purpose would wear him out. Time was a fierce enemy in this kind of situation. A quick scan of the churning surface provided nothing but a pelican fishing nearby. Floating with the ring for a second, he studied left then right toward the horizon.

A hand breached, flailing. About twenty feet away, she surfaced, gasping.

He kicked furiously. Swimming faster than he thought possible, it still seemed like miles before he'd be near enough to pass her the ring. He lifted his head and took a gulp of air. "I'm coming."

No response. His heart thundered. Maybe she hadn't heard him. He swam harder. She went in and out of view with the churning swells.

He called again. "Ellie, I'm almost there. Hang on."

Her head turned, and her blue eyes caught his.

Relief spread through him. "I'm coming."

Another minute and he neared—sliding the float to her. "Here. Let's get you on, and I'll swim us back."

A small nod was her only answer as she raised one arm over the pink plastic. She must have been really wiped out. It would be hard to get her on this stupid, but blessed, girly float. Why hadn't he picked up something better? He knew why—there hadn't been time.

He'd barely made it to her as it was.

He pushed the thought away. He'd think about that later.

Swells pitched them up and back down. He inched closer until they were face to face, still holding on.

"Are you okay?"

She nodded. "The boy?" Water dripped from her hair and eyelashes in small streams.

Gusts of wind roared in his ears, and salty water filled his mouth. "He made it. Let me help you on the ring. You have to be exhausted."

"What about you? These swells."

"I wasn't caught like you were. I'm good. I'm sure someone called 911, so help should be along."

"I'll get on with one condition." A fierce gaze caught him. "Do not let go."

"I won't ever let go of you."

A small smile lifted her lips. "I meant the float."

"I know what you meant."

~~~

Strong hands pushed Elinor over the edge of the swim ring, and she twisted to sit in the middle. Her exhausted muscles relaxed. She took a deep breath but sputtered and coughed. Thank God she was alive. And Sam. Her eyes fixed on him as they bobbed in the waves. He'd said he'd never let her go. He'd saved her life. Was this God waving a sign in front of her? To let Sam in her heart…to love again?

"I'm going to start swimming back to shore. Just rest." His voice trickled warmth and safety over her.

After only a few feet, a boat approached, seemingly out of nowhere. Thank God. As much as she treasured the Gulf, she needed dry ground right about now. The water slapped its sides as a man in a blue fishing shirt leaned over. "Heard on the radio y'all needed some help. Can you make it up the ladder on your own?"

Sam pushed her raft close to the metal rungs. "She may need a hand. She's a hero, though. Saved a boy caught in a rip
~~~

current."

The man stepped down partway and held out his hand. Elinor let him pull her to the ladder. Each step up took massive effort as though her body were a bulk weight she wasn't used to carrying. Her legs quivered when she stood on the deck of the small vessel. A flash of pink appeared, then Sam lifted her, and she found herself in his lap. When he wrapped her in an embrace, she sank into his chest and closed her eyes. Maybe she'd never let him go either.

~~~

In Elinor's guest room, Sam changed into a pair of Roy's red swim trunks and an enormous T-shirt. The clothes swallowed him, but he was lucky her father kept anything at all here. It beat trying to wear a woman's outfit for the ride back to Mobile. He threw his wet clothes in the grocery bag Elinor had given him and collected his soggy wallet. At least he hadn't had his phone in his pocket.

Elinor waited on the sofa in the living room, keys in hand. Her tired eyes met his. "Cute ensemble, but a little baggy."

"I don't like to flaunt my body like some guys." He struck a bodybuilding pose which summoned a laugh from her. It was good to hear her laugh. The vision of her struggling in the waves flashed through his mind. *Thank you, Lord.*

"Let's go then." Her steps fumbled when she stood, and Sam rushed to steady her.

"I'm driving, so you can sleep on the way back."

She caught her lip between her teeth and seemed to consider her answer. "Okay. I should probably rest a little before I go back to the hospital."

"I can take your turn. You should see a doctor. You took in a lot of salt water out there. Can't be good for your lungs."

"I'm going. And don't you dare mention this to my father." That defiant chin tilt reappeared, reminding him of the first day they'd met.

Sam couldn't help but chuckle. "Okay. But I'm going with you."

"Why are you laughing?"
~~~

"You *are* adorable." He nuzzled her nose with his own. Something he'd actually never done with anyone. In the past, he'd pretty much gagged when he saw his friends behave with such sickening affection.

Her smile made the whole goofy display worth it. He'd embarrass himself any day for that.

As he drove, Sam glanced over periodically, just to make sure Elinor was still breathing. Not something he'd ever worried about with anyone before.

When they arrived back at the house, he woke her with a peck on the cheek. Boy, he was smitten. "I'll just go change out of my *cute outfit*. I don't want to turn too many heads at the hospital."

"I'll check Mr. Darcy and Dashwood and then meet you in five minutes."

"Got it."

His phone rang the second he set foot in the boathouse. His father. He may as well get this over with. His heart was here now.

"Hello."

"I hope you've come to your senses."

"I have, Dad. I hope to go to PT school. If I can't get in, I'll find other work to support myself."

A string of curses spewed through the cell. "You'll…you'll regret this." His father's voice went from yelling to frighteningly in control. "And after all I've done for you."

"I'm not coming back to Oxford or the bank." His heart was here now.

"Then you can forget you have a father."

The words knifed into Sam's soul, but the lessons Roy had been teaching about God's love came to mind. "That's your call. Goodbye, Dad."

Sam ended the connection and pinched the bridge of his nose. This was the moment he'd always feared. All his life, he'd tried to win his father's approval. But whether on the sports field or at the bank, no matter how well he did, it had never been enough for Teddy Conrad. And it never would.

~~~

Once Elinor settled onto the hospital sofa and they'd received an update on Ruby's condition, Sam caught Roy's arm. "Can we have a word before you leave?"

"Sure, son."

"Out in the hall?"

Elinor's head snapped their way. "Why? You're not…" Her eyes speared him.

"It's business." No doubt she feared he'd spill the beans on what happened today, and maybe he should, but he'd promised to keep quiet.

"Oh." Her posture relaxed.

Sam followed Roy out the door and into the hall. "I'll walk you down to the car. Don't want Elinor with her ear to the door, snooping."

Roy chuckled. "That's a hard dog to keep on the porch."

"Sure is. How are you holding up?"

The big man sighed. "Fair to middlin'. My Ruby's been feeling poorly today, and bless it, I wish it were me in that bed and not her. I'd do anything for that woman."

He'd discovered that feeling firsthand today. "I'm sorry. I think I understand, and it's one of the things I wanted to talk to you about."

Curiosity lifted Roy's brows and stopped him in his tracks. "Do tell?"

Where should he start? "Ever since I arrived, I've been intrigued, and frankly, a little exasperated by your daughter. At first I thought she was stuffy, a bit of a bossy brat." Sam checked Roy's expression before he continued. His words might not have been coming across too well.

But Roy just nodded.

"As I've been around her more, I've found that her prickliness was more of a shield, a shell that protected a soft, sensitive heart." Sam wetted his dry lips. "I've grown to care very deeply for Elinor, and I'd like to ask your permission to take her on a date."

"Well now. Isn't that something?" Roy gazed off into the
~~~

distance and ran his fingers across his bearded chin.

What was Roy thinking? Was he reliving the mess with Craig? Sam bit the inside of his cheek and waited.

"Does she know about your feelings?"

"I believe so."

"And she's not throwing a hissy fit over it?"

"No, sir."

"Are you lookin' for a wife, or do you just want a pretty lady to have on your arm? She's been through a mountain of hurt."

Goodness, what was he looking for? Suddenly, it hit him square in the chest. "I think I'd like to share my life with her. But I thought we might just start with dinner."

One side of Roy's mouth lifted. "Well, I'll be a monkey's uncle. I reckon if you promise to be an honest and faithful man of God, you can have my permission to ask her out. Doesn't mean she'll say yes, though."

"I'll do my best on all the above, sir."

Laughter shook Roy's chest, and he clunked one big arm around Sam's shoulders. "Alrighty then. Good luck."

"Sir, earlier today, I told my father I wasn't coming back to the bank or to Oxford, so I'll probably not be making much money for a few years. I've got savings, plus a house I can sell in Oxford, so I'll look for my own place to live. An apartment or something."

"No sense getting in a tizzy to move out, unless you're uncomfortable."

"I'm not, but Craig lived in the boathouse when they dated. Too many bad memories for her, I think."

"I see." Roy squared his gaze on Sam. "How'd your father take the news?"

That lump in his throat just kept growing larger. "Says we're done."

"I'm sorry, son. You know, I've been there. We both have the Perfect Father looking out for us, though." Roy squeezed his shoulder. "You have me, too. I won't desert you, but I might smack you if you mess up with my daughter." His grip tightened.

Warmth and a good bit of fear filed through Sam. "Thank you, sir. Tomorrow, once I get Elinor home, I have a meeting with the steering committee. Then I'm going to start my observation with the therapist at Memory Oaks." He snapped his fingers. "Oh, and I've been trying to get with your financial advisor, but I can't catch him. I'll try again tomorrow."

"Sounds like you're busier than a one-legged cat in a litter box. Look after my girls, but get some rest tonight, son."

The care in Roy's gaze helped to both clean out and fill the hole his father left. Plus, Roy was right. They shared a Heavenly Father. If only he'd understood that a long while back.

~~~

As the newness of sitting next to Sam on the couch lessened, Elinor relaxed her back and sank deeper against the cushion.

Her mother's light snore eased Elinor's mind a bit. At least she was resting well.

The weatherman on the television announced that the hurricane looked to be veering its trajectory toward Texas. Which was a good thing for Mobile, despite the fact that she'd spent hours preparing for it to hit nearby.

"You've had a tough day." Sam handed her one of the pillows he'd brought the night before. "You should rest."

His eyes roamed her face, bringing warmth to her cheeks and a tingle to her lips. Their kisses came to mind, adding a slight ache in her arms to hold him.

His mouth made a slight upward curve as he placed the pillow in her hands. "I can move to the chair or…you could lean against me."

A deeper question lay in that offer. Were they moving closer, forming something more than a kiss or two?

Elinor glanced at her mother. Their quiet talk didn't seem to be bothering her. "Why would I? I…I mean, what are we doing?" Maybe she should write her questions so they made sense. She was better with words on paper than in real life.

Sam took one of her hands in his and brushed her knuckles with his thumb. "I like you, and despite our horrible track
~~~

record with first dates, I'm willing to try again. With you."

Could she try again? Trust again? She'd kissed him. And she didn't just kiss anyone, but still.... Her heart raced as his fingers traced her knuckles. And he *had* saved her life today, after all. Maybe she'd give dating one more shot.

Eyes never leaving hers, he lowered his lips to her fingers and kissed each one. "Say Saturday night, dinner out? Your mother should be doing well enough for you to leave for a little dinner by then."

Emotions clogged her throat almost as tight as the ocean had earlier. "Yes." The single word came out as a whisper, and Elinor grabbed the pillow in an effort to regather her senses. "I'll rest now." Her eyes met his for a moment. "You don't have to move." She mashed the pillow into his shoulder, folded up next to him, and shut her eyes. A second later his arm wrapped around her.

Everything about Sam holding her teemed with wholeness and home. A feeling she'd never experienced with Craig, or anyone else for that matter. Maybe their first date would be her last first date.

She forced away that thought. She was jumping way ahead of herself. Her romantic notions worked for a novel, but not real life.

Morning welcomed Elinor with the bright florescent lights overhead. Blinking as a nurse entered the room, Elinor shifted away from Sam to the edge of the couch and worked to push down her hair. Did she have a breath mint in her purse? She gave her mother a smile, and then fumbled through and found a pack of mouthwash strips. After swishing the sticky mint around the best she could, she glanced at Sam.

"Can I have one of those?" A blond piece of hair stuck up on the side of his head. His sleepy eyes exuded kindness as he smiled.

She could get used to waking up to that face. She held out the package.

The nurse checked Mother's temperature and other vitals. "I hear she did well enough on PT yesterday that the doctor is letting her go home today."

"Already?" Elinor gawked.

"She was able to use the walker and get in and out of the bed." The nurse shot a look to Elinor. "I'm going to remove the IV and the drain tube from her knee. If you're squeamish, you may not want to watch."

"I'm fine." After nearly drowning the day before, she should be able to face a little gore. Except this was her mother. Her rib cage squeezed her chest for a second. "I can hold your hand if you want, Mother."

Coolness replaced Sam's warmth as Elinor slipped away and took her place beside the bed. She covered her mother's smaller fingers with hers.

"Would you like some privacy, Miss Ruby?" Sam stood and inched to the end of the bed.

"You can stay, hon. Roy says you've been a lifesaver."

Elinor eyed Sam and quirked her lips. If Mother only knew how true that was.

The nurse stripped away the tape holding the needle in her mother's other hand. Once that horrid task ended, she uncovered the knee and removed various bindings. "Mrs. Bosarge, this might hurt a little. There's a small incision here. You'll feel some pressure when I remove the tube. Once we get it out, I'll cover it with gauze and butterfly strips."

Eyes clamped shut, her mother nodded. "I'm ready."

Air hissed through her mother's teeth, and she squeezed Elinor's hand. Tight. Obviously, hurting a little was relative to whether you were the one enduring the pain as opposed to the one causing it. Seeing her mother like this was so hard.

"All done."

Sam hovered over the bed, staring at the knee. "Don't you think that incision is too red?"

The nurse pressed near the redness, earning a wince from Mother.

Good grief, weren't these people supposed to make you feel better? "Be careful."

"It is a little angry. I'll add a note to the chart for the doctor to check it. He'll make rounds this morning." After applying the strips, the nurse re-covered the knee. "PT will be by to inflict their torture before you leave. They'll have you practicing with the walker you'll take home, give you an exercise program, and possibly a cold compression ice machine."

"What?" Elinor's mouth fell open.

Her mother squeezed her hand and gave her the most forced smile Elinor had ever seen. "We'll figure it all out."

"Of course we will." Elinor returned her own strained smile.

Once the nurse cleared out, Sam moved beside them. "I have observation hours this morning and the steering committee meeting, but I could reschedule if you need me."

Elinor glanced at her mother. "Daddy will be here soon. He and I will take Mother home together. We'll be fine."

Lord, help us be fine.

Chapter 29

Knots formed in Sam's shoulders, and he twisted his neck from side to side before entering Memory Oaks. He'd hated leaving the hospital. Worry needled him about the surgery, the red incision, Elinor's near drowning… But she'd told him to go on. He pushed through the door and signed in at the desk.

On his way to the physical therapy room, he took more mental notes of improvements that could be made. He checked his watch. Only five minutes late, but already Mr. Hammill lay on the table and lifted his leg toward his chest. "How are you doing today, Nubbin?"

"Doing pretty good for a young man." The same answer and smile the old guy sported every single time.

"Sorry I'm late." Sam shook hands with the therapist. "Sam Conrad, here for the observation hours."

"Thad Barnes. Traffic can be brutal this time of day."

Barnes seemed to be an appropriate name for the broad man. Probably another former athlete.

"How's our patient?"

"Following instructions." Thad grinned and patted Mr. Hammill's knee. "As long as I'm here to remind him. Switch sides."

Complying, Nubbin stretched out the bent leg and pulled the other knee toward his chest. "Boys, do y'all know Jesus, and do you know He loves you?"

Sam glanced at Thad before answering. "I sure do. Thank you for reminding me."

"The Lord's been good to me letting me live this long. Did you know they say I'm ninety now?"

A chuckle came from Thad. "Ninety-two, but who's counting?"

Sam smiled at his elderly friend. Maybe Nubbin could distract him from worrying about Elinor and Miss Ruby for a moment. "How about you tell us another funny story from your life?"

Nubbin began a long tale of a raccoon and a snake that had chased him around the woods.

By lunch, all the patients had filed through and completed their exercises. The physical work would've been hard enough without the added element of being elderly. Getting old certainly wasn't for sissies. Sam walked out to his car to grab his computer bag. At least he'd thought to move the steering committee meeting here to save time. It made sense anyway, because they could do a walk-through of the property as they discussed their proposals.

A small staff room held a conference table and a coffee pot—all they'd need. He opened his bag and pulled out a protein bar he'd snagged at a gas station. Too bad he hadn't packed some of the food the Bosarge's neighbors had stocked in the fridge. But he'd been in such a hurry to change and get over here. He unwrapped the bar and took a bite. Coffee might help the plastic-like meal replacement taste better. After filling his cup, he sat to wait for the rest of the committee.

The first to arrive was the nurse, Tara. Of course she'd only had to walk down the hall.

Sam stood and shook her hand. "I'm glad you're here. Have a seat."

A smile lit up Tara's face. "Do you mind if I eat my lunch, such as it is?" She held up the same bar he'd just eaten.

Sam displayed his empty wrapper. "Goes down better with a warm cup of brew."

"Ah. I knew there had to be a way to swallow these fake candy bars that taste of metal."

Chuckling, Sam poured coffee into a Styrofoam cup and delivered it to her. "Cheers."

"Thank you, Mr. Conrad." She took a sip. "That is better. I can swallow now. So, tell me how the Bosarge family is. I take it Elinor won't be here for the meeting."

He didn't want to unload on the woman, but she was a nurse. Sam described the past couple of days to Tara in full detail, including his worries about the red incision.

"I'll take my husband and visit tomorrow evening when he's off call. We'll both have a look."

"Your husband's an orthopedic surgeon?"

"An ER doc, so he sees it all. A good one, too, if I do say so myself."

Made sense. "I'd feel a whole lot better if y'all did come by."

"You really care about the family." Her lips twitched as she seemed to hold back a smile. "And about Elinor?"

"I do." He'd probably get his heart broken, but why not let the whole world see it? Again.

Other members filed into the room before he had to admit more. Sam stood to greet each one. He shifted into business mode, and they went over proposals, weighing the pros and cons, along with the amount of dollars available.

Tara led them around the physical areas under discussion. "I like your ideas. Especially soft colors and music. Oh, and the circular wandering path. Some Alzheimer's patients have to walk to burn off energy."

The older gentleman whose father currently resided down the hall nodded. "My father's one of those. Constantly roaming around. I like the idea of the new handrails and security monitoring system. I'd hate for him to sneak out the door."

The committee seemed to be in agreement. They could vote on the proposal today, except they had to be unanimous, and of course, Elinor wasn't here. He hated to trouble her right now. "How about we vote on the approval for those present, and when Miss Bosarge is able, she can review and cast her vote. If she agrees, there's no reason to meet again." But her not going along with the crowd remained a possibility. The woman had her own ideas about most everything. He could hope their newfound relationship would help. As long as their date went well. Maybe he should've waited until they'd finished the business at hand.

~~~
~~~

Alternating waves of nausea and numbness made rounds through Elinor's body as she watched Cindy, the therapist, torture her mother. How long could Mother keep going? They'd been at it for almost an hour. It seemed cruel to force someone who'd just had surgery to walk. But everything she'd found online confirmed the therapist's actions.

"Let it hang over the edge a bit. We'll ice it before you leave." After helping Mother get situated, Cindy retrieved an ice pack.

Tears ran down Mother's cheeks, and she'd looked as if she'd been holding her breath almost the entire session. Probably squeezing in screams of agony.

Elinor laced her fingers together and clutched them tight. She had to be strong. Her father would be back soon with the discharge paperwork, and they could go home.

Her mother completed her time with the ice just as he walked in. "How's my sweetheart?" After one glance at his wife's face, worry etched crinkled indentions in his forehead. "Oh darlin', I hate you're feeling so poorly." He gently took her hand to his lips. "Did they give you the pain medicine?"

"I'm just being a baby, crying like this."

Cindy shook her head. "You're doing much better than many of my patients. I've heard screaming and cussing like you couldn't imagine after knee replacement. You'll get through the recovery." She pushed the walker to the side of the bed. "Take this with you until you can walk with a cane in a couple of weeks. You'll need to wear compression hose like we talked about. You can rent an ice machine for your knee if you want. It's kind of expensive but really helps with swelling."

"We'll take one." Elinor stood and gathered her mother's things. "When can we leave?" The sooner the better.

But then she paused. At home, no medical personnel would be around in an emergency. Just her and Daddy. But they had Sam. The thought of him being at the boathouse loosened some of the tension running across her midsection.

"They'll send an aide around with a wheelchair. Sometimes it takes a while, depending on how busy they are. Keep at it,

Mrs. Bosarge, and all of this will be over before you know it."

That sure was easy for young Cindy to say. Elinor blinked to stop the eye roll she really wanted to give the girl.

An hour later, the orderly arrived. Elinor followed him as he rolled her mother down the long hall. Her muscles felt soggy and heavy. Why did sitting around make one so tired? Part of it might have been the intense swim from the day before, but still. And she thought she'd felt a little wheeze a time or two when she breathed. Stupid asthma.

Father took off to bring the car around. Maybe she should drive, though. The man loved to talk and had a hard time not looking at his passengers while doing so. Traveling with him had rattled her nerves more times than she could count.

An elevator ride and a few turns down the hall led them to the glass, automatic doors. Wind blasted through, whipping Elinor's hair into her face.

"Goodness, that's a gale." Mother shielded her eyes with her hand to block the sun and wind.

"Sure is." Elinor fumbled through the overnight bag. "I saw your sunglasses when I packed up." Her fingers touched the case. "Here." She set them on her mother's face.

"Thanks, hon. You don't have to baby me, though."

"There's Daddy." Elinor pointed down the circular drive. Once the car stopped, she opened the front door and scooted the seat back as far as it would go.

Her mother struggled to stand and staggered.

"Wait for me to assist you, Mother." Elinor held her steady and helped her in. Getting her situated with the knee pain proved to be the first challenge. Finally, Elinor strapped the buckle around her mother's waist, hurried to the driver's window, and knocked.

Her father let it down. "Did we forget something? She left her pocketbook at home."

"We didn't forget anything, but I can drive, so, um…you can watch Mother."

"Darlin', get in and rest. You've been up all night while I was home and had a good night's sleep. You've got to be exhausted."

Elinor caught her lip in her teeth. Her eyes were a bit heavy. Maybe it would be safer to let him drive. At least he was alert. "Take it soft and slow."

"Good idea. I'll be as soft as a cloud."

From what she remembered about her last airplane ride with him, clouds could be bumpy. They'd probably regret this decision.

The first turn out of the lot confirmed her theory. He whipped across two lanes of traffic and then slammed the brakes at a red light.

Her mother's eyes squeezed shut, and from the look of it, she'd gritted her teeth. "Oh." A long exhale followed.

"Daddy, pull over and let me drive. I know you mean well, but you're not used to…driving like a woman would if her mother had just been released from the hospital."

He slowed the car and glanced back at her. "I'm sorry, and I'm fixing to do better. Slowing down now."

"Soft and easy turns."

"Got it."

Her mother groaned. "Get me home in one piece."

When they arrived at the house, Elinor flopped her head back on the seat. "Thank you, Lord." No wonder Mother didn't want Daddy to drive her to therapy. That her father had never had a wreck in his whole life surpassed all odds. Once she'd regained her composure, she exited and rounded the car. "Daddy, can you get the walker while I unbuckle Mother?"

"Sure as shootin'."

Maybe her father should go into the office this afternoon. She could use a break from the Royisms and perkiness. She leaned across and pressed the metal buckle. "You okay, Mother?"

"Tired."

"You can rest soon." The next few minutes terrified her. If her mother fell… God, help us.

"Here you are, young lady." Her father smiled, but worry lined his face.

"Okay, just give me a second." Her mother sucked in a breath and then stood.

Elinor placed a hand behind her back. "That's good. No hurry."

One slow step at a time, Mother pushed the walker forward. Despite the gusty winds, the sun beat down in typical Mobile fashion. Hot and muggy.

At last, they made it to the door, and her father hurried ahead to open it for them. Dashwood whined and bounded toward them, prancing in circles at their feet.

"No, Dashwood. Sit." Elinor used her sternest voice.

Shunned, the dog crouched and ducked its head. But a second later, it was sniffing at their legs again.

"No. Get!" This dog would be the death of her mother.

Then, Mr. Darcy found them and wound around Elinor's legs, whining. The cat sniffed and batted at the walker.

Elinor huffed. "These animals are going to the boathouse for a couple of days. Sam will have to deal with them. I won't have them tripping you."

With singular focus, her mother kept a slow but steady pace until they reached the bedroom. She didn't speak or nod acknowledgement, just trudged forward. Pain contorted her face, and more tears gathered in her eyes.

Poor, sweet Mother. She was in so much agony.

They made it to the bed, and Elinor helped her in. "Let me put a pillow under your foot like they had at the hospital."

Mother gave a small nod, her lips still pressed together.

Elinor lifted her mother's lower leg and adjusted the pillow. "Would you like something to eat or drink?"

"I just want to sleep."

"Okay. I'll set a timer for the next dose of pain medicine."

No answer. A soft snore lifted her mother's chest already. This surgery had really taken a lot out of her. Out of all of them.

Mr. Darcy swished in between Elinor's legs and purred.

"Come here, sir." She lifted him up to her shoulder. "Sam's going to have company tonight."

Chapter 30

Sam quietly tapped on the Bosarges' back door. Spending the afternoon logging more hours with another therapist left him beat. Especially after the long day and night before. Still, he wanted to run before dark. He stretched his legs and knocked again.

No answer, so he let himself in. He tiptoed through the living room, glancing around. An overnight bag and pharmacy receipts lay on the couch, which meant they'd been home, but the house was still. Everyone must be napping, and he didn't want to snoop down the hall to the bedrooms. His stomach growled and echoed in the silence. The protein bar from lunch was long gone. No reason to let all that good food the neighbors had brought go to waste.

Sam made his way to the kitchen and worked quietly to fill his plate with a sampling of the entrees. He placed it in the microwave. As soon as he ate, he'd make sure everything was okay. The smells of the savory ham and casseroles cooking caused additional growling—more like roaring in his stomach. The back door creaked open, and he turned.

Roy came through and gave him a tired smile. "Look what the cat dragged in." He sniffed. "That smells mighty good."

"Here." Sam took the plate and offered it. "Your neighbors brought a ton of food. Sit and eat. I'll make another and join you."

Roy eyed the food and licked his lips. "Goodness gracious. I believe I will. Thank you, Sam-man."

"What were you doing outside?"

"Trying to stay out of Elinor's way and let them rest."

Chuckling, Sam filled another plate. He could well imagine what led Roy to sit outside. "How are the ladies?"

"My Ruby's not feeling good at all, and Elinor was tuckered out, so she had me blow up an air mattress and lay it beside our bed." His mouth quirked. "I'm booted to the guest room for a while."

"I see." Sam couldn't stop a grin.

Roy pointed his fork at him. "Don't get too amused. Elinor's put those animals in the boathouse with you."

Animals? Plural? "Both of them?" Not the cat. Not the weird, naked cat.

"Yessiree. You'll have 'em both to cuddle up with for a week or so, I reckon."

"Nice."

Another reason to look for his own place. The microwave beeped, and Sam retrieved his food. He sat at the table and dug into the lasagna first. The gooey cheese and meat melted in his mouth and hit the spot. Once he came up for air, he set his fork down on his plate. "The steering committee's recommendations are ready. We're just waiting for Elinor to look them over and vote. She hasn't been able to make many of the meetings with the death of her teacher friend and the surgery."

Roy swallowed the last hunk of ham in one bite. "Woo, I'm full as a tick." He pressed a napkin to his lips. "Good work, Sam-man. You've about finished all the assignments I had for you."

"Except your investment analysis. I've been trying to catch your financial planner, but he hasn't returned any of my calls." He was starting to wonder if the man was avoiding him.

"He's fixing to retire, I hear. We'll have to get that settled and set up with a new broker."

Maybe Boyd Watson had already cut his hours back if he was ready to retire. "I'll track him down."

They cleaned their plates, and Sam headed across the backyard to the boathouse. He opened the door, and both animals bolted out past his feet.

"Oh, shoot." He sprinted after the cat first. The thing would be much harder to find after dark, and it looked like it'd make easy gator bait. "Here, kitty, kitty."

A pack of bacon and an hour later, he'd caught both animals and corralled them in the bedroom of the boathouse. He shut them in together and slammed the door. "May the best man win." Sweat dripped from Sam's brow as he inched around the patio furniture stored in the front room to retrieve his running shoes. He wouldn't need to jog near as far after his escapade with Darcy and Dashwood.

His phone rang as he walked out. Dad? Supposedly he'd been written off. What now? Sam clicked to answer. "Hello."

"If you're going to be an idiot, at least you can send clients my way." His father's voice sounded more like a growl.

"What are you talking about?"

"I'll pull a few strings to get you into school in Jackson, and you cozy up to as many doctors there as you can. Talk up our wealth department. Reel them in for us."

Now Dad's okay with me going to PT school? What brought on that change? Getting into school a year earlier would be nice, but did he want his father's help after all that had happened? The school would be three hours away from Oxford, but almost four hours north of Mobile…and Elinor. Plus, there would be another debt he'd owe to his father. "You're saying you can get me in PT at the University of Mississippi hospital this fall?"

"Are you deaf now, too?"

"I'll get back to you."

When the curse words began, Sam ended the call. He really needed a good long run now, so he took off at a sprint down the road. The heavy wind heaved against him and whipped the tops of the trees in a circular motion. Small sticks littered the road. He hoped no branches would fall on his head. At least not a big one. No one knew for sure when and where the big storm would make landfall, but the wind had sure picked up.

He settled into his pace and ran his father's words—the clean ones—through his head. In one sense, his father had accepted his decision and reached out. Sort of. With strings attached. But he'd still have to answer to the man, probably giving a blow by blow of every medical professional he met.

Dad always had an agenda.

Still. Acceptance into school and finishing a year earlier was tempting. What should he do?

One answer came to mind. One he was going to start doing more of.

Pray.

He looked toward the windy sky. "God, I don't know where You want me. I've decided to be Your man, though, so I'm asking for wisdom and strength as I make career decisions." His mind went to Elinor. "Decisions about every part of my life. Please be with Elinor and Miss Ruby, too."

Back at the boathouse, Sam entered quickly and slammed the door, even though he'd trapped Darcy and Dashwood in the bedroom. One animal chase for the day had been enough. Maybe he'd just text Elinor to see if they were okay instead of going back to the big house. She could read it whenever she was able. After sending the message, he showered and settled onto the bed with his computer, since patio furniture crowded the living room. A second later, the bed bounced, and a bald animal with huge green eyes inspected him.

"I don't sleep with animals, Mr. Darcy. Shoo." Sam clapped his hands and waved the animal away. The cat merely sauntered to the far side of the bed. Meanwhile something wet nudged his leg. Dashwood's nose and wooly face plopped on Sam's thigh with begging eyes. "You either, boy. Sorry."

If he turned off the light and went to sleep, would they leave him alone? He needed to do more praying anyway.

~~~

Elinor woke to her mother's groans. She scrambled off the air mattress to her feet. Morning already? She checked her phone and yawned. It had been a hard night, especially when her mother had needed to get up.

There were five minutes left until the next dose of pain medicine. Close enough. She fumbled with the childproof lid until she got the bottle open and plucked out the pill.

"Here, Mother. Take your pain medicine." Elinor held out the medicine and the glass of water she'd prepared earlier.
~~~

Shaking fingers grasped at the pill, so Elinor helped hold the water while her mother drank. "We'll need to get you dressed for the therapist visit this morning."

"Not yet." Her mother lay back and closed her eyes.

"We can wait until you have a bit of relief. I'll make breakfast and get myself dressed first."

A slight nod from her mother, then nothing.

Poor thing was in so much pain. Elinor took quiet steps out of the room and up the stairs to dress. Worry picked at her the whole time. She threw on yoga pants and a T-shirt and then rushed back down the stairs to peek in at her mother. The quiet snore returned. That was better than the groaning, so she headed for the kitchen. A piece of that ham on a biscuit sounded good. She turned the stove on to preheat. There was usually biscuit dough in the freezer. A note on the refrigerator caught her attention.

Ran down to the office. Be back soon. Love, Daddy.

At seven o'clock? Wasn't he the early bird.

The back door opened, and Sam walked in dressed and clean shaven. "Good morning. How was your night?"

Oh no. Elinor combed her fingers through her hair. She hadn't even brushed the mop in her hurry to come back down. "Mother was in a lot of pain."

"The first night home from the hospital is always hard."

Did that mean tonight would be better? "How was your evening?"

One side of Sam's mouth quirked down, and he rolled his eyes.

What was that look? "Did something happen with your dad? Or your school application?"

"My dad called a couple of times. Still trying to control my life. Nothing new."

Elinor grappled with what to say. Her social skills were so lacking. A character in her book would try to comfort the hero. Maybe. "Want to have a cup of coffee and talk about it?"

His brows crinkled as if he couldn't decide. Was he holding back something?

"Maybe later tonight."

Now what? "Did you at least sleep well?"

This time he gave her his smirk. Which she was beginning to find more cute than annoying.

"What?"

"Woke up with your cat wrapped around my head and Dashwood spooning me, but other than that, fine."

The mental picture brought up a giggle, then a full-fledged, squealing laugh. "I would love to have seen that."

"You're welcome to come over tomorrow morning and wake us if you need a chuckle." His gaze warmed her. Or maybe it was the idea of waking him.

"I'm making biscuits with ham. Want one?"

"How long will it take? I have to get to Memory Oaks for my observation hours."

"Maybe ten minutes if you make the coffee."

"Deal. I'll take two."

Elinor threw eight biscuits onto the baking sheet in case her father came back soon. He'd always eat the leftovers.

As Sam started the coffee, he caught her gaze and smiled, unearthing more unlikely visions. Visions of a husband, a partner, someone to make breakfast with, laugh with, share a life with. Someone she could trust and depend on.

Chapter 31

The last patient left, and Sam made a quick exit to his car. The day observing with the therapist had been fulfilling, though his mind wandered to his father's offer. And to Elinor. He'd texted her a couple of times but received no answer. His gut told him that was a bad sign. He checked his phone again before he drove off. Nothing. Just that same old crack on the screen he'd never made time to have repaired.

Before heading home, he'd drive to Roy's financial planner's office again. The guy hadn't answered his calls, and the other two times he'd stopped by the brokerage firm, the manager claimed Mr. Watson was out.

Sam parallel parked across the street from the building. He'd looked up the broker online, so he knew who to look for. Maybe he'd wait a bit and see if Mr. Boyd Watson exited. It was five-fifteen. A man getting ready to retire probably didn't work late hours.

Sure enough, five minutes later, the clean cut, gray-haired man strutted toward a silver convertible parked sideways across two spots in the back of the lot. It figured. From the guy's online profile, he looked to be divorced and in a long-term midlife crisis.

Sam hopped out and strode toward him. "Mr. Watson. I need a word with you."

"Did I forget a meeting?" Mr. Watson checked his Rolex.

Sam inserted himself between Watson and his car. "In a way. I'm Sam Conrad, an associate of Roy Bosarge." He squared his shoulders. "You haven't returned my calls."

"I don't make a habit of talking about my clients."

"But I faxed over the appropriate paperwork, and Mr. Bosarge called your office to give you permission to speak to me."

"We'll have to set up a conference." Watson fiddled with his watch. "I'm late to an appointment."

For what, a massage? Filter. "I have questions about the Blue Mile Mutual Fund. I can't find it online. I want to see a prospectus and a full earnings report first thing in the morning."

"Fine. If you'll excuse me, I'm going to be late."

Sam let him through and returned to his car. Nothing about Boyd Watson sat right with him. But Roy had said they were friends, and the other investments looked good. Over the years, the broker had made a nice sum of money for the Bosarges.

Sam sighed. The cheesy online profile had probably just ruined his opinion of Watson. It didn't mean he wasn't legit. But he'd still check out the fund. He punched in his friend's number at the Securities Exchange compliance department for the second time. When he'd called earlier, his friend had been on vacation. Maybe he was back now.

Voicemail picked up. Sam left a detailed message before he started the car.

Once he hit the freeway, he drove as fast as traffic allowed until he reached the Bosarges' home. A Jeep Cherokee was parked in the drive. Hopefully not another old suitor of Elinor's. Their relationship had just started moving in the right direction. The last thing they needed was another disaster.

After Sam parked, he went straight to the back door and knocked. No sense having to chase those nutty animals in the boathouse yet.

A second later, Tara answered. "Hello again, Mr. Conrad."

"That's right. You said you'd bring your husband for a visit." Sam followed her into the dining room. "Have you seen the patient?"

"We've just arrived." Tara motioned to the man ahead of her, dressed in scrubs. "Meet my husband. Grayson."

"Nice to meet you." Sam extended his hand.

"Same here." Grayson stood a few inches shorter than Sam.

His grip was firm and his manner exuded confidence. Looked like he'd easily manage an emergency room. "Heard you're looking at a new career in the medical profession."

"Working on it."

"If you need any recommendations, let me know. Tara says you're a good man, and that's gold."

"Thank you." Sam turned his attention to Tara. "And you, too."

Elinor entered with her father. They each carried trays with an assortment of foods, no doubt from the brimming refrigerator. "Please help us eat this. I can make plates for you to take home, too." She offered a tired smile to Sam when she noticed him there. "I didn't hear you come in."

"I'm sneaky that way." He moved to her side. "Let me help." He took the tray to the table. "What else can I do?"

"Plates and silverware would be nice, if you don't mind."

"I live to serve." He flashed a broad smile he hoped would lighten her heart. From the looks of it, he'd been right about her having a bad day.

After ferreting out a stack of plates and as many forks, knives, and spoons from the kitchen, he set them at the table. "Next?"

"That's good. Daddy's grabbing the tea, and I have the napkins." Elinor laid one at each place. "Tara and Grayson, please, have a seat."

"You didn't need to feed us, my friend. We came to visit and perhaps help you." Tara complied, but shot a pointed look at Sam.

"They could look at your mother's incision. She's been in so much pain."

Elinor sat and toyed with the edge of the place mat. "That might make me feel better. Mother really does seem to be suffering, but I hate being an alarmist."

Laughing, Tara chose a chair beside Elinor. "Since when, child?"

Sam struggled to keep a straight face. Exactly what he'd wanted to say.

A slight smile lifted Elinor's lips. "I could always be worse if I didn't contain myself."

More rich laughter followed. "I suppose you could."

Roy returned with a tray of glasses filled with sweet tea, set them around the table, and took his place at the head. "Would you say our blessing, Grayson, along with a prayer of healing for my Ruby?"

"Of course, sir."

Sam bowed his head while Grayson lifted up the family in prayer. He silently added his own pleas to God.

A beep sounded from Roy's phone as the prayer ended. "Blasted thing. Let me see what that's about." Roy held the screen near his face and squinted. "My buddy on the weather bureau says the hurricane is making a turn. Not sure where the new projected path will be." He aimed a look at Elinor. "Maybe putting up the shutters wasn't in vain, but I sure hope it misses us."

Unease swirled around Sam's insides. He'd never ridden out a hurricane and didn't plan to. "When would we evacuate?"

"This isn't our first rodeo. Most of these storms just blow in a bunch of rain. We won't evacuate unless the local law enforcement says we have to go."

"I'm not much of a rodeo man."

Tara and Grayson chuckled.

He'd forgotten about working on his filter.

"Smart man, Sam Conrad." Tara patted the table. "That reminds me. We're working on a new evacuation plan for Memory Oaks and are updating our list of volunteers."

"What kind of volunteers?"

"Should we have to evacuate, we may need help doing so quickly. Volunteers would assist the patients onto the buses and other vehicles."

"I'll do it." Sam shrugged. "I'd help everyone and then hit the road until the storm passed. No sense hanging around to see if a tree falls on me. I hope none of us has to leave, though."

"But are you staying here? In Alabama?" Elinor's question

held more layers beyond those seven words.

His father's offer came to mind. Every time he thought of being in Mississippi, still answering to the man, his chest tightened. While the thought of living here gave him a sense of peace, no matter what his career.

"I'm staying." One way or another.

Elinor's tired eyes brightened a bit. "Of course, I'll volunteer, as long as we get Mother settled somewhere safe."

~~~

So Sam had decided to stay. Elinor held in a sigh of relief as she cleared the table. His decision shouldn't please her so much. The choice could have little to do with her. He might just want to be five hours away from his father and that Tiffany woman. Did he still have feelings for his ex? They had been engaged after all.

"Thank you for feeding us." Tara's voice broke into Elinor's deliberations.

"All courtesy of our good neighbors."

"Good indeed. Shall we visit your mother now?"

"I'll go tell her you're here. She was sleeping so well when you arrived, I hated to wake her."

"Rest is good for healing." Tara held up a clean plate. "Eating is, too. I'll prepare her dinner while you go check on her."

"You're a godsend."

A huge smile lifted Tara's cheeks. "I do my best."

Having Tara and Grayson visit might be just the thing to perk up Mother. Elinor scuttled down the hall into the bedroom.

"Mother, you have guests. Tara and her husband are here." Elinor turned on the lamp beside the bed. "Mother?"

"I don't feel good." Words crackled in her mother's throat, and she shivered.

"Are you cold? You're shaking." Elinor bent and pressed her cheek against her mother's forehead. Burning hot. Fever. "Oh, Momma. I'll get help."

Fear exploded in Elinor's chest, driving her feet to the living
~~~

room. "Sam, Grayson, Momma's sick!"

Both men rushed toward her. Grayson continued, but Sam stopped to brace her with his arm. "What's happened?"

"Fever. Shaking."

They continued to the room with her father and Tara right behind. While Grayson checked her mother's pulse and felt her head, Sam moved toward her legs.

"Is it okay for me to uncover the incision? Let Grayson take a look?"

A small nod answered the question.

Elinor joined him and removed the blanket. Red streaks made an ugly appearance, and her mother shivered harder. Looking at the swollen leg made Elinor feel as if she had fever, too. "It wasn't like this when the therapist was here earlier, but she did complain of terrible pain."

Her mother's eyes fluttered, and she groaned. "Let me go home to my momma. I can't do this anymore." Sobs shook her chest even more than the shivering. Her head writhed from side to side. "Oh, Lord Jesus, help me. I can't fight. Fight for me." Her breathing slowed. "Thank you, Jesus." Tears squeezed from her closing eyelids.

"Tara, call 911." Grayson spoke with calm decisiveness. "I'll ride with her to the ER."

"What's wrong with my Ruby?" Her father's big voice trembled.

"Infection. A severe one from the look of it."

Elinor crumbled into Sam's chest. "It's my fault."

"No. No. Shh." His arms held her up. "You didn't cause an infection, and plenty of medical professionals have looked at her. These things just happen."

"I should have known." After all, it was her mother.

Chapter 32

The flashing red lights of the ambulance sliced into the evening sky, adding to the aura of horror roaming over Elinor's face. Sam stayed close behind the emergency vehicle until they reached the unloading bay at the back of the hospital. He helped Elinor out of his car, and they both gaped as paramedics lifted Miss Ruby onto the stretcher. Roy had insisted on riding with his wife. He shuffled out and followed her and Grayson into the ER.

"Ready to go in?" Sam rested his fingers on Elinor's elbow.

She stood dazed and motionless.

Tara drove up in the Jeep and hopped out. "Come on. I know my way around here."

Blinking, Elinor snapped to attention. "Show us what to do." She took Sam's hand and squeezed. "Come with us."

"Whatever you need."

Inside, medical personnel rushed here and there. Tara navigated them through it all to a curtained area where Grayson updated his colleagues on Miss Ruby's condition. A few began asking questions of Elinor and Roy, and she managed to come up with the answers.

Plastic tubing from IV poles had already been attached to one of Miss Ruby's hands. Roy held the other.

"Sir?" A nurse pointed at Roy. "We need to have room to work. Would you and the family mind waiting in the chairs down the hall?"

Grayson neared. "I'll stay and keep you updated. We need to get her stabilized and run cultures on the infection. It could take a while."

Reluctantly, Roy took a step back. Then he seemed to change his mind and leaned over his wife. He kissed her forehead. "Get well, my Ruby. I need you." Then he turned to Grayson. "Take care of her."

"Yes, sir."

Elinor's grasp on Sam's hand tightened as they followed Roy out of the room and into the waiting area.

Tara spoke quietly, the words drifting in and out of Sam's attention as he studied Elinor. Something about assuring them Miss Ruby was in good hands.

They sat staring, waiting. An hour passed. Worry plowed through Sam's chest. And frustration. Being helpless didn't sit well with him.

Finally Grayson approached. The grim expression the doctor wore triggered a red flag in his mind.

Elinor bristled and sat straight up. "What is it?"

"There's an infection in Mrs. Bosarge's bloodstream. She was going into septic shock with an extremely low blood pressure, so we've moved her to ICU and started broad spectrum antibiotics, fluids, oxygen, but…" He took a deep breath. "Amputation is a definite possibility if the bone's infected or if the shock causes her organs to begin failing. We're fighting with every weapon we have, but it's serious. You may want to call in your immediate family."

"No, God, don't let Momma die." Elinor fell into Sam's chest, and he wrapped his arms around her.

This was all happening so quick. Like a nightmare. He needed to do something.

"You amputate whatever you want, just save my Ruby." Roy's voice cracked as he covered his face with his hands.

Grayson placed a hand on Roy's shoulder. "I promise, we're doing everything we can for her."

Sam released one hand from Elinor to search his pocket. "I'll call Cassie, if that's what you want. I have her number."

Elinor nodded her approval.

Answer enough. He pressed the contact.

It rang twice before she answered. "Hello there, Sam." Cassie sounded way too perky.

Giving bad news would be hard. "Cassie, your mother's

come down with a dangerous infection. You and Emma should get down here as soon as possible."

"But they sent her home. We thought…"

"We're back at the hospital now."

"You're saying she might…"

"The doctor says it's very serious. She's in ICU. Your father and Elinor are here."

"I'll get Em and charter a plane. We'll be there. Tell them… Just tell them we're on our way."

"Will do."

The call ended. An urge nagged at him. More like badgered him. "We should pray."

Roy's watery gaze met his. "Would you lead?"

"Sure." Sam's throat tightened. What would he say? He bowed his head and hoped words would come. Elinor's cool hand slid into his. "God, we're scared for Miss Ruby. She's such a lovely lady and a good mother and wife." Words and courage filled him as he went on. "We ask for complete healing. Beat back every bit of the infection. We know you have the power to do miracles. Grant her favor as your loving servant. Show us how to help her. How to help each other. Calm and comfort us in your love, God. In Jesus, we beg for your healing power. Amen." Expelling the air from his chest, he sighed. Where had all that come from?

"Amen." The others spoke in unison.

Elinor's teary eyes peeked up at him. "Thank you."

~~~

Fear threatened to crush Elinor into a blubbering mess, but Sam's prayerful words flowed over her, sunk into her soul. God was in control. She had to believe that, or nothing in life made sense. This should have been a routine operation. Infections were normally curable in this day and age. But now they were calling in the family as if death were imminent. Her mother had been God's faithful servant like Sam had said, but did that mean God would heal her?

She'd heard heartbreaking stories of tragedies that had happened to other families. Good people who'd died from
~~~

some freak accident or strange illness. Elinor sank further into Sam's shoulder and squeezed her eyes shut. Tears rolled down her cheeks. She'd never imagined her family would be the next to endure such a tragedy. Her stomach twisted. But really, why should they be immune?

"Don't give up," Sam whispered next to her ear. "They'll find the right combination of antibiotics."

The hospital air felt stale as she sucked in a shaky breath. "I'm scared."

"Understandably." He squeezed her tighter. "I'm here. Not going anywhere."

"I'm thankful. More than you know." For once in her life, she had someone besides just her parents to lean on. And when she needed it the most. Sam Conrad, her rock. Who would've guessed when she'd met him that first day in the boathouse? She sure hadn't wanted him around…hadn't wanted to trust him. Or love him. Elinor stiffened. She did love Sam—the annoying, maddening, rude man.

She couldn't think about that. Her mother was all that mattered right now. What if she didn't make it?

In a sudden panic, Elinor wrenched away and stood. Her chest felt so tight she could hardly breathe. "I need to walk and pray for a while."

Sam stared at her, holding out one hand. "You want company?"

"No. But keep praying."

Her father lifted his gaze from the floor. "You okay, darlin'?"

"Just need to move a bit. I've got my phone, and I won't be far." She squeezed her knuckles as she left the room and paced to the far end of the hall.

Lord, heal my mother. Please. I know I shouldn't try to bargain, but I'd take her place in a heartbeat if it were a possibility. She does so much good for others. Emma needs Mother.

What would her sweet father do without his Ruby? She continued wandering and praying until she reached the lobby. A sign before her indicated a chapel, and she stepped toward the door. Inside the small room, the quiet clashed against the noise of her frantic thoughts. Thankfully, no one else was around. After inching into the back row, she draped herself over the seat in front of her, and bowed her head. *I don't know what else to say…what to ask. Hear the plea of my heart, Lord.*

Tears spilled down her cheeks as she sobbed there on her knees. Time passed without notice until exhaustion weighed down her shoulders.

Chapter 33

Sam's fingers hovered over his phone for what had to be the hundredth time. The debate raged inside him—go find Elinor or let her be? People dealt with stress in different ways, but it had been a while since she'd left. How was she holding up? Periodically, Grayson or a nurse appeared and gave an update, which amounted to nothing, since there'd been no change.

Roy tried to share a favorite story about his wife now and then, but in the end would tear up and drop his head into his hands again. Somehow word of Miss Ruby's illness got out, because friends and neighbors trickled in, offering snacks and a needed distraction. Doubtful Elinor would've appreciated the chatter, though, if he knew the woman as well as he thought he did.

They really weren't that different. He'd never been good at chitchat. A purposeful conversation or a business project, yes, but he often struggled to not offend in nonessential talk.

Like when he'd met Elinor.

His mind detoured back to when she'd walked in on him that first day in the boathouse. He chuckled inwardly. Her and her crazy-looking cat. The thing had insisted on cuddling up next to his head the last two nights.

Seeing Elinor and Roy broken and hurting like this, not to mention Miss Ruby so sick, twisted his insides…wrenched his heart. He would do anything for them. He loved this family like his own. Well, his feelings for Elinor were not that kind of *familial*. His love for her… *Love* for her?

He was completely and utterly in love with Elinor.

The realization pinged around his mind, accelerating his pulse. In love with a woman he'd never even taken on a date. In fact, their first date was supposed to have been in a couple of days. As usual, his timing couldn't be worse.

A group of people rounded the corner, and a flash of red hair caught his attention. Sam stood as they came closer. Not Elinor, but Cassie and her husband, followed by Em and Cassie's son, Benjamin.

"Have you heard anything else?" Cassie rushed to her father's side and took his hand.

"Still waiting, darlin'."

Tara stood and offered Em the chair on the other side of her father. Em took it without speaking, her eyes wide and red. The girl had likely never been this silent in her life.

Sam shook hands with Dylan and Benjamin. "You made it fast."

Worry cut a line in Dylan's brow. "This is just unreal. She has to make it."

"We're praying, and the doctors are doing everything they can. Tara's husband is an ER doctor here and is staying with her, monitoring her care and reporting back to us."

"Where's Elinor?" Twisting around, Cassie glanced across the room.

"I'll text her." Sam took out his phone. *Oh man*. More cracks filled the screen. He must've sat on it or something. He could barely read the thing. "She needed to walk around for a while."

A really long while.

~~~

The ping of a text jolted Elinor. Her neck muscles ached from her twisted position. A wave of terror rushed through her as she fumbled through her purse for her phone. Was there bad news? It slipped from her fingers to the floor, and she bumped her head as she tried to reach it. "Come on." She read the text.

Your sisters are here. Are you okay? Can I walk you back?

She exhaled slowly and texted back. No bad news on Mother. Thank God.

I'll be right there.

Sam was kind to offer to come to her, and he'd given her space when she'd asked for it. She stared at his message and
~~~

then typed another.

Thanks.

After tucking the phone in her purse, she backtracked her way toward the ICU waiting area. The faint scent of coffee mingled with antiseptic tickled her nose. Maybe she should ask for a cup of warm brew. Not sleeping the last few nights had caught up with her. She kept walking, though. She hadn't meant to be gone so long.

As she rounded the corner, Grayson stood encircled by her family and other worried faces. She recognized friends of her parents and members of their church. Something must be wrong. She picked up her pace to a jog. Her sandals slapped against the floor, causing all heads to turn her way.

"What's happened?"

Cassie stepped out of the group and embraced her. "They may have to place Mother on a ventilator. She's getting worse. We're about to pray together."

Numb, Elinor nodded and allowed her sister to lead her to the circle. Sam repositioned himself next to her and took her hand.

"Grayson," Elinor pleaded, "isn't there more that can be done?"

"We are doing everything we can."

Tara touched Elinor's shoulder. "Praying is doing something, too. Something powerful."

Of course Tara was right, but things seemed so hopeless.

Again, Sam whispered against her ear, "Don't give up." He squeezed her hand.

She fought tears, and as the others implored for healing aloud, she prayed in her soul as hard as she could and more. Over and over, three little words. *Save my mother.*

Chapter 34

Just after dawn, light crept through the hospital windows. The aroma of coffee hovered under Sam's nose. He blinked through the blurriness of the sleepless night in the waiting room and let his cheek be caressed by Elinor's hair, which lay against his shoulder and chest. Neither of them had rested, and an achy weariness settled in his bones, as if he'd spent the night playing tackle football. And losing. That would've been preferred over the nightmare of Miss Ruby being so ill.

What time was it? If he wasn't going to do his PT observation, he'd need to call in soon. Elinor shifted, and he pressed a kiss on the top of her head. Though she was awake, she hadn't spoken for the last couple of hours. She'd kept her gaze glued to the hall where Grayson periodically passed through with an update—as if she could will him to come and announce her mother had been healed.

That would take a miracle, judging from all the reports so far. Did he believe in miracles? Sam let his eyes close.

God, I want to believe in miracles. Help me believe.

"Look!" Elinor pulled away and sat up. "Grayson's back, and he's smiling."

Chills ran through Sam's core. Was he hallucinating? Because Grayson did appear to be smiling as he walked briskly toward them.

All the family stood and waited, anxiety marking each face.

"Good news." Grayson let out a long sigh. "She's responding to the antibiotics. She's conscious. The fever's down, and her white counts have improved. She'll be on the medications awhile, perhaps months, but I feel much better about her prognosis."

"She's gonna make it?" Roy stood and took Grayson's

shoulder, his eyes pleading.

"No guarantees, but I believe we're going to beat this infection."

"Thank you, God." Elinor's hands covered her mouth, and a tear slipped down her cheek. Her gaze found him, and she offered a smile that reached her eyes, livening the pools of blue that had looked so defeated all night. "It seems like a miracle, doesn't it?"

"It sure does." Sam slipped his arm around her and squeezed. "It sure does."

Her knuckles swept away the wetness on her cheeks. "I know you're supposed to be doing other things besides taking care of me. You should go home. Get a shower and do your observation."

"I can call in and explain."

Her chin jutted up as she pulled away. "Oh, no. I don't want you to go back to Oxford and the bank, blaming me because you skipped your hours." Her lips did that little quirk of a smile.

Warmth spread over him when she added a wink.

He chuckled. "Are you trying to boss me around?"

"Just a little." Her eyes suddenly widened as a stricken expression froze onto her face. "The animals in the boathouse. The dog needs to be let out. I hope there's not a big mess."

The thought of what could be waiting for him made his empty stomach quiver. "Yeah, I better go."

"Thanks for everything. You've been like an anchor in this storm." Her fingers caught his and squeezed. "I mean it."

"You are more than welcome. I'll see you as soon as I finish."

"You should rest some, too. No need to hurry back."

"Trying to get rid of me?"

Her lips neared his ear. "No. I need you too much." She placed a soft kiss on his cheek and blushed. "Go, before Em starts picking on us."

His step lightened as he practically bounced out of the hospital. A miracle and an impromptu kiss on the cheek. Not how he'd thought this day would go.

The steady chirp of birds filling the windy sky caught his attention, and he fought the urge to cover his head and run. They looked as if they were on an important mission, so maybe they'd steer clear of him and his clean vehicle. At the end of the parking lot, he found more good news. The Mazda still sported a spotless shine. He climbed in and punched on the radio. The sound might keep him awake.

A storm warning message blared, and his stomach plunged. Though still possibly three days away, the weatherman projected the hurricane's course would hit the Alabama coast. The evacuation plan for the assisted living patients might be put to the test sooner than expected. He gunned the gas as he merged onto the interstate. He'd hurry to check for the pet damage and then go to Memory Oaks. At least renovations wouldn't start for another month or more. Who knew what kind of damage could happen if the storm blew in?

~~~

Something about having her sisters and church members at the hospital boosted Elinor's spirits. Enlightened her. She'd never realized how important family and friends were until this crisis. Em sat beside her telling funny stories. Cassie's calm and strong demeanor always offered wisdom and peace. Her father kept hugging everyone in sight. The affectionate man couldn't stop himself, he was so happy for good news.

Elinor studied each face in the waiting area. These were her people. Along with the neighbors who'd helped prepare the house for the storm. And Sam. The thought of him brought more warmth to her full heart. Maybe he was her person, and she was his. Did she dare hope?

Cassie took Elinor's hand and squeezed. "Go home. You need to rest. Dad says you've been at Mother's side for days now."

"I hate to leave." But she was exhausted.

"Just sleep awhile and come back. We'll all take turns."

"I'll take Elinor home." Tara appeared at their side. "We can talk about the evacuation plan on the way. We might need
~~~

it soon."

"Okay." Elinor nodded. "I'll come back after a nap."

On the way home, Elinor and Tara talked through the procedures of relocating the residents. From the radio reports of the weather, they may actually have to go through with the plan in another day or so. Moving dozens of elderly patients who were either ill or suffering from dementia would be a difficult task. Elinor's chest squeezed as she pictured the scared faces of her friends at Memory Oaks having to move. From her years of volunteering, she knew how upset older people became when life disturbed their routine even in the smallest ways. This would be a huge task, but she had to be a part of helping.

Once Tara dropped her off, Elinor checked on the pets again. No pungent odor assaulted her in the boathouse, so Sam must've cleaned up any messes there might have been. She let the animals back into the main house. Sadly, her mother wouldn't be home for days, maybe longer, so Sam may as well have some peace. She'd take the portrait, too. A chuckle shook her shoulders as she pictured Mr. Darcy curled up by Sam's face. Her thoughts stayed on Sam as she grabbed a bite to eat. There was so much food to choose from. She filled her plate with a scoop from several casserole dishes.

Once she finished, she picked up Mr. Darcy and trudged upstairs for a nap. After another quick prayer, she let her eyes shut. Thunder clapped outside, rattling the windows. *The storm must be moving closer.*

Chapter 35

Sam's phone vibrated over and over as he helped patients with their therapy. Calls from his mother. *Right.* His father's little trick wouldn't work this time. During lunch hour, he checked the screen again while sitting at a dining table with Mr. Hammill. Nineteen calls so far. Dad might be going nuts. His stomach tensed. Unless it was his mother who was calling. He hated to cut her off because of his father's attitude.

The phone vibrated in his hand. His friend Jess's name appeared this time. Sam accepted the call. "What's up?"

"Sam, it's your dad. He's had a heart attack, and your mother said she couldn't get you."

Sam's fingers shook as he squeezed the phone and pressed it closer to his ear. Moisture blurred his vision. "How bad is it? Is he…?"

"He's alive and at the hospital. The doctors are running tests. Your mother mentioned a blockage and a stent. I don't know much else right now."

"Oh, man."

"I'm praying for him to bounce right back. If I know Teddy Conrad as well as I think I do, he will recover."

"I don't know. We've argued so much lately… I better come up there. I'll leave now. Thanks, Jess." Sam cut the call and turned to Nubbin. "My father's sick, a heart attack, and I think I need to go."

Nubbin's sagging eyes lifted, and he nodded. "The Bible says, 'Honor your father and mother.' It's the first command with a promise. 'So that it may go well with you and that you may enjoy long life on the earth.'"

No matter how bad things were between them, Teddy Conrad was his father. He'd be there in case…in case his family needed him.

He made quick steps to find Thad Barnes. He wanted to let him know he was leaving. After a search of all the areas he could think of, Sam paced near the entrance. The man was nowhere in sight.

Sam pushed open the door. Outside, the wind howled as he scanned the parking lot. No sign of Thad's truck. Thunder rumbled and fat raindrops pinged the sidewalk in front of him. Sam stared at his car as the drops became a downpour. He wanted to be with his family, but he hated to leave Elinor. At least Miss Ruby had a good prognosis now. A debate raged within him. There was the storm and the evacuation, too.

Lightning split the air not far away. He could go check on his father now and then come back in the morning. It'd be a lot of driving, but he could do it. He took off toward his car, which was parked at the back of the lot. He could call Thad once he got on the way.

Another driver wheeled in going way too fast. Sam jumped out of the way behind the fender of a Mercury. His hand hit the metal edge, knocking his phone from his fingers.

"Slow down!" Sam shook a fist at the young man driving.

The car drove on through the lot and out the other side.

What a jerk.

Crouching to the ground with rain pelting him, Sam stared at his phone which had landed in a small pothole full of water. A black blur covered all but a small corner of the screen. Water ran off in all directions. That couldn't be good. The air buzzed around him as lightning struck way too close. Thunder cracked like the slap of a whip. Instinct and fear sprang his legs into action, and he was in his car in seconds, his heart pounding. He'd deal with his phone later. Drenched, he started the engine and headed toward Oxford.

~~~

Elinor woke with a start while Mr. Darcy purred and licked her face. Her head swam with fatigue, but she needed to get up and go back to the hospital. Blinking, she stroked the cat's bare head before setting her feet to the ground.
~~~

How long had she slept? The dark skies outside the window gave no clue. She looked to the nightstand for her phone. Only the folder that Sam had handed out that first meeting about Memory Oaks lay there. She hadn't even looked at it. Some help she'd been on the committee. Elinor ran her fingers across the paper, and then she picked it up. Flipping through the pages, she found page after page of research studies on how to better serve Alzheimer's and dementia patients in their environment.

Acoustic stimulation, visual stimulation, safety, and diet. She was flooded with appreciation. Sam must've spent hours putting this information together. No wonder he'd said no bright yellow paint. Soothing pastels were recommended…light blues.

A head nudge from Mr. Darcy interrupted her reading. He demanded more petting. The little man was so spoiled.

She really needed to find her phone and get going. Rain pattered on the roof, so she grabbed a raincoat from the closet and pulled it over her shoulders, then slipped her feet into a pair of sandals.

Downstairs, she filled the pets' food and water dishes. She let Dashwood out to do his business and then back in. After scanning the room, she spotted her phone on the dining table where she'd eaten. A red number stood over her phone icon, indicating she'd missed a few calls. *Please let Mother be okay.* Only one from Cassie, the others were from neighbors. And it was much later in the afternoon than she'd expected. She'd call Cassie on the speaker in the car. She grabbed her keys and headed for the door.

Outside on the porch, the wind whipped the branches of the ancient oak near the drive. Elinor chuckled at the thought of Sam's bird-desecrated car. The look on his face when he'd seen it… The man did love his vehicle, which made it all the more humorous.

After raising the hood of her coat, she sprinted toward her Lexus. A gust blasted through the trees, and a limb from a pine fell with a crack onto the drive. Elinor jumped at the racket, opened the door, and plopped onto the leather seats. Water dropped from her coat as she took it off and set it aside. Good grief. The weather wasn't helping matters. Having someone in the hospital was tough enough without a hurricane threatening.

Once she started the engine and drove onto the main road, she pressed the call button on the steering wheel. "Call Cassie."

A beep sounded, then a mechanical voice. "There is no one in your contacts named Lassie. Should I look for locations by that name?"

Stupid machine. "No. Call Cassie."

The wipers swished back and forth with a little squeak as she waited to see if the call would go through.

"I'm sorry. I don't recognize that command. Can you repeat that?"

"Call Cassie." Elinor groaned.

Nothing for a full minute.

"I'm really sorry about this, but I'm not able to complete your request at this time."

"Fine. You're a lot of help." She wanted to know how her mother was doing, but with all the rain, she wouldn't chance looking at her phone while driving. Plus, heavy traffic covered every road. Why were so many people out in the storm?

Elinor wheeled into the hospital garage and parked. A space close to the elevator for once. She glanced around. The lot wasn't nearly as full as it had been earlier.

She hurried inside and up the elevator to the waiting area. The family stood in a tight knot talking with a nurse. Elinor's heart sped up. Had her mother relapsed? She set a course to Cassie's side. Her older sister would give the best explanation.

"What's happened?"

"It's the hurricane. It's speeding up, and evacuations have started. The hospital's found a bed for mother in Birmingham."

"Evacuate already?" No wonder there'd been so much traffic.

Cassie nodded and took her hand. "We've got everything figured out. Em and Benjamin are flying back to Oxford.

Dylan and I will go with Daddy to Birmingham now, following the ambulance. We rented a place we can all stay for up to a month if need be. When you finish, there's room for you." Her sister's brows knitted. "Unless you had another plan?"

They were leaving now? "Finish what?"

"Daddy said you were helping evacuate Memory Oaks tomorrow, but you're welcome to come with us now, if that's changed."

"I did volunteer to help them, but…" Elinor's head spun with this new turn.

"I'm sure they'll understand if you want to be with Mother."

If Cassie, Dylan, and Daddy were with Mother, they'd do fine without her. At least until she helped the residents at Memory Oaks. She and Sam could leave after that. "I'll come as soon as I finish tomorrow. I better tell Sam the plan so he doesn't bother coming up here." She punched in the number. It went straight to voicemail. Maybe his battery was dead. Elinor tried Tara's number. If he was just down the hall, her friend could give him a head's up.

The line rang twice. "How's our patient?" Tara's rich voice answered.

"She's being evacuated to Birmingham. I wanted to let you and Sam know, so you didn't bother coming up here. I'll stay and help you tomorrow and then join them. Can you tell Sam?"

"I would, but he disappeared this afternoon. The therapist was looking for him. I thought maybe he was with you."

"No." And his car wasn't at the boathouse, either. Strange.

"If you need to go with your family, we'll make it."

"I'll see you in the morning." Elinor cut the call. Where could Sam be?

"Excuse me, Big Roy." Her father's secretary made her way into their circle. "An investigator from the FBI has been trying to get in touch with you about some money someone was trying to wire from your brokerage account." Her lips twisted. "Unless you tried to make a large wire transfer overseas today. I've been trying to call you."

Twin lines formed in the center of her father's forehead. He pulled his phone from his pocket. "I turned the ringer off this thing and forgot to turn it back on. I haven't made any transfer."

The secretary held out a message slip. "I thought it sounded important."

All the oxygen escaped from Elinor's lungs. "A wire from the brokerage account?" And Sam was nowhere to be found, either. What a fool she was. Her heart wrenched and tears swam across her vision. "Just like what happened with Craig." She had to get out of here.

"You think Sam…? No." Her father shook his head. "Sam wouldn't—"

"That's what we thought last time." Her voice cracked. "I'll come to Birmingham as soon as I can tomorrow. I hope you rented a place that allows pets." Because Mr. Darcy and Dashwood were the only males she'd want around in Birmingham other than her father. She'd known better than to trust her heart to another man.

Chapter 36

Cool air smacked Sam as he burst through the doors of the Oxford Hospital. He squeezed around two women talking just inside and jogged to the front desk. He rubbed his slick palms together and found his voice. "I need to locate a patient."

The older woman looked up from her computer and offered a smile. "Little Sammy Conrad. What brings you here?"

Mrs. Corson? His babysitter? He couldn't deal with the Little Sammy name she'd dubbed him right now. "My dad. He's a patient. I need to find him."

"Oh, I'm sorry, honey. I didn't know." Her brow wrinkled in all sorts of directions. Flustered, she focused on her computer. "I just started my shift, and I'm new at this."

Tension zapped down Sam's arms. If she'd scoot over, he'd find it for her. He leaned over the counter to scan the screen.

"I don't think you're supposed to see—"

"There it is." His finger hovered near the small letters. "Room 338." He rotated toward the elevators and jogged to reach the button. He pressed once…then a dozen more times. "Come on."

"Praying for y'all, Sammy." Mrs. Corson's voice wobbled as she tried to yell.

"Thank you." The elevator doors opened. Five people filed out. Slowly. *Come on, people. Move like you have a purpose.* He should've taken the stairs, except he didn't know where they were and didn't want to ask Mrs. Corson. It might take longer than waiting for the elevator.

Finally he stepped on, and the elevator lifted him toward the third floor. His right foot tapped with nervous energy as if he'd been caged with a wild hog. The drive had been rainy for the first half and just plain long for the other half.

His dad had to be okay. And he needed to get back to Elinor.

The doors slid open, and he stepped out. He scanned room numbers on the signs with arrows pointing various directions until he found the right one. He fought the urge to run but kept a brisk pace down the bright halls.

The room came into view. He stopped short of bursting through the door. It could be the wrong one, so he'd better knock.

As the door swung open, his mother appeared. A smile lifted her cheeks, and she stepped out and embraced him. "Sam, you came. I've missed you so much." She held him tight, then stepped back and placed her hands on his cheeks. "You look so tired, honey."

Why was she carrying on about him if his father was near death?

"How's Dad?" He craned his neck to see into the room.

"I've been trying to call you. He's going to be fine. The stent is in, and he'll be released tomorrow."

"But he had a heart attack, right?" They'd better not have been tricking him to get him back. Surely they couldn't rent a hospital room.

"The blockage caused a mild heart attack, and we were scared out of our wits. But he was lucky. No damage, and he really does feel great now. Ready to leave this place, of course." Her blue eyes searched his face. "I know you two had a falling out… You're coming in, right?"

Exhaustion spread through Sam's limbs. With it came relief and a bit of annoyance. He'd driven all this way when… He had to let that go. His father would be okay. That was good news. The prospect of talking to his father was another story. The man better not harass him to go back to the bank because of this.

But was his father really going to be okay? *Should* he go back to the bank to help?

Sam nodded at his mother and took slow steps into the room toward the bedside.

His father looked up from his newspaper. "Sam?" A perplexed look lifted his father's brows. "You came?"

"I'm going to get something to drink and let y'all talk." His mother slipped out and disappeared down the hall.

"You're my dad. I was worried about you." Sam smirked. "I should've known nothing would get you down for long."

A small smile lifted his father's lips. "True." His eyes darted around the room. "It did give me a scare, though. Thanks for showing up."

Sam pulled a chair near the bed and sat. He needed to speak his heart—set things right as best he could. "I'll always care about you, Dad. I love you. I've tried to be what you wanted, but it wasn't me. I need to be my own man now. I may screw up." A chuckle slipped from his lips. "I may even have to ask for your help or advice, but I've got to find my own way." Moisture rimmed his eyes. "That doesn't mean I don't love you."

His father's eyes met his for the briefest moment, and he nodded. "Makes sense, I guess."

Sam swallowed hard. It was a crumb, but he'd take it.

They sat for a while without speaking. His mother came in juggling two large cups of coffee and a Sprite.

Sam stood and rushed to help, relieving her of one of the coffees. He smiled. "Is this for me?"

"Just like you like it, nice and strong, no sugar."

"Thanks, Mom. I need it. It's been a long day." He lifted the lid and sipped the hot steaming liquid, savoring the possibility of a bit of energy.

His mother patted the couch. "Sit and tell us about Mobile."

Hesitant, Sam forced his feet to obey, and he sat beside her. How much did they want to know, and what would set Dad off?

He'd begin by describing Elinor's cat. That would surely bring a laugh from his father. He went on telling them about the ball, the nursing home project, and the former swindler. He worked his way up to sharing about Elinor and her family. He explained her mother's surgery, the scare, and the infection.

His mother patted his shoulder. "Sounds like this Elinor is important to you."

Warmth scalded his cheeks. He'd hate for his father to think his whole career decision was based on his feelings for a woman. Not that she didn't play a part in the *where* of his new career. Sam let out a cleansing breath. He couldn't control his father's thoughts. "She's really important."

His father nodded toward the television monitor. "Been watching the weather down where you're staying. Looks like that storm's gonna blow in pretty hard in Mobile. Coming in faster than expected now, too. Good thing you're up here."

Faster than expected? A jolt of adrenaline shocked Sam. How bad were things in Mobile? He wanted to be here for his parents, but they seemed okay. Were they? Should he ask to speak with the doctor? Because if this situation was stable, Elinor really needed him.

"Are you sure you're in no danger with your heart now, Dad?"

His father shrugged. "So they say. And I actually feel much better than I have in a while."

Sam pulled his keys from his pocket. "I've got to go back and help evacuate the nursing home where I'm logging hours."

"This late? Why in the world would you do that? You're safe here." His father's face screwed into a familiar frown.

"I committed to do it. I just wanted to make sure you were okay first."

The frown loosened. "Well, if you've got people depending on you…"

His mother caught his hand. "Shouldn't you catch a quick nap?"

"If you're sure y'all are going to be all right, I'd rather not try to sleep. But I'll come back up here as soon as I can to visit y'all."

"Your momma would like you to visit." His father's lips twitched. "Me, too."

Another crumb. And it lifted Sam's heart—gave him energy to head back into the storm. That and the coffee beginning to work its magic. "I love you, Dad. And I'll be back soon." Now he just had to keep himself awake for the five hour drive back to Mobile.

Chapter 37

Elinor's jaw ached from clenching her teeth between bouts of robust, ugly tears. She'd flopped on the couch with Mr. Darcy in her parents' house last night and hadn't had the will to move. What a fool she had been. Again.

Her chest squeezed tighter and tighter. Just seeing the boathouse when she'd driven home enraged her. If it didn't belong to her parents, she'd have the vile dwelling leveled, burned, and hauled away. Or sunk. Along with the remains of her heart. First Craig and now Sam. She'd never step foot in that place again. That was for sure.

The sound of diminishing rain pulled her attention to the back door—the lightest the deluge had been in hours. She should walk Dashwood while she had the chance, the poor dog. He'd been sweet to plop his head near hers when she was crying. His big brown eyes seemed to offer condolences and a wish to help. He hadn't left his position beside the couch since.

Elinor rubbed his wooly head and disentangled herself from Mr. Darcy. He mewed his displeasure at being disturbed, of course, as if she'd been born to be his personal pillow.

"Come, Dashwood. I need to let you out for a minute while there's a break in the storm."

He obediently followed and waited while she opened the door. Maybe dogs were good pets after all.

Outside, precipitation streamed from the clouds, but not near the downpour it had been only minutes before. Still, not even a sliver of sunlight made it through the early morning sky. Elinor grabbed a parasol from the old milk can by the door. She pushed her feet into her mother's garden boots. They were three sizes too small, but she'd endure the pain long enough to let the dog take care of business. Dashwood looked about as doubtful as she felt when they ventured onto the waterlogged grass and whipping wind. The umbrella was no match for the gales. He sniffed the air and ran beneath an old oak. In no time, he scurried back toward the house, and Elinor followed. She shook out the inverted umbrella and went inside.

If only she could shake her feelings for Sam.

She'd believed in him. Let her heart love again. How could he steal from her parents? After all they'd been through…and right at their most vulnerable time with her mother in the hospital. Of course, that's when it was easiest for predators like that to strike. At one's weakest moment. She would let Cassie have it for sending him to Mobile. Her sister had always been a good judge of character. Elinor rolled her eyes. Except for Cassie's first husband. He'd been just as bad, if not worse.

Elinor slipped off the rain boots, and trudged back toward the stairs. Since she was up so early, she'd pack and prepare the inside of the house the best she could in case of flood waters.

Once she'd put her clothes in her suitcases, she moved as much as she could carry up the stairs. Deciding where to put everything proved frustrating. If the roof were damaged, some areas on the second floor would be vulnerable, but downstairs, there was the threat of flooding. Elinor traveled up and down carrying small pieces of furniture and boxes, covering things with garbage bags or plastic. By the time she was ready to head to Memory Oaks, she was sweating and exhausted. She could barely catch her breath. Her legs ached from so many trips on the steps with heavy loads.

Thunder shook the house, and torrential rain pounded the roof. She looked down at herself in her rumpled jeans and blouse and shook her head. With all the rain, it would little matter how she looked to help evacuate. It wasn't like Sam would be there for her to impress.

Elinor groaned. Why did that thief even run through her thoughts?

~~~

The urge to roll down the window and let the water hit his face pressed on Sam for the hundredth time. Exhaustion and
~~~

sleepiness weighed heavily on him, and his eyes stung and blurred as he stared straight ahead, trying to make out the road. The torrential rain would soak the inside of his car if he even cracked the glass. Like it mattered. The few times he'd stopped for coffee, he'd gotten drenched.

Thoughts of his father nagged him all night. What if the heart attack had been worse? In the hospital, they'd had what felt like their first conversation since…ever. He hadn't realized how much resentment toward his father he'd built up over the years. Roy would tell him to let all that go for his own good, and he'd been trying. Seeing Dad in a hospital bed made that a tad easier. His new truce with the man gave him hope for a more peaceful future. Not that their relationship wouldn't still need work, but it could be salvageable. If nothing else, he'd learned lately that life was too fragile to waste time harboring bitterness. Or chasing after wealth. He'd made a good choice going to Mobile.

Other than the timing with this weather disaster.

The sky ignited with lightning, and the downpour worsened. He'd never seen rain this hard, and his knuckles tightened on the wheel. The radio announced that the outer bands of the hurricane were to blame. If these were the outer bands, he'd hate to be in the middle of the thing. With the rising of the sun, some light broke through, but with the heavy, dark clouds and the angry torrents of water pouring from them, it hadn't helped as much as he'd hoped.

Finally he reached the last stretch of highway. He'd have to go straight to Memory Oaks. There wasn't time to stop by the hospital or go to the Bosarges to check on Elinor's family. Traffic crawled as Sam neared Memory Oaks. He lost count of the number of wrecks he'd passed.

Thank you, Lord, for the safe trip. Between the weather and his own exhaustion, things could've been worse.

Sam leaned forward. The wipers smacked back and forth in a vain attempt to clear the window. He had to be near to Memory Oaks' drive. Ahead of him, two buses stopped with turn signals flashing. They slowly turned into the parking lot in front of him. His shoulders relaxed. He'd made it.

While the buses lined up behind several ambulances near the door of Memory Oaks, Sam parked and looked around the inside of his car. Should he bother bringing anything inside besides himself? He didn't even have an umbrella. Outside, the rain pounded harder with the wind thrashing it sideways. It reminded him of the day he'd left Oxford. Elinor's Lexus pulled up beside him, and a laugh rippled through him. This whole trip had been one big storm, really. But in a good way somehow.

He couldn't wait to pull Elinor into his arms.

Chapter 38

Elinor threw open her car door and sprinted toward the entrance of Memory Oaks. Seeing a car that looked like Sam's struck like a bullet ripping through the hull of her soul. Even his stupid brand of vehicle taunted her.

There was no use opening her umbrella with this wind. Her earlier experience had taught her that, but she'd tucked it under her arm as she ran anyway. She leaned it against the brick column and glanced down at her drenched clothes. Would Tara have dry scrubs she could wear? A howling gust twisted the limbs of the live oaks near the drive. *Please, Lord, protect these sweet residents. And me.*

"Well, hello." A deep voice spoke next to her ear above the sounds of the storm, and two arms wrapped around her waist. "I've missed you. Sorry, I had to—"

"Sam?" Elinor jerked away and spun to face the scoundrel. "How dare you show your face here."

His brows scrunched to meet above his nose. Water dripped from his forehead and hair and ran down his face. "I told you I'd be here." His blue eyes gazed into hers, all sappy as if nothing had happened. He was more devious than she'd imagined. Of all the nerve. Did he think he could get more money? Or maybe he thought he'd get away with the scam…and was still trying to date her. He was sadly mistaken. "Leave now."

His face screwed into a frown. "If I'd known you'd be so upset, I wouldn't have left last night, but I felt like I had to—"

"There you are." Tara held open the entry door. "I thought you'd changed your minds." She glanced at the mass of undulating clouds inching closer. "Not that I can blame you. Let's hurry, though. The storm's coming in faster than predicted. I have the ambulatory patients lined up for the first bus."

Behind Tara, scared faces of residents peered toward the skies. Elinor's throat squeezed. They'd be so afraid to leave the place they knew. She'd focus on them and ignore that crook Sam Conrad.

"Tell me what to do." Sam stepped up all confident and strong with his wet shirt stuck to his chest.

A vision of the first day she'd met him—shirtless—at the boathouse popped to mind. "No. Halt."

Both Tara and Sam turned to stare at her. "What?" They spoke in unison.

She'd meant to keep that thought inside her own mind. "I was practicing for unexpected traffic."

Tara wrapped an arm around her shoulders. "You're a tired and stressed-out young woman. Are you sure you're up for this?"

"Of course. If anyone's ready, it's me. Whatever has to be done." She shot Sam a hard glare. *Including sending criminals to jail.* As soon as they got the patients settled, she'd call the FBI.

~~~

Maybe Elinor had some sort of personality disorder. It would explain a lot.

Sam escorted another elderly woman by the elbow toward the door of the bus. "This way, ma'am. We'll wait our turn for the steps, and I'll be with you all the way."

Mrs. Chism clutched his arm tighter as they paused. "Weather looks real bad out here. Good thing I didn't go to the beauty parlor today." Her free hand went to fluff her hair. "Does it still look good, Jimmy?"

Sam smiled and surveyed her hair. "It's as lovely as always." He'd answered to a number of names today—Robby, Dale, Bart—all of which sounded better than the tone in Elinor's voice when she'd spoken his name earlier.

He gripped the golf umbrella tightly and helped her navigate the bus's steps. This group moved slowly, but at least they moved. The next group would be more difficult. Staff would
~~~

handle the bedbound, but the in-betweens would need assistance.

In the charter bus, Sam steered Mrs. Chism to a seat. "Here you are."

She struggled and gave a slight groan as she sat. "The atmosphere has my rheumatism flared up something awful." She patted the seat beside her and lifted an eyebrow. "I need one of your special massages, Jimmy."

Who exactly was this Jimmy? Sam swallowed back a chuckle. He'd better make a quick getaway. "I have to help the others."

A bolt of lightning flashed near the window and thunder boomed.

"What?" Her lips quivered. "You're leaving me? I'm afraid of the storm." Moisture shone in her eyes.

He glanced sideways while he fumbled through a few responses.

Elinor glared at him from only inches away, Nubbin holding her arm. "We need to pass."

When had she slipped up behind him? He scooted into the seat. "It's okay, Mrs. Chism." He placed a hand over hers and rubbed her knuckles. "We'll be fine. God's taking care of us."

A slow nod came from Mrs. Chism, and she pressed her lips together. "Yes. He is."

"Come on, Brother Hammill. Let's find you a seat." Elinor's voice sounded pleasant but exhausted.

Fatigue made one of his sisters really cranky. Maybe that was all that was going on.

Sam stood. "Nubbin, you want to sit here with Mrs. Chism?"

The elderly preacher's eyes met his, and a look of recognition settled there. "Sam, how's your daddy? Did you go see him in the hospital last night?"

Sam's mouth fell open. Nubbin had said his name *and* remembered about his father. A miracle for sure. "Yes, sir. He had a mild heart attack, and the doctor put in a stent. I just drove back in from Oxford this morning."

Nubbin's gnarled hand gripped his shoulder. "I was praying for him. And you."

Sam couldn't stop himself from hugging the old preacher. "Thank you, sir. It worked."

Once they released each other, Nubbin took a seat with Mrs. Chism.

Sam started to walk away when the old man stopped him. "Wait. Sam."

He turned. "Yes, sir?"

"Did you happen to bring back any cookies?"

~~~

This was truly appalling. Now Sam was lying to a poor elderly preacher. Saying his father had a heart attack. Of all things. Sam didn't even like to talk to his father. Surely he could think up a better lie.

Sam waved a broad gesture for her to go ahead of him off the bus. A sort of cute smile lifted his lips as he promised to try to get Brother Hammill some sweets as soon as possible. If only that was the real Sam. The one she'd fallen in love with. "No. Halt."

"Are you really planning to direct traffic?" The gentle press of his fingers caressed her shoulder. "Because I don't think that's a good idea. It's too dangerous. They have police for that."

She twisted away from him with a jerk. "Why do you persist with this charade? Pretending to care for our family?"

~~~

Elinor spit the words at Sam. If they'd have been razors, he would have been fish bait. When she finished, her chin jutted out, and she clamped her jaw shut.

"Charade? Of course, I care." Sam reached toward her but stopped. She may've had a complete break with reality or short-term memory loss. Did mental illness run in her family? Or had she been replaced with an evil clone? "Why would you even say that, Ellie?"

"Do *not* call me that. We know about the money. You should get out of town while you can. Run off to the Caribbean or wherever you'd planned on hiding."

"What money?" Did she think he was Craig? Wasn't she too young for dementia?

"As if you don't know." She huffed. "Since you're here and there's work to do, restrict your remarks to only those pertaining to the evacuation."

Boy, she was stressed. He'd be quiet for a while. Not like there wasn't plenty to do.

The soggy ground refused to accept more of the liquid tumbling down from above, and small ponds and fast-moving streams formed on the parking lot. Sam slogged through the water to the next patient. If they'd let him, and if he knew he wouldn't hurt the patients, he'd have carried the last of the elderly to the vehicles, but apparently that would break protocol. And probably freak the residents out, too. They were frightened and disoriented enough just leaving the building.

Another twenty minutes passed, and he descended the bus steps one final time. The last ambulance rolled away with one of the most fragile women he'd seen. Sympathy shredded his heart as he'd watched her shriveled form on the stretcher. Life's last stages could be brutal. He said a quick prayer for her and the rest of the patients and staff.

Tara directed him inside, where they spent the next hour preparing the facility for the storm as best they could. The staff's frantic expressions, along with the racket outside, gnawed at his stomach. Or maybe he was hungry. He hadn't eaten much in the last twenty-four hours. A voice came over the PA with an announcement that they should all exit the building. They'd done all they could, and the weather was becoming even rougher than predicted.

Where was Elinor? He went out to the parking lot in search of her Lexus.

Endless rivulets of water ran down his face, and a flood inundated his shoes. His thoughts turned to that last patient. What had the woman's life been like? Did she have family? Where were they now? Had she ever been in love?

Fifty years from now, would he be satisfied with the mark

he'd left on this earth? One thought struck him with a vengeance—he didn't want to imagine life without Elinor. Even if she was a bit eccentric. He wanted family and a lot of it. He wanted to be a good father and husband, like Roy. He even wanted that hairless cat curled up with him every night if that's what it took to be with his Ellie.

"What in the world are you doing just standing there in the rain? We're done. I'm calling back the FBI to tell them where you are as soon as I get in my car." Blue eyes nailed him. Overpowered him.

FBI? "I'm not Craig, and I don't know what you think I've done, but I love you, Elinor Elizabeth Bosarge." He lifted his arms to embrace her, but she jerked back a step.

"What?" The wind yanked away her umbrella and launched it toward the bay with extraordinary speed. Despite the gale force winds, she remained focused on him, unmoving other than the quiver of her chin.

"You folks better get a move on." A deep voice broke their trance, and a police car pulled beside them. "Storm watching is dangerous, and I just got word on the radio. This lady is coming faster and harder than expected. You need to evacuate now."

The wind gusted as if confirming the man's announcement. "Yes, sir." Sam took Elinor's arm. "We need to go."

"Yes. No. Officer, you should take this man—"

The police car rolled away, and she wrangled her arm from his grasp. "I'm not leaving with you. And I have to go get Mr. Darcy and Dashwood." Elinor spun and ran, splashing toward her car, never once giving him a backward glance.

Chapter 39

"Wait." Sam pounded on her passenger window with his palm. Tree limbs cracked nearby, and he flinched as more water than he'd thought possible hammered him. "Let me go with you."

The Lexus's engine started, and the headlights came on. The windshield wipers activated with a frenzy, and the car eased backward. He stepped away to avoid being run over. Raising his arms over his head, he jogged beside the vehicle and waved. "Hey! Let me go with you."

But she just put the car in drive and left the lot.

Lightning rent the air again, and Sam sprinted to his Mazda. She really had gone crazy in all this madness. He'd have to follow her, though he wished they could leave town and pray that the pets survived. She'd never go for that. And if he were honest, he wouldn't either. There had to be time to get to the house, throw two animals in the car, and then evacuate. There had to be.

Because he didn't want to imagine the alternative.

The AC blasted, and his wet shirt and pants pressed cold against his skin, sending knifelike shivers through him. Goose bumps rose on his arms, part from the wetness, part from anxiety about hurricanes. He scoffed, cut off the air, and shut the vents. What else was he supposed to do but go on? Leaning forward as far as the seatbelt would allow, he tried to see through the waterfall coursing down his windshield.

He drove toward the Bosarges' home with almost no visibility, thankful for the white line on the right side of the road. Cars, trucks, boats on trailers, and emergency vehicles passed traveling the opposite way, and the closer he got to the Bosarge home, the more deserted the road became. He reached for his hazard lights and pressed them on. How was Elinor faring in this mess?

Mile after mile, he squeezed the steering wheel until he reached the southward turn. Shingles littered the road in one section. At least he was getting close. He blew out a long breath as the car curved onto the old road near the river.

That's when he saw her. The Lexus hit a patch of water, sprayed moisture high in the air. The car fishtailed, hydroplaned sideways, and slid off the road and into the drainage ditch.

~~~

Elinor's heart beat in her throat as she scrambled to press the gas. Her ribs squeezed her lungs like a vise. Water rushed across her feet. "Oh, Lord, help! What do I do?"

Her fingers shook as she fumbled to unbuckle the seatbelt. After wrenching it free, she pivoted to grab her purse. A knock on her window jarred her head back. Her breath seemed to be caught in her throat.

A strong profile hovered there, banging, shouting something.

Sam. Would the man never give up?

He pointed frantically at the window.

Fumbling, she pulled at the lock, pulled the handle, and pushed the door. Something weighed against it. The water? Her chest squeezed harder.

She pressed the power window, and it lowered. Thank God.

Sam held out his hand. "Come on! Hurry!"

She hugged her purse under one arm and climbed through, trying to avoid his touch. As her feet felt for the ground, a rushing torrent pulled at her legs, and she fell forward. Muscular arms caught her, gathered her up, and lifted her off the ground. Sam was carrying her.

"I don't need your help."

"Of course, you don't." He kept his gaze on the ground as he navigated the slippery bank of the ditch, which was quickly becoming a river.

The rain blowing sideways tasted of salt. The brackish water of the bay must've been spraying along with the precipitation.
~~~

Thank the Lord they were nearing the driveway. She may as well let Sam drive her the rest of the way to the house.

He set her on her feet but held one arm around her waist while he opened the door of his Mazda. He grabbed her purse and pitched it in the back.

Of all the nerve.

After she got situated, he shut the door and sprinted to the driver's side. Without speaking, he drove toward the house, the downpour and wind outside so loud now, it little mattered. All she wanted was to get home, get the animals, and leave.

Her car, though. She'd have to call a tow truck. But would they come out in a hurricane? By the time they did, it would probably have floated who knew where. She'd have to drive one of her parents' cars to Birmingham.

Sparks flashed in front of the windshield, and Sam yanked the wheel left to avoid a falling power line. The seatbelt clutched at Elinor's chest and the air caught there. Were they going to die out here? Her last moments on earth would be spent strapped in a car with a man who had ripped her heart in two.

A whistling sound accompanied her breath as she exhaled.

Not now. Not an asthma attack.

~~~

Adrenaline rushed through Sam's body and ignited fire in his limbs. That power pole had been far too close. He focused on the road. He couldn't chance a look at Elinor. The distraction would be too dangerous. But she had to be scared out of her wits by now. Between being trapped in her car and the flying objects…

At least she hadn't screamed. In fact, she'd said nothing. Which was odd. *For her.*

That's when he heard it just above the thrash of the rain. *A gasp.* More like a crackling grab for air.

No. This couldn't be happening. Was it the stress of the situation bringing it on? He pressed the brake, pushed the gear into park, and whirled to look at Elinor. "Do you have your inhaler?"
~~~

Her chest lifted and lowered as she struggled for air. Her index finger pointed to the backseat.

He unbuckled his seatbelt and reached over the console. He'd been annoyed when she'd brought the purse from the flooding car and had thrown it probably a little too hard into the back. The contents were strewn across the floor. The wind roared louder as he fumbled through the clutter of items. His fingers felt the smooth plastic. "Got it!"

Soft hands ripped it from his grip as he turned around. Elinor shook the inhaler, depressed the canister once, sat up straight, and released a ragged breath. Placing the canister in her mouth, she inhaled slowly, then held her breath. Her eyes slid shut.

"Are you okay?" Fear crept over him like a tidal surge. *Please, God, let her be okay.*

She nodded, repeated the routine, and then opened her eyes. "We can go." Her voice was barely an uneven whisper.

"We're going to make it. Don't worry." He took her free hand and caressed it before turning back toward the road.

A crack and a rustling clatter jerked their attention forward. A tree smashed across the road in front of them. Its branches scraped and landed on the hood of his car.

"Lord, help us." Could this get any worse?

Another tree clattered to the ground behind them.

Yep, it could get worse.

Chapter 40

How are we going to get out of here? Elinor hugged her arms around herself.

She knew the answer. They'd have to walk to the house and hunker down for the duration. She'd have to ride out a hurricane with Sam Conrad.

"Good thing you're a runner." She glanced at him. "We better hurry before another tree falls."

His eyes met hers. Tenderness dwelled there as his hand touched her cheek. "Do you need me to carry you? Can you breathe?"

Even if he was a swindler, how could he be all bad? No one would go this far and be a total loss. He'd gone through the surgery with her mother and now a hurricane to help her save her pets. Maybe it was his father's verbal abuse that caused Sam to go down the wrong path. "I'm good now. Let's do hurry."

He smirked. "Let's do."

They scrambled out of the car and climbed over the downed tree. Wind and pine needles walloped them. Various cracks and booms sounded in the woods. Sam grabbed her hand, and they ran faster than she'd thought possible. She pictured herself swimming laps, keeping pace, kicking hard against the water. She could do this.

At last, the ancient oak near their house came into view. Though the wind howled, it stood firm against the onslaught. She hoped her parents' home would do the same.

Another whirlwind of leaves came toward them, slapping against their legs. Between the roar of the wind and the popping limbs, it seemed they were on a battlefield.

~~~

They had to hurry. The storm was getting worse. Sam
~~~

whisked Elinor off her feet and took off at a run for the last yards between them and the house.

Instead of fighting, she clasped her arms around him and clung tightly. She ducked her head to his shoulder, giving him a clear view of his path.

They reached the door, and he set her down. She stared at him without moving. Sam cleared his throat. "Are you going to open the door?"

Her eyes widened. "I left my purse in your car."

His throat clogged with emotion. What if she had another asthma attack? "What about your inhaler?"

"I have it in my pocket, but no keys."

Oh…no keys.

His hand went to his wet jeans pocket. Whew. "I have keys."

"Thank the Lord. I may even visit you in prison."

She was a strange one. "Let's talk more about that inside."

She stepped out of the way, and he unlocked the door.

He followed her inside. The dog shook and whimpered under the coffee table, and the cat lay curled up beside his head. Pieces of a shredded silk flower arrangement littered the floor. "What are the procedures for making it through a hurricane? Where do we go?"

"My mother's walk-in closet. It's large and in the center of the house. There are batteries, a flashlight, and a radio in there, plus the blow-up mattress. In tornado warnings, we open a card table and put the blow-up mattress on top to try and shield our heads from falling objects. You do that, and I'll gather a bunch of pillows to make a nest under the table. I need to get the animals once we get everything together."

"That's all?"

"We have food and water. A generator to keep it cold. Enough to last weeks. I did everything else I could before I left this morning."

They worked to prepare their *nest*. Blowing up the air mattress without the pump proved to be the biggest challenge. Of course a small hole kept leaking air, making it difficult to fill the thing.

Elinor came and went. She brought water, snacks, and pillows. She turned on the radio and gathered the pets. All the while, the haunting howl of the wind circled the house. Booms and cracks of falling trees alternated with thunder shaking the roof. Worry for Elinor niggled at Sam as he pushed out another puff of air.

"Haven't you finished yet?" She bit her lower lip and wrung her hands. "You only had two things to do." Her tone was accusatory.

"There's a hole in this thing." He pointed at the mattress.

"We need duct tape." She dropped to her knees and reached under the hanging clothes. "It's here someplace." Crawling around the large walk-in closet, she felt along the baseboards, frustrated sighs accompanying the action.

Another colossal boom sounded, and they were plunged into darkness.

Chapter 41

Had a tree hit the house? Elinor froze under the rack of her mother's skirts. "Sam?"

"I'm right here. I'm going to sit down where I am so I don't step on you or one of the animals."

"Okay. I'll crawl your way. We'll have to get into the nest without the air mattress." Her fear and frustration sharpened each word.

"Sorry." His voice sounded deflated, as if she'd injured him.

Perhaps she'd used Sam's father's severe tone. Elinor sighed. "You are not responsible for the punctured mattress. It's not your fault. Probably Mr. Darcy's." Clothing of some kind tangled on her head as she made her way out from under the closet rack. She awkwardly pulled at the fabric as she crawled. Until she hit something solid. "Oh!"

"That would be my shoulder." Something prodded her face. "Is that you, Ellie? Your hair feels weird."

"I think one of my mother's skirts is caught on my face." Good thing, too, or he might have poked her eye out. "Where's the flashlight?"

"I'll help you." The prodding continued, and he jerked at the clothing covering her head until she was free.

Disoriented, she fell forward. "Oops."

Two strong arms caught her, cradled her. Hands made their way to her cheeks in the darkness. "Are you okay?"

"Other than being trapped in a hurricane, I'm fine."

A chuckle shook his chest. "Me, too. Because if I had to be trapped with anyone, I'd choose you." Something soft and warm pressed a kiss against the side of her head.

Sam's kiss.

Exhaustion and fear seeped through her, and sustaining her

anger at him suddenly seemed like too much work. The security of his arms was more than she could fight right now. Abandoning her bitterness, she snuggled closer in the dark. She sighed and rested against his chest. The truth of what he'd done—she couldn't push that away so easily. "Why did you try to steal from Daddy's brokerage account?"

~~~

Sam's muscles tensed. "What are you talking about?"

"The large sum of money that *someone* tried to wire from Daddy's account yesterday."

"Boyd Watson." The man had been avoiding him for good reason. The visit to his office and the call to the SEC must've spooked the swindler into action. The way Elinor had been acting today… Now all the pieces fell into place. Sam scoffed. "I knew that guy was slimy. That's why I called my friend from the SEC."

"The football league?"

"The Securities and Exchange Commission. He must have called the FBI."

~~~

Elinor shifted away to face him, though she couldn't see anything in the pitch black. "What are you talking about?"

"Your father's investment broker, Boyd Watson, had recently invested some of your father's money in a mutual fund I'd never heard of. I'd tried calling to ask about it. I even went to his office."

"You did?" Her muddled brain tried to make sense of the new information.

"I'm sure your father wasn't the only one he tried to steal from. I've seen it before. Embezzlers are like addicts, they blow through money. It's never enough. They keep going until they're caught."

"*You're* not a thief then?"

Sam's arms slid around her and pulled her closer. "I'd give up every last dollar I have for you to trust me."

"Your father really had a heart attack?"

"He did. He was lucky, though. They put in a stent, and he

seemed to be feeling better, so I came on back to help evacuate and…for you."

"Why didn't you call to tell me where you were going?"

"My phone got busted when I was leaving. I didn't have access to anyone's number without it. I just figured I'd be back by morning."

The truth slapped her like a cold wave. Sam had driven to Oxford to see about his estranged father, and then he'd turned around and traveled all the way back down to Mobile in the middle of a hurricane for her. For Memory Oaks, too, of course. And the way she'd been treating him… Her hands scrambled up, fumbling to find his face. "Where are your lips, sir?"

"What?" His voice wavered.

Finally, a shadow of stubble tickled her fingers. Rain still pounded on the roof above them, but that was nothing compared to the way her heart pounded in her chest. Sam *did* love her. He *was* an honest man. She'd been acting crazy, and yet he'd stayed.

"I'm sorry I thought… I love you, too, Sam Conrad." Soft lips met her fingertips, and she angled her head in the darkness. She lingered, caressing his mouth with her own. His breath tickled her lips as he let out a small sigh.

Ripples of warmth and light washed over her as her kiss lengthened, exploring, tasting the man that was Sam, woodsy and linen and strong. She ran her fingers through his hair. She sunk deeper into his chest, cocooning into his embrace. The booms of thunder seemed more like fireworks exploding inside her. Honest and steadfast. Her heart had found its hero.

Elinor stayed cradled in the shelter of Sam's arms while the storm raged outside.

With no phone service, no electricity, and cut off from the outside world, she should have been fearful. But deep within her spirit, she knew she and Sam were safe…somehow.

They slept on and off, Mr. Darcy and Dashwood snuggled against them, the past days' fatigue taking its toll. Eventually, the echoes of the gales and torrents grew softer.

Quietly, Elinor lifted Sam's hand to slide out of his grasp, then replaced it gently, so she didn't disturb his sleep. She wriggled free and felt around. Why had they never located that flashlight? She stood and took slow steps to where she hoped was the entrance of the closet. She stuck her hand out. Her fingers found the indentations in the door, slid down midway to find the knob, and opened it. Light seeped through a crack near the sill of a covered window across the bedroom. Had they slept the whole night?

Dashwood bounded past her and out of the bedroom. "No. Wait."

"What is it?" She felt Sam's presence beside her. "Are you all right?"

"I am indeed all right." She turned and slipped her arms around him. "In fact, I am happier in a storm with you than I have ever been."

"Me, too."

She soaked in the feel of his lips pressed on her forehead, breathed in his scent.

"Do you think it's safe to peek outside yet?" he asked. "See about the damage?"

"There's no water at our feet or dripping on our heads, so let's try it." But she hated to let him go.

Hand-in-hand, they made their way down the hall and through the living room and kitchen. Still no moisture on the floor. A really good sign. She cracked the back door.

Sam's fingers rested on the small of her back. "The big oak tree's still there."

She opened the door wider, and they looked toward the bay. The devastation made her blink twice. "The boathouse." Elinor sucked in a breath. "It's…it's…"

"Toast. Gone. Sunk." He squeezed her closer. "I'm so sorry. I shouldn't have said it that way. I try to filter, but sometimes, my mouth—"

"Your mouth is perfect." She pivoted and pressed a kiss to his lips, then caressed his cheeks. "It's my fault. I wished its demise. If that's the worst of the damage, Daddy will survive.

But your belongings were in there. I'm so sorry."

Sam shook his head and nuzzled her nose. "All I need is to wake up to your blue eyes for the rest of my life, however short or long that life may be."

Her cheeks buzzed as she pondered the implication of his words. "But we haven't even been on a date."

"I think we've both had enough *bad* dates to know when we've got a good thing." The corner of his lips quirked into that adorable smirk of his.

"So we'll skip dating and…do what?"

Sam dropped to one knee. "I know this isn't a fancy proposal like in one of your novels, but Elinor Elizabeth Bosarge, will you skip dating and marry me?"

Happiness sprang up inside her, flooded her chest, lifted her lips, blurred her vision. "On one condition."

"Really?" His brows rose. "There's a condition?"

Elinor giggled. She did sound like a baby dolphin. "You have to promise to love and adopt Mr. Darcy as your own son-cat."

A bark of a laugh came from Sam's throat. "For you, I'll do anything. Even love your Sphynx."

"Then I will happily marry you, Sam Conrad."

Chapter 42

In the bedroom of her freshly-painted beach house, Elinor stood before the full-length mirror and smoothed the white satin of her wedding dress. The Regency style fit snug to the waist then billowed with soft pleats to her flat lace shoes. Her fingers went to the antique cameo Sam had given her as a wedding gift the night before. Tingles ran down her arms, and her brain buzzed with awe. She was, in fact, getting married. Becoming the wife of Sam Conrad. Living her own happily ever after. Moisture pricked her eyes, and her nose stung. There was a time when she would never have believed it possible. She'd never imagined having this much joy.

Em fluttered around her, misting hairspray. Her baby sister paused and stared at her. "Your hair looks so pretty with this dress, Nora. I could just cry. Are you going to see Sam before the wedding?"

"That would be highly improper." But she'd love to catch a glimpse of him.

Em twisted one of the curls that had slipped out of the bridal headband and sprayed more of the aerosol. "Sam is going to drop dead on the sand when he sees you."

Nice wording as usual. "I hope not." Elinor shot a hard look at Emma, but added a wink. "It took me too long to find him. And I refuse to ever date again."

Em breathed a long sigh. "I hope I find someone to love me the way he loves you."

"What about that nice fellow Bryan who's playing the music out there. I thought—"

"We're good friends for now."

Joining them, Cassie pulled them both into a hug. "Things will work out for you. And we'll always have each other. Sisters in life and in Christ. Right, Em?"

Em nodded. "Yes, we are. I've made that decision for my life. You've both been great examples of faith, just like Momma and Daddy. And we came so close to losing Momma…" Em pressed her eyes closed.

Her sister had taken their mother's illness to heart. One good thing came of that nightmare. Maybe others. She'd seen the side of Sam that was confident and strong and dependable when she needed him most.

"Knock, knock, ladies." Two of Cassie's friends stood at the door. The dark-haired one, Sarah Beth, held a pitcher in one hand and a brown-eyed baby girl in the other arm. "We brought lemonade and appetizers. Your mother said you need to eat a snack, so you don't pass out on the beach."

"You all look beautiful." The blonde named Jill held her son—Cassie's stepson—and a tray of meat, cheese, and crackers. The grinning toddler on her hip grabbed a piece of cheese and shoved it in his mouth. "You stinker."

An adorable little girl followed Jill. "I'll watch Michael for you, Momma."

"Thank you, Katie." Jill placed appetizers on the side table. The toddler squirmed in her arms and slipped down her legs. She set him on his feet. "Elinor, I'm so glad you and Sam found each other. He needed someone who'd love and take care of him."

Heart squeezing, Elinor took one of the crackers and nibbled at it. She imagined Sam, left at the altar at his first wedding. Poor, sweet man. He did need someone. And she was his someone. "Thank you for the refreshments. How are you feeling, Jill? Cassie said you'd been ill a while back."

"I'm good. In remission from the lupus for now."

Michael ran to the sliding glass door in Elinor's room. "Wa-wa. Wa-wa." His chubby fingers fumbled at the metal latch.

Jill laughed. "It's a good thing I'm feeling better. That little boy keeps me running. We're trying to keep the kids occupied and out of the guys' way next door."

Elinor swallowed hard. Knowing Sam was in the rental

house next to them getting ready for the ceremony made her heart skip. "Did you take them a tray, too? How are they over there? Is Sam nervous?"

Laughing, Sarah Beth waved her off. "Don't worry. I've never seen a man glow so much. And that's even with Jess and Nick ribbing him about anything they can think of, and his dad hanging around in there, too."

"Ribbing him? Why would they?"

Her sisters exchanged strange glances with Sarah Beth and Jill.

What was going on? Elinor checked her phone. There was no time to question them. "Let's keep praying it doesn't rain. Even with the big tents Daddy had put up, outdoor weddings are risky." Why had she chosen to marry on the beach?

~~~

Sam plucked at the strange collar once more as they walked down the deck. A sudden wave of fear hit him. Why had he decided to rent this sort of tux? It had seemed like such a good idea at the time. Elinor would probably think he was an idiot and leave him faster than Tiffany when she saw him.

"Maybe I should change."

Wide-eyed, Jess and Nick exchanged glances.

"We were just picking on you." Jess squeezed his shoulder. "You look fine. She's going to love you no matter what."

Smirking, Nick gave him a little punch. "You're a stud. And you know what she likes better than we do."

Cassie's husband Dylan nodded. "You don't have anything to worry about. Let's get this show on the road."

Guitar music and singing drifted on the light evening breeze blowing in from the Gulf. Outdoor lanterns hung from poles, and white twinkling lights had been strung around the large tents that had been set up to provide shelter in case of rain. Sam started down the steps toward the beach. A few puffy clouds hung in the western sky. Maybe the weather would stay clear. His best friends and his father walked beside him as he traveled down the aisle—for the second time in his life. He prayed this time went better, or he might just walk out into the
~~~

water and keep going.

Only a small crowd looked on as he waited for his bride. Close friends and family. Elinor had wanted a small gathering, which was fine with him, especially after the last monstrosity of the wedding that almost was. Now he thanked the Lord that he'd been jilted at the altar. He'd go through that humiliation a million times to be here today.

His heart thumped against his ribs as each bridesmaid made her way down the stairs and onto the beach. The guitar music changed to the "Wedding March," and Sam lifted his gaze to Elinor's deck. The audience stood and turned. Elinor stepped from the glass door, her hand in the crook of her father's arm. Her white gown gracefully rippled in the breeze. Her red hair was twisted into some sort of white band with pearls shimmering on it. A few strands framed her face. She smiled at him, her gaze holding his as she walked toward him. The vision of his bride stole his breath away.

~~~

Elinor's breath caught. Sam's blue gaze followed her up the aisle. Thank goodness for her father's strength. She was so giddy, she might fall over. She'd already instructed everyone that, if that happened, they were to carry or drag her the rest of the way to her future husband.

Her husband. What a beautiful sight he was. What was he wearing? She studied his tuxedo. An old-fashioned-style suit. From the eighteen hundreds. He'd dressed as Mr. Darcy, cravat and everything. She couldn't stop grinning at the sight.

The minister spoke a few words, though she couldn't seem to comprehend them. Her father gave her arm to Sam.

"I love your suit," she whispered.

"I'm glad. Mr. Darcy, the cat, *only* has a bowtie." He motioned with his head toward the cat carrier that rested in the sand near her mother's cane. His eyes sparkled in the low light, and he stood up a little taller.

With each "I do," Elinor's chest expanded. Her heart pounded wildly as they exchanged rings.

Finally, the preacher announced they were Mr. and Mrs.
~~~

Conrad. "You may kiss the bride."

The wind kicked up, and Sam wrapped his arms around her. He pressed his lips to hers then pulled back and held her gaze. "Nothing is going to steal you away from me. Not even the wind."

Elinor placed her hands on his cheeks. "If the skies get rough, storms won't tear us apart. *We* will be blown together."

Don't miss the next book

by Janet W. Ferguson.

Magnolia Storms

A Coastal Hearts Novel

Set in Ocean Springs, Mississippi

Be the first to know about the release by signing up for the newsletter at http://www.janetfergusonauthor.com/under-the-southern-sun

Dear Reader,

Thank you for trusting me with your time and resources. I hope you had fun reading this story. It's been my favorite to write. Our hearts are funny creatures sometimes, aren't they? I had my share of bad dates, and likely I'm the villain of someone's story about their bad date with me. My friends and I had fun brainstorming the dates for this book. But it was tough to end this novel, because I liked the characters so much. Miss Ruby, Nubbin, Tara, and of course Sam & Elinor. I really liked Big Roy as a loving father figure. If you don't have that, remember you have a heavenly Father who knows the number of hairs on your head and holds you lovingly in the palm of His hand. He won't fail you.

Blessings in Him who is able!

Did you enjoy this book? I hope so! **Would you take a quick minute to leave a review online?** It doesn't have to be long. Just a sentence or two telling what you liked about the book.

About the Author

Faith, Humor, Romance
Southern Style

Janet W. Ferguson grew up in Mississippi and received a degree in Banking and Finance from the University of Mississippi. She has served her church as a children's minister and a youth volunteer. An avid reader, she worked as a librarian at a large public high school. She and her husband have two children, one really smart dog, and a few cats that allow them to share the space.

https://www.facebook.com/Janet.Ferguson.author
http://www.janetfergusonauthor.com/under-the-southern-sun
https://www.pinterest.com/janetwferguson/
https://twitter.com/JanetwFerguson

Publisher's Note: This book is a work of fiction. Names, characters, any resemblance to persons, living or dead, or events is purely coincidental. The characters and incidents are the product of the author's imagination and used fictitiously. Locales and public names are sometimes used for atmospheric purposes.

Mobile, Alabama and Fort Morgan are real places, but other than the names, the events in the locations are fictional. None of the events are based on actual people. The charming cities made the perfect backdrops for my novel.